A Design of Gold

An idea well expressed is like a design of gold
set in silver.

Proverbs 25: 11 TEV

PAULA VINCE

Even Before
Publishing®

Australia

A Design of Gold

Published by Even Before Publishing; Christian books by Wombat Books.

www.evenbeforepublishing.com

www.wombatbooks.com.au

© Paula Vince 2009

Cover art and photography © Sarah Rowan Dahl

www.rowandahl.com

Design and layout by Rochelle Manners

ISBN: 978-1-921633-03-4

About the Author

Paula Vince lives in Mount Barker, South Australia, with her husband and three children. She enjoys her simple lifestyle of writing and educating her children at home.

Paula values her faith, family and fiction. She believes nothing has more power to delight and inspire people than a good story with lovable characters.

Special Thanks

To my publisher, Rochelle Manners, a talented lady with a passion for bringing good books to people. I'm delighted to be included in your list.

To my editor, Anne Hamilton, who understood how my characters tick and helped me tell their story the way I wanted to.

To Wendy Sargeant for an initial editing perusal and valuable tips that helped me keep the drama moving.

To the cover artist Sarah Rowan Dahl, for a beautiful image and photo.

Prologue

The young man knew he'd struggle to make it back to shore. Thirty minutes earlier he'd been sitting on cool sand, gazing at the stars and trying to dull his despair with a few drinks. Now he was desperately trying to save his own life.

The moonlit sea had not appeared so turbulent from the beach. It had seemed just frisky enough for him to contemplate body-surfing in his boxer shorts. He'd wanted to release pent-up energy. That energy had been burned up long ago and now, if only he could make it back, he'd collapse in the shallows without even thinking of moving for at least an hour!

Grunts forced their way out of his tight lips. He tried to stop, in case making any noise wasted too much of his stamina. But as soon as he compelled himself to stay quiet the grinding ache in his exhausted chest and limbs seemed to increase tenfold. The grunts quickly escalated to whimpers of anguish.

There was nobody to see or hear him. He'd had that stretch of beach to himself. It was why he'd ventured into the water in his underwear in the first place. The moon was a grinning sliver, mocking his attempts to reach the shallows.

A vicious cramp shot from his calf to his knee like a pistol blast. *Owww! God, please!* Flexing his foot brought tears of agony. He tried to draw the sore leg up to his chest to rub the pain away, but what it really needed was the comfort of firm ground.

A wave burst over his head with a triumphant spray of foam. The next one did the same. The harsh taste in his mouth reminded him of the salt-water gargles of his childhood. The young man spluttered up a mouthful of it just before it reached his windpipe, but it gurgled its way down his gullet instead and sloshed around inside his stomach. Now there was salt water both inside and outside of him.

With a groan, he realised that during his ten-second pause, the relentless tide had dragged him back out another twenty metres. And he'd just used every reserve of his strength to gain two metres! At that moment, he knew deep in his heart that the ocean had probably beaten him.

What was I thinking, to put my life on the line over a woman? But Nicola wasn't just any woman. He'd known her since they were children, but had never noticed her romantically until his mother and sister brought her charms to his attention. Mum and Karen had only pointed out Nicola's obvious attractions – her flawless complexion and pretty face. He'd noticed far more himself. The sparkling quickness of her good-humoured smile and the luminous glow in her green eyes had suddenly made him melt inside. Like a ninny, he'd mooned over Nicola for far too long, letting his hopes build up until he'd read too much into her open friendliness. And he'd believed Mum and Karen when they convinced him that she loved him too. Perhaps he'd just *wanted* to believe them. Fool-like, he'd spent weeks imagining signs where as it turned out, there had been none. The genuine surprise and awkwardness on her beautiful face had spurred him to buy a few drinks and retreat to sulk at the beach...*What an idiot!*

Now he'd done the most stupid thing of all. How would he ever win Nicola around if he went and got himself drowned? That dread word slipped into his consciousness like a switch immobilising his limbs. He could not move any longer. He was completely spent. Instantly, powerful waves buffeted him around. He could barely tell the direction to the pin-prick street lights on the shore.

Then his ears discerned something strange and unearthly. There had been no sound of life, but now this subtle, alluring music seemed to flow around him. It might have even been coming from his oxygen-starved brain. It filled every part of him with a symphony like a clear, melodic orchestra. The tune was an old hymn that he'd long ago forgotten the lyrics of, but now they were pouring back.

Oh, hear us when we cry to thee, for those in peril on the sea!

If he could've opened his mouth he would have tried to sing along.

Suddenly the empty surf seemed to be teeming with creatures like men. Perhaps they'd been there all along. Or perhaps he was just hallucinating. Strong, shining warriors hovered over the water, beckoning him. What did they want? The weaker he felt, the brighter they appeared.

They were holding out their hands.

Giving up and relinquishing himself to the ocean seemed to be the only logical thing to do. If this was drowning, it wasn't so bad.

His last thought was a mild regret that he couldn't share this experience with Nicola.

1

Lord, please keep Shane safe. It's so horrible sitting here trying to guess what might have happened to him. If it's anything bad, I don't know what I'll do.

The group in the Turnbull's lounge room had hit a silent patch. Many words had already been spoken but Nicola knew the others would soon begin rehashing the same ground. There was nothing new to be said. Not unless she shared what she knew. She'd stayed quiet because she wanted to convince herself that what had happened the previous evening had nothing to do with Shane's disappearance.

I can't believe he would've taken what I said so hard. If only he'd come back and talk to me.

Silence was worse in its own way than the torrent of words had been. Nicola could barely breathe in the suffocating hush. Perhaps that was why the talk-silence-talk pattern had begun. Whenever the lull reached saturation point, somebody would blurt out a remark about Shane and set the others off again.

They were showing telltale signs of strain. Karen squirmed in her seat, obviously trying to think of any clue that might shed light on her brother's disappearance. She wrapped James, her husband's arm, tighter around her. He looked uncomfortable and arched his back. Nicola's younger sister, Laura, plucked compulsively at the curls behind her right ear. Soon Shane's mother and Nicola's mother would move restlessly too. Then the talking would begin. It was a terrible, futile chain reaction and only Nicola hadn't participated.

The comments were slower to start off this time round, probably because of the presence of the policeman who sat jotting notes. Nicola's mother crossed her left foot over her right.

But it was Shane's mother who cleared her throat and began the next round of talking. 'Officer Phelps, he wouldn't have left home without telling us. He would've known I'd be worried sick. He never would've been so cruel.'

'OK.' Everyone knew this policeman didn't waste words.

'And I know he was happy at work because he told me he was.'

The officer cocked one dark eyebrow. 'Was he in the habit of telling his mother everything that was going on?'

Nicola's mother, Ruth Price, said, 'Pam has an excellent relationship with her son and she knows him as well as anybody. We all know Shane well enough to know that he wouldn't have left without a trace.'

Well, we thought *we knew him.* Nicola felt positively sick.

'My brother was always loved by everybody who knew him,' Karen said, speaking too loudly.

James cleared his throat and added, 'Shane was a happy type of fellow. He's more than just my brother-in-law. We've been next-door-neighbours and friends from the time we were this high.' He raised the palm of his hand about a metre from the ground.

'Shane's the most easy-going guy I've ever met,' Laura declared.

'He was best man when James and I got married.' Karen's raspy voice made her sound like a stranger.

Poor Karen. Nicola couldn't bear to contemplate how she'd feel if their situations were reversed and James, her own brother, was missing.

Officer Phelps placed down his pen and looked up. 'Are you all quite certain there have been no sudden changes in Shane's life?'

'Definitely not.' Mrs Turnbull's eyelids were so red and heavy, she appeared to be squinting. 'I'm his mother. I'd know.'

Sparky, the Turnbull's cat, sprang lightly onto his mistress' knees and pushed his head beneath her hand. Mrs Turnbull absently stroked his head and Sparky's loud purring filled the room.

'I get the picture. When a man of routine goes missing for no apparent reason, it makes our job more difficult. Any insight at all into his frame of mind might be useful.'

'But there was nothing,' Shane's mother persisted.

'Well, there *is* one thing!' Nicola's voice sounded more distorted to her own ears than Karen's had. After hours of keeping quiet, it seemed to break like old elastic. Six heads swivelled to look at her.

'Go on,' the policeman said.

She watched her own fingers twisting in her lap. 'Last night when we walked home from the bus stop, Shane didn't go straight inside his house. He got into his car and drove off. And I know he was hurt and upset.'

'Nicky, *now* is a fine time to speak up!' Ruth Price didn't try to conceal her exasperation.

'I know. I'm sorry.' Nicola looked up at the mantelpiece and focused on her coloured sketch of Shane. She had captured the twinkle in his blue eyes perfectly. Everyone who knew him had said it was a good likeness. She'd chosen Shane for her project because she thought he'd be easier than anyone else. Shane's distinct features; square jaw, thin blonde fuzz of a moustache and blue eyes, were easy to replicate. Her Art teacher had asked to meet each of her students' models, so the class could assess the accuracy of each portrait. Obliging Shane had visited Nicola's Art College with no objections. *I wonder if that was what he meant by the 'signs.'* Her stomach swirled, although she'd barely eaten all day.

'Tell me what happened, young lady. Don't leave anything out.'

'OK.' Nicola had to concentrate both on keeping her voice steady *and* on what she was saying. 'When we were on the bus home from work...'

Officer Phelps jerked up his hand. 'Hold on. You work with him?'

'No, we work at different places in the city but catch the same bus home.'

'Go on.'

'Shane asked me if I'd like to go out with him... on a date. And I tried to tell him that I don't think of him as someone I'd like to date. I love Shane but he's more like a brother to me. He really surprised me by asking. I always thought I was like a sister to him, but I could see that he was disappointed and embarrassed. That's really all there was to it.'

'So he didn't take kindly to being refused?' the policeman asked.

Nicola was acutely aware of Karen's eyes, blue like Shane's, blazing at her.

'I wouldn't have called it an actual refusal. I was trying to explain; to bring him around to my way of thinking. He didn't seem to take it too badly… at first. Shane has always been a gentleman. That's why I didn't think his disappearance could have anything to do with…'

The officer's hand shot up again. Nicola fought an urge to wrench it from his wrist.

'I've already been given five other character profiles. I wasn't asking for another one. Just tell us what happened.'

'Well, when I told him I couldn't get my head around him asking me out, he said, "I see." He looked out the window for the rest of the way and didn't speak until we got out. And I didn't know what to say either. Then, when we started walking, he said, "I think I've wasted my time for the past six months."' Nicola would have been unable to describe the tightness in Shane's voice if she'd wanted to try. 'I told him he's always been one of my very best friends and he said…' She paused to swallow. 'He said that he didn't spend all that time talking with me on the bus because he wanted my friendship.'

'Then what?'

'He asked me why I was giving him signals if I wasn't attracted to him. And I told him he'd made a mistake. I wasn't giving him any signals. By then, we were outside our two houses. Instead of going inside, Shane pulled out his car keys. Then he said, "I'll probably be apologising to you next time I see you, Nicola, but just now I'm too wound up to think straight." And he got in his car and reversed really sharply. I've never seen Shane drive like that before. And that was the last I saw of him.'

'That was the last *anybody* saw of him!' Karen cried.

Officer Phelps glared at Nicola. 'You should have told us this before. Instead of an abduction we might be dealing with a grown man licking his wounds.'

'What do you have against Shane?' Mrs Turnbull was looking straight at Nicola.

'Nothing! Shane's great. It's just...'

'*Great?*' Mrs Turnbull shoved the cat off her knee. 'If you thought he was *great,* you would've agreed to go out with him. And Shane would be here sitting with us now instead of this cop.'

Two blurry, fierce images of Mrs Turnbull shimmered before Nicola's eyes. 'I *love* Shane. I just never thought of him that...'

'Is there someone else?'

'*No!*'

'I meant is there someone *you* prefer? Of course we all know you've never had another man in your life. You haven't had the gumption.'

Nicola's mother touched her friend's arm. 'Pam, take it easy. Don't say that.'

Mrs Turnbull twitched her arm away. 'I won't regret *anything* I've said. If your girl has sent my boy running off heartbroken...'

'This really isn't the issue here.' The policeman's authoritative tone soared above the woman's shrill voice. 'We have a twenty-four-year-old man who's simply disappeared and we need to find him.'

Somebody knocked on the door. It broke the pattern of talk-silence-talk and Nicola guessed by the brisk volley of raps that the caller was no member of the family. Karen fairly leaped off her seat to answer it. She returned to the lounge room followed by another policeman and Nicola's heart lurched at the sight of his face. The pattern was about to end and she guessed from his expression that she wouldn't want to hear what he had to say.

'Any leads on Shane Turnbull?' Officer Phelps asked with inane calmness, as if he couldn't read disaster spread across his colleague's face like a map.

The second policeman gave a regretful nod. 'I need to speak to Mrs Turnbull alone.'

Pale and trembling, Shane's mother stood up and beckoned the newcomer to follow her to her sewing room. Nicola's chest had tightened so every heartbeat ached. The sewing room door closed and silence set in again. Karen hid her face on James' shoulder.

For a moment that felt like eternity there was nothing. Then they heard a guttural groan of despair. It sounded more like a wounded beast than an elderly woman and the hairs on the back of Nicola's neck rose. Her eyes locked with Laura's wide, green shocked ones. With a muffled sob, their mother pressed a hand over her mouth.

The policeman stepped out of the sewing room. 'Which of you is Ruth? She's asking for Ruth.'

'That's me.' With a squeeze of Laura's hand, Nicola's mother rose to her feet.

When the door had closed behind them, Karen raised her face. 'Nicola.' Her chin wobbled so she could barely speak. But she managed to force out, 'Whatever's happened to my brother is your fault. And I'll never speak to you again.'

*   *   *

Nicola heard her mother return home. Even when Ruth tapped on her bedroom door, she couldn't bear to lift her sore eyes from her pillow.

'Nicky, look at us.'

Us? Nicola turned her head. Laura had followed their mother into her bedroom and stood behind her. Ruth sat on Nicola's bed and stroked her hair. 'They found Shane.'

Nicola closed her eyes and moaned. She couldn't bear to ask for details.

'Where did they find him?' Laura's voice trembled.

'They found his car first, parked in a car park on the coast near Port Elliot. Then they found Shane at a beach about two kilometres from it.' Her face twisted with agony. 'He was washed up on the shore.'

'But Shane was a *good* swimmer.' Laura looked as appalled as Nicola felt.

'They don't think there were suspicious circumstances,' Ruth said quickly. 'Shane was in his boxer shorts. His shirt and jeans were folded neatly on the front seat of his car.'

Those small details seared Nicola's heart like red hot wire. 'He always folded his clothes neatly whenever we went for a swim, ever since we were kids.' She remembered James teasing him about it and Shane just smiling.

'Last night was very hot,' Ruth said.

Nicola nodded. Her legs and the back of her neck had been perspiring on the bus.

'He'd been seen at a pub,' her mother was saying. 'They're guessing that he must've had some drinks and then decided to drive to the beach. The autopsy will tell. Maybe when he got there, he decided he'd like a swim. Who knows? But the tide must have swept him out. And then…'

'Stop!' Nicola begged. She wanted to blank out thoughts of Shane's terror when he realised he couldn't return to shore. But an image of fatigue etched across his broad forehead was clear in her mind. She knew Shane's features well, the way his face appeared quite flat until his forehead seemed to turn two abrupt corners, one on each side. She'd sketched it!

Laura's brows were knitted together, still perplexed. 'But Shane wasn't a heavy drinker.'

'It doesn't take many drinks for a person to lose his judgment. Especially a moderate drinker like Shane.' Ruth's voice was too thick with tears to go on.

'I'm sorry! I'm sorry! I'm so sorry!' Nicola found it was easier to talk than to swallow.

Ruth drew her into her arms and smoothed Nicola's fringe back from her sticky brow.

'But why wouldn't you go out with Shane?' Laura demanded.

'I just knew I'd never feel that way about him.'

'But *how* would you know that until you'd given him a chance?'

Ruth placed a finger against her lips. 'Sssh, Laura, it's too late for this.'

Laura began sobbing too. 'But we've all been hoping he'd ask her for months. We thought they'd be a perfect match. Mum, you said so yourself. You know how we'd sit and talk about it, you, me and Karen. You know Nic's not like me. She'll never find another fellow as good as Shane. She can't get guys to look at her. And Shane was so bashful it was the bravest thing in the world for him to ask her.' Laura's pretty, flushed face glared at Nicola. 'Why'd you have to cut him down?'

'I didn't mean to cut him down! I just knew… I felt… it wouldn't work for me. And I tried to explain it so he'd understand.' As she spoke, a picture of Shane carefully folding his clothes before his swim flashed through her brain. Nicola wanted to tuck her head into her shoulders and die.

'I'll bet it was because he wasn't as picture-perfect as those models in your Art lessons! Why don't you get real, Nicola? All you do is pore over paintings and read romance novels! Those guys don't even *exist* except in art. Even the models in magazines are jazzed up with computer tricks. And if anyone *was* that good-looking, he'd have tickets on himself anyway. Shane would've been worth *ten* of those pin-up boys.'

Their mother seized Laura's rigid hand and pulled her down onto Nicola's bed. 'She needs to vent her spleen,' she told Nicola, and cupped Laura's face between her hands. Ruth always made excuses for Laura's behaviour. That, at least, stayed the same.

'I can't pretend I wasn't disappointed myself,' she went on. 'Shane was always polite to me, ever since he was a little boy. And I thought you might've been interested. You're twenty-two years old now. That's a perfect age to settle down with a lovely person like Shane. The way you asked him to pose for your picture, I'd just hoped…' Ruth trailed off. She knew she'd made her point clear.

'I'm a total idiot,' Nicola said.

Laura was flexing her hands into fists, over and over again. 'You'd never have found anyone better for you!'

'Maybe I *should've* said yes!' Nicola shot back. 'He took me by surprise. My first instinct was just to blurt out how I really felt. If there was some way I could go back to Friday night…'

Ruth kissed the top of her head. 'We could talk around in circles all night but that would get us nowhere. I've left James over there doing his best to comfort both Pam and Karen at once, but he's never had to deal with anything like this before. It's terrible for him, too. We need to help Pam through the next few weeks. There'll be loads of practical details, including a funeral to plan.' Ruth stopped to dab her eyes. 'How terrible it is to be talking about planning a funeral for a boy Shane's age. Nicola, we need you to be washing your face and coming down to the kitchen.'

Although it was the last thing she felt like doing, Nicola lurched to the bathroom. Her green irises appeared lost in pools of jelly. She'd never seen herself like that but it didn't matter. Nothing mattered now that Shane was dead. She pulled a comb through her hair and ran a wet cloth over her face. An outside door slammed. Somebody had either come in or gone out. Her mother and Laura were already in the kitchen and Nicola could hear Karen's voice. She braced herself to join them.

2

'How long will you be? You said I'd get to use the computer as much as you when you finished school.'

'That doesn't mean I never get to use it ever.' Jerome Bowman tried to ignore the warm breath tickling the back of his neck. His younger brother, Sam, was bending down behind him, squinting at the screen.

'What are you doing *now?* You've already searched for Gareth Edgley's second book and couldn't find it. Why don't you just give up?'

'I'm not giving up. Now I'm trying to find Gareth Edgley himself. I'm searching through the British telephone directory on-line.'

This statement elicited a loud groan from Sam. 'That'll take *ages.* He's probably dead, anyway.'

Jerome felt his temperature swell like mercury in a tube. The high pitch of Sam's voice grated on his nerves. 'The longer you nag me, the longer I'll take.'

'This is my bedroom too and it's my turn on the computer. You were using it for an *hour* when I got home from school.'

Jerome had lost track of what part of the screen he was perusing. The names and addresses were blurring into each other. He flicked the computer back to the Start menu and flung himself onto his bed. 'There, use it! Are you satisfied? You only want to play computer games, anyway.'

'Do you want to play a game with me instead?' Sam swivelled around on the computer chair to look at him. 'How about Star Wars monopoly?'

Jerome shook his head without bothering to answer.

Sam's eyes narrowed. That was the first sign that his crestfallen expression was on its way. Sure enough, the corners of his mouth drooped next and his eyebrows drew together in a scowl. 'You *never* want to do anything with me *ever! Why* won't you play something? You're only gonna lie on your back doing nothing.'

'Well, I did have something to do before you nagged me off the computer. Wish Mum and Dad would let me use the Loft instead of looking for a boarder.' Jerome would turn twenty years old in another few months and thought it high time he stopped sharing a bedroom with his eleven-year-old brother.

'They want to help you save money. You couldn't afford to pay rent like a boarder *and* save up to join a mission.'

'Thanks, Mr Know-it-all. I already knew that.'

'Then why'd you say it?'

'I didn't expect an answer. I was just letting off steam.'

'Yeah, you're always whinging,' Sam said.

Jerome stared at him. He was too irritated to laugh and too depressed to say, 'Look who's talking.' He scrambled up and pulled on his shoes.

'Where are you going?'

'Out for a jog.'

'Why?'

To fill in time. I want to be doing something meaningful already. I'm tired of being stuck in limbo-land.'

'Whatever.' Sam's shoulders were hunched over the keyboard as he started killing computer aliens.

Jerome had wasted countless hours over the years playing mindless games himself. *How long is it going to be like this? I can't stand much more. I wish something would happen.*

*   *   *

'*She* can't come across,' shot from Karen's mouth as Nicola walked in. 'Mum wouldn't want to see her.'

'That's OK,' Nicola blurted. Karen's hostility made her heart quicken.

'Karen, please listen,' Ruth pleaded. 'Shane's accident was not Nicola's fault.'

'It *was* her fault. I don't understand what he saw in her, anyway. She's so fat and frumpy.' Karen clearly wondered if she'd said too much. Her gaze darted from one face to the next, challenging anybody to rebuke her. When nobody spoke up, she went on, 'What makes her think she'd be such a great catch?'

'I didn't think that!'

'He thought the world of her and I *encouraged* him to. For weeks I've been telling him to just ask her. Now I could rip my tongue out. I hope she never, ever finds anyone to love her! And I hope some day she'll feel the same way she made poor Shane feel.

'Karen, just stop it!' James demanded.

She whirled around to face him. 'I *won't* stop it. My brother is dead and it's her fault. *You* stop it! How dare you tell me to...'

'I'm telling you for your own sake. You're not behaving like yourself. It's hard enough coping with Shane's death. You don't need the extra problem of regretting all the angry things you say.' Although he'd never cried since he was ten years old, James' face was pale and blotched from rubbing it.

'The only thing I regret is being her friend for all these years. I can't believe she had the nerve to think she was too good for my brother.'

'Karen, I *never* thought I was too good for Shane.'

A prickly pause followed, during which Karen pursed her lips and sneered.

'Did you hear her?' James prompted gently at last.

'I'm not talking to her.'

'Karen, that's just making things harder.'

'It'll make things easier for *me*. I'll never talk to her again.'

'How will *that* make things easier? You'll have to speak to her some time. She's my sister.'

'Don't tell me what I have to do!' Her voice was rising to hysteria.

James made a move toward her but his mother intervened, stepping between them and seizing his wrist. 'James, don't you make things harder either. You can't reason with her yet.'

James drew his breath to respond, then shook his head and lowered his forehead into his palm. 'Well, what am I supposed to do?'

Ruth hugged Karen. 'Just keep supporting your wife as best you can.'

'He'll do that easier if I get out of here.' Nicola's voice came out in a whisper.

'Where will you go?' Ruth asked.

Nicola already had her purse and keys but not an answer. 'Just for a drive. Don't worry.'

Karen's voice followed her to the front door. 'Don't you people get it? My mother is my main priority now. And she'd go off the deep end if she had to look at *her.*'

'Yes, we know. Ssssh.' Ruth was soothing Karen and holding her close.

James stepped outside with Nicola and screwed up his eyes in the late afternoon sunlight. He swivelled his shoulders and stretched, groaning as if he'd been wrung out. 'She's been like this for hours. Don't hold what she says against her. It's just the shock. She doesn't mean half of it.'

Although Nicola knew that Karen really had meant everything she said, his words settled like healing dew on her raw heart. James, like her, had regarded Shane with the fondness of a brother. It felt as if they were supporting sorrow between them like a beam. 'That's OK. I know.'

'Nicola, there's one thing I wondered about.' His eyes were streaked red and heavy with the grief he hadn't shed through tears.

'What's that?'

'Why *wouldn't* you go out with Shane?'

He'd dropped his end of the beam and left her bearing the weight. Nicola couldn't manage a better reply than, 'I don't know, James. I guess I think of him almost as much of a brother as you!' Nothing she could say would bring Shane back to them, anyway.

After an aimless drive, she parked on the side of a road adjacent to a city beach. When she closed her eyes the murmur of the sea made her head ache.

This is it! A tragedy. Nicola had always followed her mother's example and prayed to God to keep misfortune from their lives and now He'd let a major catastrophe rock them to the core. She was still breathing because there was no alternative. *It'll get worse, though.* It'd been only a day since Nicola had seen Shane or heard his voice and on one level, his death still felt unreal. She'd lived for far longer than that without seeing him. Her tired mind tried to grasp the idea of never seeing Shane again. With the passing of a week, a month, six months and a year, she was certain the pain would press sharper and harder. Time would rip her wound deeper.

Shane Turnbull had been reliable and steady, like a comfortable piece of furniture. Nicola hadn't realised until she lost him that he occupied such a warm, brotherly spot in her heart. She was fond of the baggy plain trousers that made his sturdy figure strangely shapeless; his shuffling walk; the way his eyes lit up when anybody began to discuss politics or sport. It was all endearing but *not* romantic.

What made him feel that way about me? Karen's words had hit hard but they reinforced the truth that Nicola knew well. She was overweight and too aloof. She'd lived with Laura for a lifetime of seeing how alluring girls were supposed to behave. Their mother had counselled Nicola to study Laura's actions and make her younger sister a role model. Nicola had tried but whenever an opportunity to behave like Laura had come, she almost always crashed and burned. *Why wasn't Shane interested in Laura instead of me?*

The sunset over the horizon had almost reached its zenith of scarlet perfection. Nicola had studied enough sunsets for art lessons to know that this one would quickly fade. It was particularly lovely. Was God celebrating because He had Shane with Him in heaven? More intolerable memories bombarded her senses. They had to come sooner or later, so she braced herself to deal with them.

Shane never got uptight when he lost games. Nicola had always enjoyed him as a team member. He'd praised her mother's cooking whenever he shared a meal at their house. He'd always offered to lend a helping hand and he'd laugh at anybody's jokes. She'd been glad whenever she heard that Shane would be anywhere she might be expected to talk, because his presence would take off the pressure. Nicola would have loved to be able to say 'yes' to Shane. She wished with all her heart that she'd said it anyway.

The sun was fading fast. She watched the nimble feet of two small girls twinkle across the sand. They reminded Nicola of two other little girls who had run along other beaches. They used to call themselves best friends. One had been lean with sandy blonde hair and an orange bikini. The other was plump with two rows of pink lace stitched around the waist of her one-piece bathers. She'd been so proud of the pretty lace, she never realised that it drew attention to her thick waist.

One afternoon while they waded in the shallows, the taller girl said, 'Nicky, what do you think of this idea? When we grow up, I'll marry your brother and you can marry mine.'

'Hey, that'd be great!' The plump little girl liked to please people. The marriage planning game had lasted for weeks. They dragged it out to annoy their brothers. But the tall, slim girl had ended up keeping her side of the old pact.

Fifteen years had swept that memory to some dreamy place. After such a long time, memories and dreams merged together. Nicola wondered if Karen had kept that dream-memory too.

The darkness thickened and more people left the beach. Nicola searched in her tote bag for her mobile phone. She dialled her own number and waited until her mother answered.

'Nicola, where are you?' Ruth was breathing heavily.

'Somewhere near Brighton or Glenelg. How is everyone?'

The moment of silence that followed was heavy with grief. Silence spoke clearer than words over the phone.

'Pam has fallen asleep. I don't know how she'll act when she wakes up. She might fall apart when it comes rushing back. Karen and James have gone home and Laura's gone with them to help look after Karen. I'll be going next door to spend the night with Pam so she won't be alone.'

'Wouldn't Mrs Turnbull sleep in our spare room bed?' Nicola wondered if being away from Shane's familiar surroundings would make his mother's grief ever so slightly easier to bear.

Ruth's silence was different this time; sticky and awkward. 'She'd rather keep away from... other people.'

'You mean she'd rather keep away from *me?*' Nicola would be the only other person in the house who Mrs Turnbull would need to avoid.

'Now, Nicky, just...'

'That's OK. I don't blame her. Mum, maybe I should move out for a while.' She hadn't thought any such thing until that moment. Then she realised that in a corner of her mind, she'd been thinking it ever since she parked by the beach.

'Listen honey, Pam and Karen are both reacting from their emotions. They'll come around.'

'I still think I'll go.' She wasn't as certain as her mother. Pam Turnbull would probably not blame her, at least when she'd had more time to think about it, but Nicola wasn't sure that Karen would ever come around.

'Nicky, I know you care about the Turnbulls but...'

'Mum, it'll be the best thing for them not to see me. They'd be reminded of what happened every single time.' The firmness of her own voice surprised Nicola.

The next pause meant that her mother was grappling with a new idea. 'Where would you go?'

'I don't know. Last week at work Vicki was telling the rest of us that she knows a nice family in the Adelaide Hills who are looking for a single boarder. I could check them out first.' Nicola amazed herself that in the middle of the hugest tragedy of her life, a storehouse in her brain still reminded her of trivia.

'The Hills are so far away! I don't want you to go.'

'It's not all that far. And I'd still come and see you, Mum. Anyway, it might not even be available anymore. I might go somewhere else.'

'But I want to see you now. You've got to come home tonight. I want to talk to you before I go back to Pam's.'

'I know. I'm on my way.' Home was home no longer. The thought of returning to the last spot she'd spoken to Shane made Nicola shudder in the muggy heat of her car.

3

'My kids call it *The Loft*. It's like an attic bedroom and sitting room in one,' said the lady who sat across from Nicola.

Work was over for the day. Nicola's employer, Vicki, had closed shop but invited her friend Casey to come and tell Nicola about the room she was hoping to lease.

Nicola had been taught by her art tutor how to gauge details about people she met. She had practised until it came automatically. The light crow's feet around Casey's eyes and mouth were in positions that showed she smiled a lot. She was probably in her late thirties. Her hair was the colour of honey shining in the sunshine. Even before Nicola started her art lessons, her first instinct, when she met somebody with interesting features, had always been to rush off and sketch a portrait.

'It's a breathtaking room,' Vicki added. 'Take my word for it.'

'I used to be a boarder in that same room about fifteen years ago, so it's had a test run.' Casey Bowman had a way of making everything she said sparkle. Nicola was uncertain if she'd be able to capture that quality on paper but she longed to try.

'Did you end up buying the house?' she asked.

Casey exchanged amused glances with Vicki. 'No, even better. I married the guy who lived there. I was boarding with him.'

'That's a great story.' Nicola began to understand why Casey Bowman was relaxed and cheerful. She was a Laura-type of person. Details slotted into place in their lives like puzzle pieces clicking together. Some people seemed to be born with a propensity to be lucky.

'We'd like a boarder because business can be slow sometimes,' Casey said. 'We figured that since we have the extra space, we might as well try to help somebody else too. Evening meals can be included, if you like. I already cook for a family of five so one more will be easy.'

'Thank you.' Nicola hadn't expected such a generous offer.

'I enjoy cooking and you'll be busy working all day. It'll be a pleasure.'

Casey was easy to like, despite reminding Nicola of Laura. She had a family of five so Nicola figured, 'You must have three children?'

Casey dimpled and nodded. 'Two boys and a girl.'

'They're all lovely kids,' Vicki put in. 'You'll get along well with all of them. Laura is a little doll.'

Nicola turned cold inside. *Laura!* There had to be a Laura in there somewhere. It seemed she could not escape from them.

'You'll have something good for next Wednesday night, Nic,' Vicki said. She explained to Casey, 'Nicola has been coming to my new Gratitude Group.'

Nicola almost groaned. The group! Last Wednesday evening seemed so long ago. She hadn't mentioned Shane's death to anybody at work yet. She didn't think she could without breaking down. She'd probably tell them at the group. But what could anybody possibly say?

'What's a Gratitude Group?' Casey was all interest.

'It's an idea I found in a book. We all concentrate on finding positive things in our daily lives and help each other by offering uplifting thoughts and suggestions.'

'Vicki, you're one of the most innovative people I know. You've just given me something to be grateful for too. A perfect boarder.' Casey stood up and slung her handbag strap over her shoulder. 'Nicola, would you like to come and have a look tomorrow?'

She quickly nodded. 'I was hoping the sooner the better.'

Vicki gave Nicola's arm a squeeze. 'You'll love it. I can already imagine you sitting by Casey's dormer window up there doing your painting.'

'Painting?' Casey's eyes widened. 'Are you an artist?'

Nicola always blushed when anybody asked her that. 'I like to draw and paint.'

'You *are* an artist. Wait 'til I tell my husband. I have a good feeling about this, Nicola. I think this room was meant for you. It's providential.'

Nicola didn't have to force her polite smile. She'd trained herself so well, it did it itself. She decided not to tell Casey and her family about Shane for the time being. Although Nicola agreed that the Bowman's attic room might indeed be providential, she couldn't help feeling guilty for bringing intense sadness into a happy home. Even though they'd never know about it.

*   *   *

'Nicola, Casey tells me you work in a bookshop.'

'That's right.' Nicola's palms were sweating slightly. Casey's sister-in-law was making conversation but Nicola could think of nothing to say to carry it along. People's opening remarks often seemed limiting.

Earlier that evening, Casey had whispered an apology for having other guests to dinner on Nicola's first night with them.

'I never would have planned it this way. It's my husband's sister and her family. Suzanne phoned this morning. She's just come back from a holiday overseas with her husband and little girl and they have lots of photos to show us.'

'I don't mind at all.' It was true. Being surrounded by strangers with their dinner conversation helped distract Nicola's mind from thoughts of Shane. It was Wednesday, so she would have the Gratitude Group later that same evening. Nicola had prepared herself to tell the other group members about her tragedy. Keeping it crushed inside her was getting harder each day.

Vicki and Shirley would probably try to assure her, 'It wasn't your fault that he made a bad decision.' That wouldn't return Shane to his loved ones but might ease some of Nicola's intense guilt about her own part in his death.

'Well, it's good to have a steady job.' Suzanne Adams' smile was wide and gracious.

'It certainly is,' her husband added. He looked past Nicola across the table. 'Jerome, now that you've finished school, what are you doing with yourself?'

Nicola was relieved to have the attention drawn from herself to Casey's oldest son. Casey had introduced her three children to Nicola earlier that afternoon from youngest to oldest: Laura, Sam and Jerome. The girl and youngest boy were talkative and cheerful, just as Nicola had imagined Casey's children would be, but their brother had been a total surprise. Casey had given Nicola no idea of what to expect. But how could Casey have known?

He was much older than his siblings–but that wasn't it. Nicola had shaken his hand with something like shocked recognition. That boy had almost every feature she'd painted for her 'Personal Adonis.' The teacher, Mrs Reynolds, had set the class project last year. Her students each had to paint their own ideas of the perfect Venus and the perfect Adonis. 'It's always great fun to unveil all the completed paintings on the last day of term,' Mrs Reynolds had said. 'There are usually so many differences in people's ultimate opinions of true beauty.' Nicola's class had been no exception. There were laughs and exclamations as everybody gazed at each other's creations.

Nicola's Adonis had been tall and lean with an arched brow, firm jaw and strong cheek bones, like Casey's son. He'd had dark hair, just wavy enough not to be called curly, somewhere between long and short. But the Bowman boy's wide, friendly smile was an improvement on Nicola's Adonis, who merely gazed out of the canvas with the most intelligent expression she could give him, handsome and tight-lipped.

'I've just started working at McDonald's,' Jerome Bowman said, responding to his uncle's question.

'McDonald's? That's a waste of your time and study. What about those Uni offers you had?'

Jerome looked down at his plate. 'I didn't accept any of 'em.'

'Isn't that a bit irresponsible after all that work?'

'Why is it irresponsible?' Jerome sounded polite but vaguely defiant. Nicola admired his nerve. Eric Adams reminded her of some of the more intimidating customers she'd faced in the shop.

'Why do you think? Because so many school leavers would appreciate your opportunity but didn't get an offer.'

'Well, now maybe some of 'em will get one. It'd be even more irresponsible if I accepted one of those offers and kept out somebody else who really wanted to get in, don't you think?' Jerome's white knuckles around his fork displayed his tenseness.

'He can always get in later,' said Casey's husband, Piers. He winked at his son.

'I'm working at McDonald's because I'm saving up for something else, anyway.'

'What might that be?'

Jerome nervously licked his lips. 'I want to go to Asia or East Europe and help a mission.'

Casey and Piers sighed and glanced at each other in a way that made Nicola think they'd heard that story before.

'What sort of mission?'

'This guy I've been reading about called Gareth Edgley started a Christian mission looking after the very poorest people. They feed them and clothe them and give them medicine and books and help them learn to read and look after themselves. I'd like to find one like that.'

'Real Mahatma Gandhi stuff,' Casey added. 'Bare feet, vows of poverty, the whole deal.'

Jerome glanced at his mother askance. 'I think they're allowed to wear shoes.'

'Why on earth would you want to do that, Jerome?' Suzanne looked across at Casey and Nicola with a shake of the head. 'It's always the good looking ones who want to do some outlandish, sacrificial thing. You should stick around instead. There's enough of a shortage of attractive young men as it is. Do the girls a favour.'

Jerome blushed and smiled.

'He'd only be able to do *one* girl a favour anyway, Suze.' Piers Bowman seemed to be enjoying the conversation.

Casey added, 'Unless he decides to be like Eric.' Her comment drew a laugh from the adults.

Suzanne patted Eric's knee and explained to Nicola, 'My dear hubby here used to have quite a reputation as a lady's man.'

'But never all at once,' he added dryly.

'And I don't know if they'd agree that he did them a favour.' It was now clear that Piers *was* enjoying himself.

'Anyway, I've had a great idea,' Suzanne announced. 'Jerome doesn't even need to go to University. There's more to life than swotting over books. We're going to need a new paper-work person soon so I can spend more time at home with Olivia. Why don't you come and work for us, Jerome?'

'Hold on!' Eric objected. 'You can't make an offer like that without consulting me!'

She sucked an impatient breath between pursed lips and drew her pencil thin brows together. 'Well, you're sitting right here.'

'And I say no! We want someone serious and responsible who'd have their heart in the job. He wouldn't do at all.'

'Thanks anyway, Auntie Suze,' Jerome put in quickly.

'*I'll do it!*' nine-year-old Laura shrilled. She had held the floor several times already. Although Casey had rebuked eleven-year-old Sam for interrupting and then for talking with his mouth full, both she and Piers seemed to smile indulgently every time Laura raised her voice and took over. Their double-standards stood out a mile to Nicola, who'd lived for many years with similar behaviour from her own pampered sister.

'You're the best option I've considered so far,' Eric told her, 'but unfortunately I can't wait another ten years until you're old enough.'

'Nicola, are you happy at your bookshop?' Suzanne asked. 'Our photo studio might make a refreshing change.'

Eric shot his wife an exasperated look. 'What did I just tell you? You can't go asking…'

'Alright, alright!'

'Nicola wouldn't be right either.' Eric glanced at the newcomer. 'I'm sorry, I know I've only just met you but I can tell. We need a people-oriented person. You're not right at all.'

'Well, I'm sure she's glad she didn't even ask.' Piers gave Nicola a sympathetic wink and she found herself smiling back. The more he said, the more she felt she was going to like Piers.

'They hired *me* long ago,' Casey told her. 'Suzanne talked Eric into it and he never felt I was quite right either. That's probably why he's being so extra cautious now.'

'But see the good that resulted from it,' Suzanne beamed. 'I got Piers and Casey together.'

'The person I want needs to have a careless, bubbly attitude,' Eric said, getting the conversation back on track.

'But didn't you say before they would need to be serious and responsible?' Nicola asked, putting in her word without thinking.

There was a slight pause followed by a general roar of laughter. Even Suzanne and Eric's four-year-old Olivia laughed until her brown curls bounced, though she didn't understand the joke.

Jerome's smile lightened the table. 'That's Uncle Eric for you. The person he wants has to be serious *and* bubbly.'

Eric held up his hand for silence. 'OK, you've all had a laugh at my expense. Let's just say the person I want would have to be someone like Suzanne.'

Piers spluttered around his dessert spoon even more. 'It'll be *impossible* to find anyone, then.'

Nicola looked at Piers' immaculate, vivacious sister and didn't doubt it. Suzanne Adams was the sort of person Nicola despaired of ever capturing adequately on canvas. The dark, flowing hair might be easy enough, the flash in her dark eyes would be slightly harder but her sweet cloud of perfume would have to be left to the imagination.

After dinner, Nicola dried dishes for Casey while Suzanne sat on a kitchen chair and talked.

'Is Jerome serious about going off and being a missionary?'

'Completely serious. But he needs to raise enough money to get anywhere so I don't know if the idea will burn itself out before he manages.'

'Doesn't he remind you of somebody?' Suzanne asked, with an arch of her eyebrows.

'Who were you thinking of?'

Suzanne glanced toward the door before she murmured, 'Anna, of course.'

Casey kept washing cutlery. 'I hadn't really thought about it.'

'Come on, you're joking! It hadn't occurred to you at all?'

'Maybe briefly,' Casey admitted. 'Piers mentioned it out of the blue a few days ago and I told him he was being paranoid.'

'Well, *I* think he was being wise. You and Piers need to keep your eyes on Jerome because he has that same blood coursing through his veins. Don't let him go the same way Anna did.'

Nicola found it difficult to tie the threads of the strangers' conversation together. Apart from not knowing who Anna was, she couldn't help wondering, *What's wrong with being a missionary?*

'There's not much influence we can have on him, at his age,' Casey said, 'except to tell him how we feel about things. I don't think we need to worry. He cares about the plight of the world, that's all.'

'Anna cared too!' Suzanne pronounced darkly. 'There was nothing wrong with any of *her* ideas to help, either! But look where they got her.'

Casey laughed but it sounded less mirthful than any other laugh Nicola had heard from her. 'Come on, Suzanne! You're worse than Piers! Jerome has a warm, caring heart. It's his personality.'

Her sister-in-law idly began nibbling chocolates from a bowl on the table. 'I'm not saying all this to upset you. You never met her so you don't see what I see. Every time I set eyes on Jerome after a long time, I get a shock because he reminds me more and more of her.'

'Anna died nineteen years ago. You hardly even knew her. Surely you don't remember her all that clearly.'

'I probably *wouldn't* remember her if Jerome didn't remind me of her. It's not his looks, Casey. It's that streak of fanaticism. It's obviously in his blood.'

Who was Anna, I wonder? Nicola was gripped by sadness at this hint of a family tragedy. Her nerves were so raw from own heartache, tears were always near the surface.

Casey was up to the large pans. She rolled her sleeves up higher and began scrubbing the bottom of a heavy frying pan with steel wool. 'If that's the case, then there's not much we can do about it.' She looked up and said, 'Nicola, there's no need to bother waiting around for this one. Thanks for your help.'

Nicola hung up her damp tea towel and went upstairs to get ready for the Gratitude Group. She re-applied her lipstick, ran a brush through her hair and dug a cardigan from the bottom of her suitcase. Then she settled onto the cosy padded window seat and searched through her handbag for her mobile phone. She would have just enough time to phone her mother to let her know how she'd settled in, as she'd promised.

But Nicola hesitated with a pounding heart before she began dialling. Pam Turnbull was still staying with her mother and it was quite likely that James and Karen might be there for dinner too. Karen might answer the phone, as she sometimes did. Nicola's own stomach responded to the thought with a lurch.

She knew that she was being cowardly but she prayed, *Please let it be Mum, or even Laura.*

4

Jerome was setting out for a moonlit jog. On his way through the passage, something made him stop short. It was a figure standing in the evening shadows with her ear pressed against the lounge room door. The person was too tall and broad across the back to be his mother. Casey was in the lounge room with their visitors, anyway. He could hear her laughing. This was their new boarder and she appeared to be listening in.

Jerome hardly knew whether he ought to be shocked or amused. Who would even want to eavesdrop on the dull conversation? His uncle Eric only ever wanted to talk about himself. He wondered whether it would be easiest to creep past her to the front door or retreat to the kitchen.

She suddenly wheeled around and he glimpsed deep anguish on her face before she saw him and it changed to startled horror.

Jerome spoke up before she could say a word. 'Hi. Are you OK?'

'Yeah, you made me jump.' She raised a hand to her chest. 'I was on my way out to a meeting and found your uncle's car parked right behind mine. I'm about to ask him to shift it. I'm just waiting for a gap in the conversation.'

'Sorry for scaring you.' He was relieved that their boarder wasn't a crazed prowler after all. 'It's impossible to find a gap once he gets going. I'll help, if you like.'

Jerome tapped on the door and poked in his head. 'Hey, excuse me,

Uncle Eric.'

'Will you give me a few moments? I'm in the middle of telling a story to your parents.' Eric's irritation was evident in his voice. Jerome saw their boarder wince beside him. He had a sudden idea.

'It's nothing. I just wondered if I can shift one of your belongings.'

'Yeah, shift whatever you like,' Eric said testily.

Jerome clicked the door shut and turned with a grin. 'Did you hear him? I have his permission to move it. I know his keys are in his coat pocket hanging over there.'

She followed him to the coat hooks by the front door. 'Maybe you shouldn't. I'm sure that wasn't what he meant.'

Jerome already had Eric's key ring. 'Don't worry. I won't move it far.' They stepped out onto the moonlit porch. 'I'll shift it behind Dad's so you can get out.'

A smile flickered around her lips. 'Thank you.'

Jerome opened the door of Eric's Porsche, relishing his perfect timing. The seat was plush and luxurious and the leg room was stunning. It was not a bad opportunity for somebody still on his learner's permit. Every couple of inches counted. The key turned like quicksilver and the car handled like magic. Jerome was too nervous to loiter in there for long. He reluctantly scrambled out of the car.

'What sort of meeting is it?'

She hesitated. 'I don't think you'd find it very interesting. It's a Gratitude Group. We all share something to be grateful for each week.'

'Cool. I've just given you something, haven't I?'

For a moment her face appeared blank, then her lips twitched into a smile. 'Yeah, I should use that one. But I hope you won't get in trouble.'

He ran his hand over Eric's gleaming red bonnet. 'It'd be worth it if I did. But I'll shift it back again and he probably won't even know. And it's not your fault if I choose to do something silly.' He was startled by the abrupt change in Nicola's expression. His last sentence seemed to have a strange effect on her. Her smile vanished and the pale, drawn frown had returned. 'Hey, what's up?'

'Nothing. Thanks for your help.' She slid behind the wheel of her own Toyota Corolla and slowly backed out until she had enough room to turn. Jerome stared down the driveway after her car. When the beam from her back lights had gone, he climbed back into the Porsche. But something was on his mind that hadn't been there at the start. It was the grief he'd seen on her face in that split second before she'd noticed him in the passage.

That can't *have been just because she was too nervous to ask Uncle Eric to shift his car.*

*   *   *

Nicola walked in to find a new member of the Gratitude Group. Shirley Henderson's teenage daughter, Bianca, sat glowering down at her own feet while Vicki did her best to welcome her.

'We're delighted to have you along, Bianca. I'm going to make it my gratitude point for tonight. It's far better than what I came with.'

Bianca Henderson rolled her eyes. 'Yeah, well, Mum's been trying to twist my arm for weeks. But I warned her it'd better not be a bunch of hopeless saddoes sitting around telling hard-luck stories all night while everyone else tries to cheer 'em up.'

The other five group members roared with laughter.

Ron Giles, the only male member, said, 'We'll refrain from the hard-luck stories tonight, just for you, Bianca.'

'We always have a very enjoyable night,' Vicki said. 'I'm sure you'll be impressed. And tonight we'll start with…' Her eyes scanned the faces. 'How about you, Nic? You always brighten us up. I don't feel like gloom and doom either.'

Nicola flushed as all eyes turned to her. She had to come up with something quickly.

'I was nearly late getting here. The family I'm boarding with have a rich, scary relative who parked his Porsche right behind my car. But just as I was trying to muster my courage to ask him to shift it, the oldest son of the family came out and shifted it for me.'

Nicola saw Bianca Henderson watching her without a smile. Bianca's left eyebrow was cocked and her nose ever so slightly wrinkled in the disdainful look some teenagers managed to perfect so well. Nicola looked back at her, unfazed, because she'd seen that same expression so many times on other faces. *Does she think she's original or what?* Nicola would easily be able to sketch Bianca's face off pat but she wouldn't want to bother.

She would have to keep her grief about Shane to herself.

*   *   *

When Eric, Suzanne and Olivia left, Casey went to soak in the bathtub. While Piers tidied dirty dishes, Jerome returned from his jog.

'I take it you haven't managed to find Gareth Edgley's book yet?' Piers knew what his son's glum expression meant.

Jerome lay flat on his back on the couch and grunted.

'Has it occurred to you that if it's this hard to find him, maybe he doesn't want to be found?'

'That's what I reckon,' Sam cried gleefully.

'Of course he'd want people to read his second book,' Jerome retorted. 'Why else would he have written it?'

'Well, at least you can say that you couldn't have tried any harder.'

'I'm not giving up yet. Coming across his *first* book in that Op Shop was a miracle. I know God would want me to find the second. There *must* be some way of getting hold of it.'

'Well if that's true, you'll find it. I'm not saying to stop searching. I just hate to see you making yourself totally miserable about it in the meanwhile. Maybe he's passed away. He'd have to be pretty old. Why is it so urgent to find this out-of-print book, anyway?'

'Dad, haven't you been listening to a thing I've been talking about for the last two weeks? It's meant to tie up a lot of loose ends that I found at the end of the first book. It's all about how he fulfils his dream and sets up his mission team in Europe. I'll die if I can't get hold of it.'

Sam and Laura both burst out laughing and their brother glared at them.

'It's just a book!' Laura chortled.

Jerome aimed a sofa cushion at her face and threw it hard. 'It's not just any old book. It's his whole mind-set.' He'd read the description on the back fly leaf of Gareth Edgley's book often enough to quote it verbatim. *'Putting Gareth Edgley's priceless advice to the test will enable any reader to make a significant difference in the world. To be able to declare that you've made somebody else's life even marginally easier and happier is to have succeeded in what counts the most.'*

Sam and Laura seemed to be in stitches again and Piers couldn't help smiling too.

'Well, keep looking, but you don't need that book to be able to do all that. You can start right now.'

'How do you mean?' Jerome's voice was full of cool suspicion.

'You can start by making the people around you happier. Like playing games with Sam and Laura.'

Jerome was up off his seat and striding to the kitchen. 'I knew you'd say something pathetic like that.'

'What's so bad about playing with us?' Sam shouted after him.

Jerome poked his head back in to the lounge room. 'If you must know, it's always a cinch to win and that makes it dead boring.' He glared at his father. 'And Dad, you aren't half predictable!'

Piers ruffled Sam's tawny hair and muttered, 'So are you,' loud enough for Jerome to hear.

Sam's eyes were bright as his mind ticked over with an idea. 'It's still too early for bed. Dad, will *you* play something with us?'

Piers pretended to think it over, then leaned back for a deck of cards. 'I suppose I could. I always feel like winding down whenever Eric and Suzanne have been. How about Hearts then?' To his children's delight, he began dealing.

Jerome strode out of the kitchen sipping a hot drink. 'I might as well play too, to prove that I'm *not* predictable.'

Piers just grinned and gestured to a pile of cards across the table. 'That's your hand. I've dealt you in already.'

Jerome stared at him. For a split second his old smile flashed. Piers hadn't seen it since Gareth Edgley's book had come into the household and changed Jerome's life. For something Jerome claimed to be so wonderful, it had certainly brought its share of misery to everyone, especially Jerome himself. It had been easier in the days when Jerome spent most of his time studying his Bible rather than reading about strange missionaries.

Only once had Piers voiced his concerns. 'Anna was driven and single-minded, just like that,' he commented quietly to Casey. Piers knew he shouldn't have spoken. Now Casey was nervous about Jerome too, although she said she wasn't.

'When is our new boarder getting home?' Laura asked.

Piers shrugged. 'I don't know but she has a key.'

'She's a bit fat, isn't she?'

'She isn't fat at all,' Jerome snapped. 'Why do you like to criticise people?'

Laura put on her injured expression. '*You're* criticising *me!* I was only gonna say I wouldn't mind being fat if I could be as pretty as her.'

'You *are* pretty,' Piers responded.

Jerome shook his head with a sigh. 'Dad, why do you have to butter her up whenever she asks for it? I wish someone in this family would say or do something *un*predictable for a change.'

'That comment of yours was just as predictable as anything we said,' Piers told him.

Jerome looked thoughtful. 'Yeah, I suppose it was.'

5

Jerome heard the sound of rough sobbing first. He stopped wiping the cooking surface and glanced through the open pay window. Another team member, Michael Quinlan, was sitting in his old Holden with his face in his hands, while his shoulders shuddered.

'His shift finished hours ago. Wonder what's up.' It chilled Jerome to see a fellow his own age crying like his sister, Laura.

Ryan Fielke kept cleaning the soft serve machine. 'Don't pay any attention. It's always something with him.'

'But he's pretty upset.' The hollow coldness was eating through Jerome.

'You're still too new to have woken up to him. Mike's a drain. He'll take any sympathy people offer but he never tries to clean up his act. According to him, nothing's ever his fault. He just keeps coming up with new dramas.'

'What if this is something really bad?' Jerome couldn't bring himself to believe a grown man would howl over a trifle.

'Hey, J, take my advice and don't buy into it.' The team workers at McDonalds were each given nicknames by their supervisor and Jerome's had been shortened to his first letter on his very first day. 'Trying to help Mike Quinlan is like stepping onto a treadmill. Rick's been on the verge of sacking him except that Mike works that twisted sympathy thing on him, too. Pretend not to notice. Just get on your bike and ride home. You don't need his problems dumped on you.'

On his way out to get his bike, Jerome couldn't help glancing back at the lone car. Michael was still crying. Jerome hesitated with his hands on his handle bars. Approaching the guy would be awkward but taking Ryan's advice didn't sit well with him. Jerome believed that too many people were reluctant to get involved with others' problems. As far as he saw it, he didn't really have a choice.

He moved over to stand by Michael's half open window. 'Hey.'

The young man almost jumped out of his skin. 'What the hell…?'

'Sorry, man. Are you OK?'

Michael hunched his shoulders and sniffed. 'What does it look like?'

'Yeah, I know, dumb question. There's probably nothing I can do but…'

'It's all Ryan an' Jack's fault, really. This mess started when I went to the pub for a game o' cards with them after work last Monday.'

Jerome looked uneasily back over his shoulder to the kitchen, where he knew Ryan was still finishing off the tidying-up before leaving. Theirs was still one of the outlets that didn't stay open around the clock.

'There was this great, mean thug called Boris. Dunno if that was his real name but that's what he called himself. He won money off all of us. A hundred dollars from me. Must've been cheating, I reckon, 'cause Jack an' me are pretty sharp. Hey, you might've even noticed him coming into Macca's. Big fat guy with dreadlocks and tattoos. Every day he's been finding me and telling me if I don't pay him, he'll hurt me real bad.' Michael wrapped his own fingers around his throat and pulled a lugubrious face. 'Anyway, I promised I'd pay him when I got paid but that wasn't good enough for him. He started saying it had to be by this Wednesday. And there was no *way* I'd have it by then.'

'Well, tonight's Friday and you seem to be in OK shape.'

Michael ran a shaky hand through his fair hair. 'I borrowed the money from my brother's wife.' He began plucking fluff from his steering wheel cover. 'I live with 'em, you see. Anyway, I promised Claire I'd pay her back by tonight and asked her not to tell Blake. He's my brother.' Michael rolled a fluff ball between his hands. 'And I *would've* been able to do it, if Boris hadn't completely stuffed me up.' He pressed his eyes into the balls of his hands and moaned.

Jerome shuffled on his feet. It had taken only a few words from his side to get himself involved. 'What happened?'

Michael made a watery sounding slurp through his nose. 'When I paid Boris the hundred bucks, he swore I owed him *two* hundred!' His hazel eyes bulged at Jerome. 'He's a filthy liar! But his mates were standing there backing him up. I'd *never* gamble that much away! I'm not *stupid!* So he took my last hundred bucks and now I'm bankrupt 'til next pay. But Claire will be expecting me to come home with the money!' To Jerome's dismay, those eyes pooled up and overflowed.

'Now she'll tell Blake an' they'll both be on my back thinking *I'm* a useless liar when it wasn't even my fault. And I can't face 'em. They *always* go on at me!'

Jerome felt it was time to put an end to the misery. 'Look, I'll lend you a hundred bucks until next week.'

For an instant, Michael's restless fingers and wheezy breathing stopped. '*Would* you?'

'Yeah, that'll be OK. Do you want to come across to the easy teller with me to get it?'

'You bet!' He scrambled out and kicked the door shut behind him. Michael stumbled over the curb and seized Jerome's arm to regain his balance. 'I won't be putting *you* out of pocket, will I?'

'Naw, I'll be alright. I've been saving.' Jerome hoped Ryan and the others would not hear about it. He would just be careful to lend him no more until he was paid back.

'Saving?' Michael's voice rang with incredulity. 'How do you save on our lousy salary?' His lanky body seemed to be zigzagging across the footpath.

Jerome shrugged. 'I don't have a car to run. And I live at home with my folks.'

'I used to live with my folks, but Mum died a few years ago and Dad's a useless no-hoper.'

When they made it to the teller, Michael almost ploughed into the wall. And when Jerome handed him the crisp note, he fumbled for his wallet and seemed to have trouble finding the note compartment. He finally crumpled it in with his coins and Jerome had an uneasy feeling that he might not be doing Michael a favour after all.

'Have you had a few drinks tonight?'

'Just a few. I went to see if I could talk Boris around. I couldn't.'

'Well, you're probably not in much shape to drive home.' There were others on the road to think about apart from Michael himself.

'I do feel a bit dizzy.'

The lights of McDonald's were out. Ryan had gone home.

'Guess I could drive you. Where do you live?'

Michael muttered a suburb that was not too far from Jerome's.

'Well, hop in the passenger's side.' As Jerome slid behind Michael's wheel, he mumbled, 'I shouldn't really be doing this without my "L" plates.'

Michael gaped at him. 'You mean you don't even have your licence?'

'Not yet.'

'Why not?'

'I was concentrating on my studies.'

Michael shook his shaggy head with a snort.

'Hey, don't complain. I'm good enough and I'll have it soon. I still think that out of the two of us, I'm the safest option to drive.'

Michael slumped over and pressed one cheek against the window pane. 'At least you got a responsible adult driver sitting with you.' He laughed until he drooled on the glass.

'Yeah, sure.'

They'd travelled for some time before Jerome spotted the worst possible sight. He clutched the steering wheel and muttered an exclamation as the policeman waved him over to the side of the road. Michael didn't seem to realise what was going on.

'Hey, what's up?'

'Breathalyzer!' Jerome hissed.

Michael closed his eyes and chuckled. 'You beauty! Sometimes I think my brother must be right and there *is* a God. If *I'd* been driving, I'd be history.'

Jerome sat waiting his turn. 'Yeah, that's great for you, but what about me?'

'You haven't been drinking. Have you?'

'Course not, but what if he asks for my licence? I haven't *got* one!'

'Oh, yeah.' Michael's head drooped.

'G'day, mate.' The policeman sounded cordial enough. 'I'd like you to blow a steady breath right into this tube here when I tell you.'

Jerome followed the instructions with a sinking heart. He wished Michael Quinlan wouldn't sit hunched over beside him with bated breath, guilt oozing from every pore. The policeman glanced at Jerome's result.

'No worries. Thanks, mate. Have a good night.'

They were off again. Michael scrambled up, beaming. 'That was a close shave. We're nearly home anyway so it would've been the most rotten luck if I'd been caught.'

'You're welcome.' Jerome couldn't help grinning back. 'I probably saved you the hundred bucks you borrowed and more.' His pulse was still racing.

Michael's house seemed to be the only one on the street with an inside light still on. As the boys stepped out of the car, the screen door flew open and a young woman stepped outside. Jerome noticed that she was pregnant, and she smiled when she saw that Michael was not alone.

'Hello. I'm Claire, Michael's sister-in-law.'

'Hi, I'm Jerome Bowman. We work together.' He felt shy, as he always did around girls. At least the long, thick plait that hung over her shoulder made it easier not to focus on her huge belly. It was so disproportionate to the rest of her. Claire wore some sort of white maternity smock that made her appear like an angel.

'Are you an' Blake still up waiting for me?' Michael sounded indignant.

'No, Ethan woke up and Blake's just settling him down again.' Claire's voice was hushed and soothing. 'But we *did* expect you home hours ago. You haven't been drinking, have you?'

Michael was digging around in his wallet. 'No.'

Claire looked at Jerome and whispered, 'Has he?'

Jerome hardly knew what to reply. He knew his hesitation spoke volumes.

'What does it matter, anyway?' Michael grumbled. 'I'm nineteen years old. I can look after myself. Here!' He handed her the cash.

Claire stared at it. 'Is this the money you owe me?'

'What did you think it was?'

'I didn't expect you'd really have it tonight,' she admitted.

'That's pretty obvious! I *promised* I'd pay you back and you still didn't believe me!' Michael looked at Jerome and rolled his eyes. 'See, I told you they never trust me.' He lurched into the house. If Jerome had been alone, he might have laughed. Michael Quinlan was unbelievable.

'Did you drive him home?' Claire asked quietly.

'Yeah, it was no problem.' She reminded him of somebody else, with her serene features and gentle manner, but he couldn't work out who it was.

'But how will *you* get home? If you don't mind waiting, my husband could...'

'No thanks.' Jerome felt he'd got in deep enough. 'I don't live far from here.'

Claire's forehead furrowed. She didn't seem entirely convinced. 'Well, if you're sure... Michael probably didn't even thank you but I appreciate your kindness. He can be a bigger handful than our one-year-old son.' Claire looked down at her own belly. 'In a few months, we'll have *three* children, counting Michael. Anyway, it was nice to meet you, Jerome.'

Only when he started walking did he realise that getting home might be more of a problem than he thought. There would probably be no buses running so late, and home was still a good ten kilometres away.

'At least it's not a bad night for a walk,' Jerome told himself. His family would not even be home. They would be staying overnight at his grandparent's home in Victor Harbor. He'd stupidly left his keys behind at McDonald's where they'd be locked in. Jerome would have to force his own way into the house, but that should pose no problem. Gareth Edgley had faced far more annoying inconveniences.

*   *   *

Home alone at 1.30a.m., sleepless Nicola was torn between grief and fear. Since Shane's funeral, her temples had barely stopped pounding with the effort of trying to hold herself together. Especially when Karen and her mother glared at her through the memorial service, making it clear that they wished she hadn't come. Now, anguish for Shane welled up as it did every night. Her mental image of his gasping, exhausted face struggling to stay alive haunted her. *Oh Shane, did the waves come up and wash you out again? Or did you totally lose your bearing in the darkness after a few drinks and not know where the shore was?* She usually wept quietly into her pillow hoping nobody would notice her swollen, red eyes in the morning. Tonight that would not be an issue. Casey Bowman had told her, 'My parents in Victor Harbor are having an anniversary dinner that will go 'til late, so Piers and the kids and I will stay there for the night.'

Having the house to herself frayed Nicola's nerves. The Bowmans lived in such an isolated spot that only the faintest hum from faraway traffic could be heard. The whisper of pine needles outside dominated all other sounds but did not mask them. She raised her ear from her pillow to listen to faint creaks and bumps from the empty house downstairs.

'It's just the normal sounds old houses make.' Telling herself this did not stop her hair prickling whenever she imagined she heard one. Nicola decided to tiptoe down to turn on the TV and kitchen light. She would lie on the couch and doze off as soon as she managed to lose her jitters.

Once downstairs, she pressed her back against the kitchen door and flicked on the light. Nothing was amiss out there. Casey's cheerful china pottery was piled on the old dresser and the room smelled like cinnamon, cloves and the Wednesday night roast.

'I *was* being over-sensitive,' Nicola mumbled to herself.

A different sound startled her. Nicola's throat constricted so she couldn't draw a breath. Something was rattling one of the lounge room window screens. She had no idea if it was a person or an animal but her overwrought mind screamed, *You've got to do something!*

The house was too far from others for anybody to hear her call for help but she whispered, 'God help me, please!' It was the first prayer for help she'd uttered since Shane's death. But Shane must have surely pleaded the same prayer as he struggled and drowned. God hadn't helped *him!* Nicola snapped her mind shut. She couldn't think about Shane now.

Her hand rummaged in the top kitchen drawer and found a rolling pin. Clutching it in trembling hands, Nicola tiptoed closer to the lounge room to see whatever was making the noise. Her forehead broke out in beads of perspiration when she discerned a wiry masculine outline behind the curtains. He had the screen off. Two fingers moved into the small gap between the window and its frame. He easily glided the sliding window pane wider and eased one leg through the window.

The kitchen door was bolted shut. Nicola knew she'd never manage to open it before he climbed all the way in. There was only one other option. If she waited until the intruder was inside with her, she would not stand a chance. Nicola took the last few steps and swung the rolling pin at his head. She heard him gasp. His hand flew up and caught hold of it just as it grazed his temple. At the same time, she let out a scream from the bottom of her lungs.

He was shouting too but she could barely hear what he said over her own scream. Without letting go his end of the rolling pin, the intruder managed to clutch hold of her wrist with his other hand so she could no longer swing her end. His strong grip burned her. He was still yelling and she discerned a 'Stop!' in whatever he said. She had to concentrate on not letting the rolling pin slide from her own slippery grip.

'GET OUT!' She was putting words to her own screams. Then Nicola needed to draw a fresh breath.

'It's me! Jerome Bowman!'

She turned limp. His features came into focus as she blinked at him, straddling the window ledge and still clutching her wrist with his eyes fixed on the rolling pin. His chest was heaving. Then her terror was washed away by something even worse. It was heavy and sticky, filling her stomach and her brain, keeping her rooted to the carpet. It tasted something like shame but far more bitter. Even though it would be agony to speak, she knew it would be far worse not to. The thickness made its way into her hoarse voice.

'I thought you were an intruder.'

6

He released her wrist. 'Well, I was sort of hoping you didn't know it was me.'

Nicola felt a laugh trying to force its way through the murky thick guilt but it didn't quite make it. Her lips managed a twisted smile, probably more of a grimace. Nicola doubted she would ever laugh again. And she still had lots of explaining to do.

'Casey said you kids would be with her in Victor Harbor!' Her statement sounded more like an excuse than an explanation.

'She didn't mean me.' He finished scrambling through the window. 'I'm a bit older than the other two, in case you hadn't noticed.'

Nicola took his remark as a reproof and her eyes prickled. 'I *had* noticed. I didn't mean you're a *kid*. I meant you're one of Casey's kids.'

'OK, I'll let you off, then.'

She looked up quickly to find him grinning at her. Although he'd managed to ward off the full force of her blow, a purple-black welt shaped like the end of a rolling pin was swelling on his eye socket. Nicola groaned.

'I really hurt you, didn't I? Come into the kitchen and get some ice. I'll make you some coffee too.'

'No thanks. I don't like coffee much.'

'OK.' She hoped he didn't sense her dejection.

'I'll have hot chocolate instead. *You* could probably do with a hot drink, too. I'll make 'em.'

'No, you grab the ice pack. Sit down.' She gushed water into the kettle knowing that fixing him a drink would not come close to making amends.

He sat quietly at the table, watching her. 'I'm really sorry I scared you.'

'It wasn't *your* fault!' She gasped, realising the implication of what she'd said. 'It wasn't your mother's fault, either. I'm just... dense.'

He flashed her one of his disconcerting, slightly lopsided smiles. 'You're really worried about putting your foot in it, aren't you?'

'I just feel so terrible.'

'Well, I can tell you, if anyone was to blame it definitely wasn't *you*. Even if you'd expected me home, I'm not usually as late as...' He paused, squinting up at the kitchen clock. '*Two o'clock!* Oh man, I suppose I should've said *early.*'

She watched his long fingers press the ice pack against his cheek bone. 'And I imagine you usually choose to come in through the door,' she added, placing the hot cup before him.

He laughed as if she'd made a joke. Her heavy, sick feeling began to lift. At least *somebody* found the situation funny.

'That's right.' He took a sip of hot chocolate. 'I left my keys behind.'

*   *   *

It turned out to be a bizarre evening from start to finish. Instead of going to bed, as he'd expected, Jerome found himself sitting at the kitchen table telling their new boarder about Michael Quinlan, trying to make the story entertaining so she would relax. When he told the part about the breath test, she let out a chuckle and he felt a flash of elation. It reminded him of the rush of delight he always used to feel before winning games against his family had grown all too easy.

As long as her clear, green eyes were fixed on him he wanted to keep talking, but the story ran out long before his enthusiasm.

'You were lucky,' Nicola breathed.

'Yeah, until I got home. But maybe you're right, I'm lucky you chose the rolling pin and not the carving knife.'

Instead of laughing again, she made a sound more like a sob. He wanted to kick himself. 'Hey, chill out. I was only joking.'

She buried her face in her hands and turned her shoulder to him.

'You're not crying, are you? Come on, Nicola, if this is all because you feel sorry for me, crying is the last thing that'll cheer me up. I've had my fill of people crying tonight.'

She peeped through her fingers and let out a spontaneous laugh.

'Yeah, that's more like it! I reckon it was far worse for you than it was for me, anyway. It was pretty brave of you to take on an intruder like that.'

'But I wouldn't have been much good, would I?' A smile lurked around the corners of her lips.

All at once, he realised who Michael's sister-in-law had reminded him of. In many ways, the two young women were not at all alike. Nicola's shoulder length hair was a shade darker than Claire's. And she was larger framed and generally curvier. Jerome shifted the ice pack to hide his red face. The similarity had more to do with the way they behaved. Nicola's gentle manner appealed to him more than the loud behaviour of the showy girls he'd known at school. 'Is *that* what's bothering you?' he asked. 'I thought you were sorry for me but maybe you would've felt better if you'd knocked me out cold. Don't worry, you could always take a few self-defence lessons.'

* * *

Nicola remained at the table after Jerome had gone to his bedroom. Her tired muscles quivered but her mind still spun too fast to lie her body down.

For once, images of Shane's drowning face were not at the forefront of her mind. Pondering what Piers and Casey might say when they saw how she'd battered their son made her cringe. And thoughts of Jerome himself made her flush. She had no business to be thinking about him, anyway. He was still a teenager. His mother had told her that he was nineteen.

His bedroom door creaked open and she heard him come back

down the passage. From her seat at the table, she could see him in the bathroom, leaning over the basin as he cleaned his teeth. He'd changed into an old t-shirt and faded track pants.

Nicola had spent hours of work inventing her Personal Adonis but her creativity had ended with his striking pose on canvas. Watching Jerome's back showed her how her Adonis' shoulder blades would glide fluidly beneath his shirt. It was OK to observe him for the sake of art. The sinews in his forearms were a symphony of movement. She watched him stoop to rinse his mouth and carelessly run his thumb through the bristles of his toothbrush to air-dry it. As he gingerly touched his swollen cheek bone, renewed guilt stirred inside her. He stepped out and saw her there. Jerome raised his hand in a 'good night' salute.

'Don't worry about any more burglars. There's a man in the house, now.'

Nicola laughed louder than his jest deserved, partly because she felt she hadn't laughed enough before and partly to cover her embarrassment at being caught watching him. She had no idea when she went upstairs that she left him crestfallen, wishing she hadn't laughed *quite* so hard.

It wasn't that funny, was it? he thought.

*　*　*

Telling Piers and Casey went smoother than Nicola had let herself hope for.

'Nicola, I'm so terribly sorry.' Poor Casey was flustered with dismay. 'I thought you knew Jerome wouldn't be with us. He always works late on Fridays. When I said the kids would be with us, I assumed you knew I meant just the younger two.' Casey smiled sheepishly. 'I sound as if I'm making excuses, but I'm not. The whole mix-up was entirely my fault.'

'That's OK. You weren't to know he'd come in through the window.'

'Wow, you got him good.' Sam's eyes were fixed on his brother's purplish bruise. 'Wish I'd been home to see it. But nothing good ever happens when I'm around.'

Casey whirled to look at him. 'Sam, do you call this good?'

'Well, I suppose it's good that it didn't happen to him,' Piers said.

'It's completely my fault for not making myself clear,' Casey reiterated, 'and I'm sorry.'

'That's OK,' Nicola graciously repeated.

'Hey, Mum, if you want to keep apologising, why don't you apologise to me? I got the worst end of the rolling pin.' Jerome winked at Nicola to show her he wasn't serious. The gesture made him look more like his father. Jerome's resemblance to Piers overshadowed any of Casey's features he might have possessed.

'*You?*' Casey cried. 'I don't think I need to worry. I'm sure you probably got enough attention and sympathy from poor Nicola to last you all week.'

Sam and Laura burst out laughing and Nicola couldn't help smiling. Their mirth was contagious but she turned to the sink to hide her flaming face.

The others trailed out of the kitchen while she washed her tea cup. Piers went to his shed and Casey to water her pot plants. Sam and Laura kicked a football on the grass. Nicola wasn't sure where Jerome had gone, but when the phone rang, there was nobody within earshot to answer it but her. She cleared her throat and picked up the receiver, slightly nervous at the thought of speaking to a stranger.

'Hello, Nicola speaking.'

7

'*I* could've baby-sat.' Angry tears were ten times harder to hold back than sad tears but Michael made the effort. He did not wish to appear totally stupid in front of Claire's parents.

Claire's father sank onto the softest armchair with a grunt. 'For Pete's sake! You should've worked all this out before we came. We're here now and we're going to stay.'

Only ten minutes ago, Michael had been enjoying a game of football on TV. Now he wanted to tear four people to shreds. It was the same blinding rage he used to fight off with drugs. He dreaded the familiar sour taste of aggression because he still hadn't worked out anything new to smother it.

How he hated Mr Parker's pompous handle-bar moustache. It pointed down, straight and stiff, on either side of his mouth, making it appear as if he was always looking at Michael down his nose. He hated Blake and Claire for not warning him that her parents were coming. He detested the simpering, apologetic smile Blake gave his father-in-law and the flash of fear in Claire's blue eyes. *How dumb can they be?* Claire's mother cradled Ethan in her arms, mumbling soothing sounds as if she was protecting him from Michael's anger. Michael wanted to spit. They were all so dense, it didn't occur to any of them that Ethan was the only person in the world Michael would never, ever hurt.

'I could've looked after Ethan! I was going to be home all night. You didn't need to ask *them!*' Michael strode outside, barely aware of leaving until he heard the screen door slam behind him. He flung himself against the stone wall and stars spun in his head. They matched the sparks of light already flashing behind his eyelids.

Then Blake was there, touching his shoulder. 'Will you calm down?'

'No, I *won't* calm down!' Tears and words flowed out in a torrent. 'Why won't you ever let *me* look after Ethan? He loves me more than *them*. You think I'm a little kid but I'm nineteen! I'm an adult.'

'Well act like one then, and pipe down.' Blake peered back over his shoulder and whispered. 'You know I've always been on shaky ground with Claire's father. It's only since Ethan was born that he'll even talk to me. So why did you have to do your block the moment he walked in?'

Michael was exasperated. Blake just didn't seem to be getting the point. 'You didn't *have* to call them! That's why. *I* would've looked after Ethan fine.' He knew his own voice wouldn't go softer so he didn't even try. During his moments of rage, Michael felt like a radio with a faulty volume knob. He didn't care if the Parkers overheard. Let them hear. It wasn't his problem.

Blake hissed, 'Don't you think we'd let you if only we could…'

'If only you could *trust* me! Go on, say it! You think I'm a cretin.'

Blake rolled his eyes. 'Michael, why do you force me to say things you don't want to hear? Ethan's very small. He takes a lot of care. You haven't been out of rehab for all that long and you're still taking one day at a time, trying to look after *yourself*.'

Michael raised his voice even louder to compensate for Blake's mumbling. 'But I got through rehab, didn't I? I'm fed up with you and Claire not trusting me. I lost all my friends when I went through that clinic so at least *family* ought to support me!'

'And that's just what we're doing. That's why you're living here.'

'And you hate every minute of it. Don't you? I should've gone to England with Sean and Angela.'

Blake just sighed. 'Don't get started on that. I know you want an argument but I won't take the bait. Claire and I are supposed to be going out for dinner. We need a break from all this rubbish. You know we want you here but…'

'Yeah, it really sounds like it! You need a *break* from all my *rubbish!*'

Even Blake's volume increased. 'Michael, if you don't believe me, then there's nothing more I can say. You'll just have to…'

The screen door creaked open and Claire stepped out, clutching Ethan's hand. Ethan slipped his small, soft hand into Michael's and looked up at him with milky-brown eyes, just like Blake's. 'Come back, Unca Mike.'

Michael swallowed and ruffled his nephew's silky hair. 'Naw, I'm going out, mate.' To his own surprise, it *was* possible to speak softly, for Ethan's sake. 'I would've stayed with you. But your Mum an' Dad don't trust me and I won't stay here with those oldies.'

Michael didn't miss the way Claire cringed. *Good!*

'Where are you going, then?' Blake asked.

'What's it to you?'

'You've got nowhere to go but the pub. And you know whenever you go there you spend all your money on drink.'

Michael bristled. 'What makes you think I have nowhere else? Do you think everyone hates me just because *you* do?'

'You never stop trying to twist my words, do you? I'm going by what you said. You told me just now that you lost all your friends.'

'Why don't you catch up with your new friend?' Claire asked quickly.

Michael looked at her, baffled. 'What new friend?'

'The boy who dropped you home last night. He seemed nice.'

Disappointment rose up in Michael, dragging his heart to his toes. 'He's not really a friend. He just did me a favour.'

'Why don't you *make* him a friend?' Claire's eyes shone with her idea.

'I can't. Not yet. I owe him money.' Michael had a vague feeling that perhaps he shouldn't have said that.

Blake shook his head with a mirthless laugh. 'How many people do you owe money to *now?*'

'You get stuffed! You're always picking on me! I paid Claire back yesterday, didn't I?' Michael's hand flew up to cover his mouth but the words had already tumbled out. Claire gasped and Blake spun around to look at her with raised eyebrows. Michael chose that moment to break away and sprint down the street.

After five minutes of running, he found himself smirking at the thought of their shocked expressions. Perhaps it wasn't such a bad slip of the tongue after all. *I hope they have a huge argument! I hope I ruin their night.* It would be the perfect way for him to get back at them for spoiling *his* night!

*   *   *

A problem remained. Where *was* he to go? Without money in his wallet, hanging out at the pub was not a cheerful prospect.

How long will those stupid, nosy-Parkers be there, anyway? Michael didn't mind Claire's mother on her own, but he couldn't bear her stuck-up husband.

He had made it into the main street of town. Michael sat on a bench, folded his arms and glowered at his feet. *I can't sit* here *all night.* Blake and Claire were out enjoying themselves and he was stuck scuffling his shoes in the dirt.

Since Michael had been through rehabilitation and cleaned himself up, his old friends did not want to know him. Jamie, Eddie, Josh and the others had gone their separate ways. Michael was not sorry to part company with them. He never wanted to be back where he used to be. But that didn't change the fact that he had nowhere else to go.

Claire's words ran through his head. *'How about your new friend?'* He thought about the kid at work they all called 'J.' Michael hadn't exchanged many words with him. Whenever they worked the same shift, Michael was out the back preparing food while J often worked in one of the Drive-Thru' pay windows. Only pretty girls or pin-up boys seemed to get their chance out there.

Michael stretched his arms behind his head and groaned. *Shows how desperate I am.* The new kid was nicknamed 'J in pay.' He was not like the fellows Michael usually chose to befriend. J never went with others to the pub after work, yet he wasn't a total nerd. Although he never participated in the goofy behaviour that sometimes went on outside of working hours, J would still grin at the antics of the others. He'd laugh at a joke.

And at least he came to find out what my problem was. Nobody else could care less. Michael felt far too lonely to be choosy.

He was on his feet, shambling across the road to a telephone booth. J had told him where he lived and Michael thumbed through the dog-eared directory. B for Bowman. There was just one address in the right suburb with a woodwork business on the following line. That had to be the right one. He knew J's dad was a cabinet maker.

'Here goes.' Michael's shaking fingers groped in his pocket for his mobile phone. If this virtual stranger rejected him too, another part of him would wither up and die. He pressed in the number and muttered, 'Dunno why I'm even doing this. Hardly even *know* the guy.' He could barely hear the dial tone over the blood pounding through his ears.

A female voice said, 'Hello, Nicola speaking.'

'Hi, can I please speak to J?' He didn't realise how heavily he was breathing until he started to speak.

'Sorry, I think you have the wrong number.'

Michael hadn't expected that. 'I was certain he lived there.'

'Nobody called Jay lives here.'

'Oh, crumbs!' His mind was always foggy. Michael searched his memory for the proper name on J's name badge. 'I mean... what is it? ... Jerome!'

'Oh, sorry, I didn't realise who you meant. I'll get him for you.'

'Tell him it's Mike Quinlan, from work.'

'Sure.'

He was in for another wait. Michael sank down on the ground and leaned against a shop front until the phone was picked up again.

'Hi, Mike.'

'G'day. I just wanted to say thanks for your help last night.'

'Hey, don't mention it.'

'Well... I'll try and pay you back this week.'

'Yeah, no sweat.'

'There's just one more thing.' Heat crept up the back of Michael's neck. 'What are you doing tonight?'

'Not much.' J sounded surprised. 'Why?'

'Can I come an' visit you?'

'What for?'

Michael felt his heart sinking. 'No reason. I got nowhere else to go. My brother's stupid in-laws are over and I hate 'em. Just thought you might be free. But forget it. I can find somewhere else to go.' Tears were blinding him but at least J didn't know that.

'There's not much happening over here but you can come if you like.'

Michael snatched the straw like a drowning man. 'Cool. I'll be right over.'

'Hold on. I'll tell you where we live.'

'That's OK. I got your address.'

'I'll tell you anyway because it's still hard to find.'

'OK, mate.' Michael closed his eyes and fazed out. Far simpler details than road directions usually tore his concentration to shreds. He would look it up in his street directory instead. While J spoke about intersections and dirt roads, he was already planning how he'd tell Blake and Claire that he'd made his own plans and wasn't entirely clueless.

*   *   *

It was very late by the time Michael Quinlan roared off in his old car, leaving a cloud of dust and thick silence behind him. They all looked at each other and then Casey shook her head with a laugh. 'What just hit us?'

She called Michael a hurricane. Her husband said he was more like a breath of fresh air and Sam declared he was by far their best visitor ever. Nicola had just smiled and said that she hadn't lived there long enough to agree with Sam. She thought both Piers and Casey were right and called Michael Quinlan a very powerful gust of fresh air. And Jerome told them all, 'I should've warned you how hyperactive he is.'

Michael had arrived about half an hour after he'd spoken to Jerome on the phone. His eyes bulged when he first saw Jerome's black eye. When he heard how it had happened, he said, 'At least it was for a good cause. You saved me from being another statistic for those cops.'

Jerome rubbed his sore face and retorted, 'Yeah, that makes me feel heaps better.'

Michael spotted Sam's cricket bat and stumps on the verandah and suggested a game out on the flattest paddock. He even talked Piers into joining them. 'C'mon, Dad, not often you get this chance,' he said, startling Jerome with how quickly his father had been appropriated. Michael, Sam and Laura just managed to beat Piers and Jerome. Piers returned to his work while the others lounged on the dim verandah.

Michael ruffled Sam's hair and said, 'I would've given an arm and a leg to have the run of a place like this when I was your age.'

'Wouldn't have done you much good, then,' Jerome said, and the others gaped blankly at him. Jerome rolled his eyes and let them. He'd given up trying to explain his jokes. It took the fun out of them.

Sam put on his best gloomy expression and Jerome guessed what was coming next, almost word for word.

'It's not much good when nobody but Laura plays with me. Jerome never bothers.'

Michael shot Jerome an incredulous stare. 'Man, are you crazy? This excellent place is wasted on the likes of you.' He swept his hand to encompass the rustling grass and clear expanse of Milky Way.

Jerome gave Sam a playful swat. 'I *do* play with him. What he meant is that I don't play as much as he'd like me to. Some of us have other things to do.'

'Not me! If I lived here, I'd always be out playing cricket or football.'

'Easy to say, but you'd get sick of bowling to Sam after the first thousand times.'

'You sound like Sean and Blake. They're *my* older brothers.' Michael grimaced as if he had a sour taste in his mouth. 'Both married now, but when I was Sam an' Laura's age, they never had time for me. Sean always had other sport practises with more *important* people. Ten years ago, he had an accident and broke his back. He's a para-athlete now. Over in England for a few months, playing wheelchair hockey for Australia. People go on about how lucky I must've been to have him as a brother when we were young. Do they reckon he'd ever waste his precious time on *me*? And Blake was always fiddling around making things or else he had his nose stuck in a book. Older brothers are just crashing bores if you ask me.'

This remark seemed to be an open invitation to Sam and Laura, who began to interrupt each other with stories about Jerome's anti-social habits.

'Even when he *enjoys* a game, he won't play it with us because he thinks we're not good enough for him.'

'Yeah, and he never gives us a chance to prove him wrong.'

'*He* goes around with his nose in a book too, and just lately, it's been only *one* book. *Distributing Heaven* by some moron called Gareth Edgley. It's all about how *he* walked around with *his* nose in books, talking about how bad the world is and how he tried to fix it. Don't know how many times Jerome's read it but it always makes him grouchy.'

Michael threw his head back and laughed as if Sam was a hilarious comedian. Jerome forced a smile as Sam's face glowed.

'I wish *you* were my brother.'

'Me too. I don't know why the people who'd make *good* older brothers never get a chance to prove it.' Michael spotted the huge log of a fallen tree Piers had hauled near the work shed. He leaped to his feet. 'Look, that log would be perfect for a game of *Knock 'em Off*. You know, two people try to keep their balance and push each other off and the one who falls loses. There are four of us. Let's have two teams and the first team that wins twenty rounds are the champions.'

Both children pleaded to be on Michael's team. Laura even scrambled on his back and squeezed his shoulders. Michael rummaged deep in his pocket and extracted a two dollar coin which he looked at with surprise.

'Hey, I'm richer than I thought I was.'

Jerome expected him to settle the teams by tossing it, but Michael had other ideas.

'Hey, you two, I know I'm the legend here but I'll tell you what. Whoever agrees to be on your brother's team gets this money.'

'Nope.' Sam shook his head. 'It wouldn't be worth it.'

A tiny smile played around Laura's lips. 'I need just two more dollars for something I'm saving for. I'll take it.'

By now, Jerome was well into the spirit of the competition. 'You won't regret it, Laura. C'mon, we'll thrash 'em.'

Darkness made the game slightly difficult. The floodlight from the verandah was not quite strong enough but competition was keen and evenly matched. Sam and Laura competed against each other and won ten rounds each. They welcomed such a legitimate chance to fight each other. At last Michael and Jerome, who had each won nine rounds, faced off for the deciding battle.

They wrestled, wobbled, and fell together on the grass. The spectators, Sam and Laura, began bawling in each other's faces about whose foot had touched the ground first. Laura shoved Sam, Sam poked her back and Jerome had to scramble up and intervene before it came to outright blows.

Michael remounted the log, scratching his head and flexing his knuckles. 'We need some unbiased person to be referee. Let's ask your boarder.'

That idea made Jerome feel foolish. 'No, she's probably busy.'

'I'll ask her!' Laura was already rabbiting inside.

'Tell her it's important!' Sam hollered after her.

Jerome couldn't help laughing. 'She'll think we're a bunch of cuckoos.'

Nicola followed Laura outside, smiling. 'What's this urgent job, then?'

Jerome let the others explain, feeling glad of the darkness. Even the tips of his ears were hot. Nicola's presence boosted his resolve to win. He placed his feet securely on the log as he faced Michael.

'OK, one, two, three, *GO!*' Nicola's voice was hearty enough to please Sam and Laura. Jerome swallowed his laugh and turned away from her. He had to concentrate. Michael had already gripped his shoulders and was shaking him hard while Jerome lurched slightly to the side, trying to yank Michael off the log using his flailing arm. Michael raised his opposite hand like a bear's paw and clouted it straight against Jerome's bruised eye.

'Hey, not fair!' Jerome gasped.

'*Everything's* fair!' Sam shouted on behalf of his champion. Jerome had learned to tune out Sam's screeches years ago.

Michael's lanky body was hard to budge. *Different to the guy who was lurching into gutters and against walls last night,* Jerome thought. He made a quick move to change the position of his feet and looked up. 'You won't...' but the words died on Jerome's lips. He seemed to be looking into the face of a total stranger. Michael's jaw was tense, his hazel eyes blazing. At that moment, Jerome knew Michael Quinlan's usual clowning act was a cover-up for a fierce warrior. He was just pretending to treat the battle like a bit of backyard fun. Michael was in it for blood.

Jerome collected his scattered wits but not before Michael used the millisecond lapse to his own advantage. Michael pummelled Jerome's chest while Jerome grabbed a handful of Michael's shirt, intending to steady himself while removing his opponent.

'Hey, *that's* not fair!' Sam cried out.

Jerome opened his mouth to remind him, 'You said *everything's* fair,' but found himself lying on the ground with Michael's hot breath in his face. Michael mopped back straggly fair hair, panting and laughing. His good-natured clown persona was firmly back in place.

Nicola waited until Sam and Laura's noise had subsided. 'I saw what happened. Jerome's foot hit the ground a fraction of a second before Michael's.'

Pandemonium erupted. Michael was on his feet doing handstands and cartwheels, punching the air and giving Sam high fives. A frown puckered Laura's brow.

'I'll never hear the end of this from Sam.'

Jerome grinned at her. 'Come on, we were so close. And you're two dollars richer for it but *he* isn't.' He raised his voice to call, 'Well done, guys!'

Michael sat heavily on the log and heaved a sigh. 'I wish my brothers could've seen it.'

* * *

Michael did not want to leave. He sat at the table munching biscuits, drinking coffee and talking non-stop. Even when Jerome went out in the dark to help Sam find his cricket bat, Michael chattered on to Nicola, who seemed to be cornered. Jerome returned to find that he'd filled her in on his grudge against his family.

'Sean and Angela keep phoning from London every week to see how I am. It's so incredibly annoying.'

'Perhaps it shows that they really do care about you,' Nicola suggested.

Michael laughed, scattering crumbs from his mouth across the table. 'There's a big difference between caring for someone and not trusting them. They're forever checking up on me. Angela thinks that without *her* around, I'm gonna sell my soul to the devil, join a drug ring and get thrown in jail all in one week.'

He took a quick glance around to see if anyone was smiling at his joke. 'Even Blake says she's a pain in the neck. He doesn't think Angela trusts him and Claire to look after me properly. Claire's a counsellor, after all, but Angela still thinks I'll be too much for her.'

'Who does she counsel?' Nicola asked.

Michael bit into another biscuit. 'She works at a crisis pregnancy centre. Helps teenage girls who have got themselves in trouble. I wish she'd stick to them and butt out of *my* life. I wish they'd *all* loosen up and treat me like the adult I am. They reckon I need to *earn* their trust? But how can you earn someone's trust when they never give you a chance by trusting you?'

At that point, Piers decided to rescue Nicola and speak up. 'Would you like to earn their trust by doing a bit of work around here? I can always use some extra help out in the work shed and I'm willing to pay for however long you choose to spend here. Cash in hand.'

'It's just drudge work,' Jerome said, deciding Michael needed to be warned. 'Sweeping and cleaning and stuff.'

'That doesn't matter,' Piers insisted. 'It all needs to be done and Jerome has earned himself a nice bit of spending money over the years. Even Sam is doing his bit. What do you say?'

Michael was off his seat, pumping Piers' hand. 'I'm your man, Mr Bowman! I don't care if it's drudge work. I'm always short of cash. Tell me a time and I'll be here.'

'Wish I got that reaction from my own boys,' Piers said.

'You will, if Michael's here.' Sam still looked at their guest as if he wore a halo.

'It's high time you were in bed,' Casey told him. 'Off you go.'

'Think I might go too,' Jerome yawned. 'I'm still a bit tired after last night.'

Then Nicola spun around to look at him with her eyebrows drawn together. Her expression clearly said, 'Help me out. He's *your* friend!' She had no idea how comical she looked and Jerome almost laughed.

'It might be time you hit the road, mate,' Piers told Michael. 'Your brother's relatives must be long gone by now and you should get some sleep.'

Michael groaned and sighed. 'OK, but I never get to sleep very easily. I hate lying still. The only way I get sleepy is to keep doing something until I crash.'

Jerome found it difficult to imagine Michael sleeping at all. Although he'd never admit it to his new friend, he couldn't help a stirring of sympathy for Blake and Claire.

8

Nicola preferred taking her book down to the kitchen table rather than staying in her room. Even though she was quietly studying, being close to others made her far less lonely. She could see through the open door to the lounge room where Jerome had his laptop set up on the floor. Lying on his stomach and resting his chin in his cupped hands, he was peering at the screen. Laura kept springing over his back in her ballet tutu but Jerome paid her no attention.

'Hey, Jerome!' Sam had to speak three times before his brother looked up.

Jerome placed his finger against the screen to mark his spot. 'What?'

'How do you pronounce this word?' Sam spelled out, 'P S E U D O N Y M.'

'Pseudonym,' Jerome told him.

Laura's foot clipped the top of Jerome's computer and she came crashing to her knees beside him. 'What's a pseudo-thingy?'

'Will you watch out? It's a name an author makes up for himself when he doesn't want people to know his real name.'

Laura looked at Sam. 'Why did you want to know that?'

His eyes were gleaming. 'I just read it in a book. Jerome, did you ever stop to think, maybe Gareth Edgley is a pseudo-numb?'

'Of course it isn't.'

'How do you know it isn't? If it *is* a fake name, you might as well stop wasting your time looking for him. I'm only trying to help you.'

69

'Yeah, right! Big help.'

'What makes you so sure he lives in England, anyway?'

'Well, I'm not totally sure, but he is British.'

'But he wrote that book donkey's years ago. He might've shifted his headquarters to America, if he's still alive. Are you gonna search through all the telephone numbers there too?'

'That'd take years,' Laura piped up.

'And even if Gareth Edgley is his real name, maybe he has a silent number to stop people like Jerome from bugging him,' Sam added.

Nicola placed a hand over her mouth to cover a smile as Jerome closed his computer with a scowl and scrambled to his feet. 'You don't even want me to find him, do you? You're as mean as...' She didn't hear the rest because the front door slammed shut behind him.

'I'm just sick of all this ever-lasting fuss about Gareth Edgley!' Sam flung open the door and dashed outside after him.

'Hey, wait for me!' Laura pulled off her satin slippers and the door slammed one last time. Nicola was left alone after all. With no distractions, she turned her attention back to the Art Course handbook that lay open before her. Although she had no heart for further study, she needed to help herself stop thinking about Shane. She had to fill her head with something so it might as well be something useful.

She circled a red ring around *First Impressions, Part 2.* It seemed the obvious choice as she'd completed Part 1 the previous year. The tutor, Mrs Reynolds, had an interesting teaching style. During *First Impressions* she taught how artists could train themselves to gauge as much detail as possible about a person's character from their physical appearance. Mrs Reynolds had told her students never to believe anybody who claimed that first impressions were not significant. 'They carry more weight than you would ever believe and we use them all the time, whether or not we acknowledge it.' That being the case, she told her Art students that understanding and using first impressions would give them an advantage over others.

Nicola's pencil sketch of Shane had been an assignment for *First Impressions.* The students had taken turns to display their work before the others while they all tried to assess what sort of people the subjects in the drawings must be. Nicola had been delighted when their descriptions of Shane proved to be quite accurate. While his blue eyes twinkled out from her sketch, people put forward, 'Mellow, easy-going, content, tranquil, phlegmatic, calm and fun.' Mrs Reynolds had given Nicola one of her rare smiles of approval and said she'd done a grand job.

The following week, Shane obligingly paid his visit to Nicola's art class to have his accuracy assessed. Nicola remembered how he had posed for everybody with his chin slightly tilted as it had been in her sketch. Her throat instantly clamped tight. The waves of heartache confused her. Sometimes after deliberately thinking about Shane for long stretches of time, she thought she'd forced her grief to run its course. Then at other times like this, sudden random memories poured back the anguish as bitter as gall.

She drew out her sketch pad. Shane would not want her to keep feeling sad. And if she was going to keep up *First Impressions,* she knew Mrs Reynolds would scold her if she found out that Nicola hadn't kept up her practise as she was supposed to. She would want to see several fresh pieces and Nicola had to think of somebody new to sketch. It had to be a person she didn't know well, so she could show Mrs Reynolds as her requirement to get into the second course. She'd already sketched every member of the Bowman family except for Jerome. Nicola felt that she had already painted *him* in great enough detail before she even met him. Then the thought of Michael Quinlan popped into her head.

Nicola chose a soft lead pencil and started a quick sketch from memory. After fifteen minutes she set the pencil down and regarded her work. She wasn't sure if the drawing was good or not. Michael was a complex boy. Perhaps it would be too optimistic to expect anybody to gauge his character from her sketch when the real Michael was such a mass of contradictions. Sadness and happiness flitted across his talking face in quick succession. He would tell a funny story one moment and gripe about his family the next. Ever-changing, never still, like a landscape in a storm, she wondered if she'd chosen too hard a subject.

Maybe his contradictions are *his character.* Nicola decided she had captured something interesting. His slightly oily hair and shaggy fringe showed that Michael didn't care much about his own appearance but his clean, neatly pressed clothes suggested that somebody did. Perhaps pictures did speak louder than words. Whatever Michael Quinlan thought of his brother and sister-in-law, Nicola felt she had proven to her own satisfaction that they were doing their best to look after him. She closed the book, looking forward to any insight Mrs Reynolds might have regarding Michael's character.

'Hi, have you got a moment?'

Nicola jumped out of her skin and whirled around. 'Sure.'

Jerome was grinning ruefully. 'I scared you again, didn't I?'

Her heart was still racing. 'Yes,' she admitted, trying to sound light-hearted. 'That's the third time since I've lived here.'

'Sorry. I never knew I had such a way of creeping up on people until you came.'

She flushed and tried not to notice his black eye but it was impossible. The bruise had turned sickly yellow-green around its edges. 'What did you want to ask me?'

He turned a kitchen chair around and perched on it back-to-front with his chin resting on the top. 'I don't know why I never thought to ask you before. You work in a bookshop, after all. I'm trying to get hold of an out-of-print book but I'm not having any luck at all. Do you think you could help?'

'I don't know. It all depends how old it is, who published it and how many copies there were. What book are you looking for?'

He handed a volume across the table to her. 'The sequel to this one.'

'*Distributing Heaven* by Gareth Edgley.' Nicola skimmed the back cover blurb. Then she opened it to check the fly leaves.

'It doesn't say when it was published so my guess would be that it was self-published.' She pointed to the logo. '*Heavenly Publications.* That sounds like a name he might have made up himself. And there isn't even an ISBN. So I think you have a hard job on your hands.'

Jerome let out a breezy sigh between his teeth. 'I thought you might say that. Lots of people have told me the same thing already. Thanks anyway.'

'Where did you find this one?' she asked.

'At a second-hand shop. Don't even know what made me pick it up. The title must've caught my eye. When I saw it was a biography I thought I'd give it a read. I like stories about people who have done some good in the world. But the second-hand shop doesn't have the sequel. It was the first place I checked.'

'Where else have you checked?'

'Where else *haven't* I checked? I've searched every library catalogue I could find. I asked dozens of librarians but none of them could help. Even the Uni library, which has storeys crammed with old books, didn't have it. And I've tried every search engine I could find on the computer. I looked for anything to do with Gareth Edgley, *Distributing Heaven* or *A Design of Gold.* That's what the sequel's called. Some links had over fifty pages but I didn't give up. I checked them all. And none of them had anything to do with him. So I've started trying to look up his address. That's pretty desperate, I know, like trying to find one particular grain of sand on the beach.'

Nicola looked at the book again. Its stark cover of black and red checks definitely appeared dated. 'This must be an excellent book to have you searching so hard for its sequel.'

He rolled his eyes to the ceiling in a way she took to mean that her observation was a vast understatement. 'I can't even begin to tell you the difference this book has made in the way I think about things! This guy is incredible!'

'Give me a run down on the plot, then,' she said.

He was laughing. Her heart quickened again. She'd made him laugh.

'I'd be happy to do that but I'm not really sure if you know what you're in for. Once I get started on this... well, just ask Sam.'

'I know, but I don't care. Tell me anyway.'

He spun another chair around to use as a leg rest. 'OK, but don't say I didn't warn you.'

'Gareth Edgley was born as the illegitimate son of a servant girl. The family she worked with weren't happy when they found out she was pregnant but they let her and the baby stay on, because her family had been working for theirs for years. So Gareth grew up helping around the house with odd jobs. And their employers, the Bradford family, had a pretty daughter called Irene who was just Gareth's age.'

'Just a second,' Nicola interrupted. 'Are you sure this isn't fiction?'

'Positive. I know it sounds like a story but every word is true. Gareth had a bad accident when he was ten years old. He'd been helping the gardener repair the roof on a wet day and slipped off and fell down on the path. They thought he was going to die but he'd just damaged his spine. He had to lie flat on his back in the big house for week after week. And they thought he would never walk again.'

'But he obviously got better.'

'He did, but the part of the book where he was lying in bed takes up a big chunk of the story. He was grateful that he and his mother had generous employers who cared for him while he was sick. Then he realised that whenever he was feeling grateful about anything, he was happier. So he decided he needed to turn gratitude into a habit for his own sake. Whenever an unhappy thought popped into his head he imagined himself smashing it to pieces with a hammer. But happy thoughts were hard to come by. So Gareth tried to think of one that would cover everything. He decided that since he'd survived the fall from a two-storey roof, God must have a plan for his life.'

'That's pretty perceptive, for a ten-year-old boy,' Nicola marvelled.

'But he was a pretty amazing boy. He promised God that if he ever recovered enough to walk again, he'd help make the world a better place. He'd do something brilliant, even though he had no idea what it would be.

'At the time, the only bright spot in Gareth's life was studying French with Irene, from his bed. Her parents let the French tutor teach from Gareth's room to help keep him occupied. And Gareth was grateful for getting the free lessons. If he hadn't fallen, he would never have learned French.'

'Hey, Vicki might be interested in this book for her Gratitude Group.'

'Yeah, she should read it.'

'Go on. I suppose Gareth fell in love with Irene.'

'Yeah, he did.' Jerome flushed. 'It might sound corny the way I'm telling it but the way he wrote it was great. He knew he had no chance with Irene because she was the daughter of wealth and he was a servant. Her parents wanted her to marry a rich kid called Arthur who was the son of some friends of theirs.'

'Of course they would.' Nicola couldn't suppress a teasing smile.

'Wait 'til you hear the rest before you make any more judgements. By the time he was thirteen he was able to move around the house almost as good as before. He went back to work for the Bradford family and his mother died when he was nineteen. By then the War had started but Gareth couldn't enlist because of his spine. He took that as part of God's plan for his life, because he was a pacifist and didn't want to be involved in warfare. But the promise he'd made to God to do something brilliant was still burning away in his heart.'

Jerome folded his arms in front of him and shot Nicola a challenging look. 'So go on, you think this is pretty predictable. Tell me what he did.'

She smiled and shrugged. 'Did he become advisor to the Prime Minister?'

'It was far more exciting than that. He joined the French Resistance and helped hide prisoners from the Germans.'

'Hey, if he hadn't had those French lessons, he'd never have been able to do that!' Nicola was too intrigued to laugh.

'Yeah, now you got it! By then, he was calling all of those coincidences part of the design of gold that God was weaving into his life. He even helped rescue some important political prisoners. He was like the Scarlet Pimpernel but real.'

'So that's how he fulfilled his promise to be brilliant?'

'That's just the beginning. After the War he spent some time in a French monastery to study his Bible and devote himself to prayer. Don't laugh, because it sounds pretty simple, but the way he wrote it was really deep and meaningful. After two years in the monastery, Gareth realised that there were plenty of people back in Britain who could use his help.'

'Wow, that *is* profound!' Nicola couldn't help her lips twitching.

Jerome grinned at her and shook his head. 'So he went back and set himself up a bit like Saint Francis. He gave away everything he had.'

'Which wouldn't have been much, I imagine.'

'It wasn't much to start with but just wait 'til you hear. He walked across the country on foot doing odd jobs in return for food and shelter. He always told people that God brought him their way to show them how much He loved them. And you wouldn't believe how many times God put him in exactly the right place where the person he was with needed to hear precisely what Gareth had to say. People started giving him money as goodwill offerings and he'd give it all away again at the next place he went. Millions of dollars passed through his hands and he never kept any for himself.'

'How did he decide where he was going to go?'

'That's the most amazing part. Every night before he left a place, he'd pray that God would guide him the following day, and then he'd settle back perfectly certain that wherever he took it into his head to go next would be the right place. And he'd always find that it was exactly where God needed him to be unless he'd forgotten to pray. Whenever he got lazy about praying he'd find that people wouldn't want him around or annoying things would keep happening to stop him working. So he learned from personal experience that he *had* to pray just to keep on track.'

A tide of sadness washed through Nicola as she wondered if Shane's death could have been prevented by something so simple.

'Gareth Edgley started with nothing and he never wanted any personal recognition,' Jerome went on. 'He started thinking of himself as one of God's ambassadors and that's why he called the book *Distributing Heaven*. That's exactly what he considered himself to be doing. And at the end, he wrote that being able to pour his energy into the world as an offering of thanks to God who blessed him more than he ever dared to imagine. He said you really need a chance to be a blessing before you have any idea what true happiness is. And here I am, hanging around, just letting the days filter through my calendar.'

With a sigh, Jerome slouched further down his seat and let his forehead rest on the back of the chair. For somebody who had discovered a book with such a positive message, his expression was the most dejected Nicola had seen that day.

9

'Do you know what's meant to happen in the next book?' Nicola asked.

'Yeah, he's got a bit of blurb about it on the last few pages. He goes back across the English Channel and starts his distributing heaven campaign in Europe. He gets other people working with him and starts a proper mission. And he manages to win Irene's heart from Arthur.' Jerome looked up with a sheepish smile. 'OK, I know that part sounds a bit farfetched but it's a true story and I'm interested to see how he did it and what her parents thought. Anyway, read this last bit for yourself.' He flicked to the very last page and handed it back across to Nicola.

She read aloud, *'If you think my story is gripping so far, you've read nothing yet!'* Nicola looked up at Jerome who nodded sombrely.

'Go on,' he said.

'God showered me with more blessings than you'd ever believe. In A DESIGN OF GOLD I share more secrets from my heart so you will be equipped to impact the world just as I've done. Hold onto your seats when you read this book. Whatever you do, don't miss out.'

'That's easy for him to say,' Jerome grumbled.

'I guess all you can do is keep searching on ebay. Or you could advertise for it in newspapers.'

'Yeah, I've tried all that,' Jerome mumbled with a tinge of frustration.

'Is this the book that helped you decide to be a missionary?'

He turned his chair around to sit on it properly. 'I guess it is. I had no idea what I wanted to do with my life before I read it. While I was reading it, the impact was so great, I *knew* I was getting a prod from God. I couldn't spend my life doing any more noble work than Gareth Edgley's. He changed people's lives. I want to be a life-changer too.'

'You don't need to go overseas to start.'

Jerome's eyes narrowed. 'Have you been talking to my dad? I can't do it *here*. It's not the same at all. People around here already have everything they want. They have everything *I* could give them, anyway. They just don't have the same needs that they have in Europe or Asia.'

I think you're dead wrong there. Nicola kept her mouth closed. Jerome's mind was obviously set. 'It'd be a great experience for you to go,' she offered after a moment. Saying what people wanted to hear was always a safe option.

'I've started saving to get over there ever since I finished the book. I wanted to go to Britain first and meet Gareth Edgley but it looks like I can write *that* off.'

'Ironic, isn't it?' she mused. 'You're carefully saving every cent so you can fly to the other side of the world just to give it all away.'

Nicola wondered if her observation had been too blunt. She was relieved to see his lips quirk in a reluctant smile.

'When you put it that way, I might as well just post it over there.'

'But then you wouldn't have the personal fulfilment of helping people face to face.'

Instead of answering, he leaned his elbows on the table and looked at her. 'Are you happy working in a bookshop?'

She hadn't expected that question. Nicola paused to think. 'I don't know. I *thought* I would be. I thought it was a miracle when I got the job, but it's not what it's cracked up to be. I've seen some fantastic books come to the end of their shelf life and never get re-ordered.'

'The end of their shelf life?' Jerome repeated. 'You make them sound like groceries in a supermarket.'

'Well, that's how they're treated. And at the same time, so much trashy literature comes in. Today I sold a book about witchcraft to a young guy who was dressed in black and covered in piercings. And I couldn't help thinking that I might be helping to send him on the road to… somewhere he wouldn't want to find himself. That bothers me a lot. No, I'm not really happy.'

He was studying her again. 'You don't get out much, do you?'

She felt herself prickle with the usual defensiveness. 'I would if I felt like it! I'm not the going out type.'

'Hey, I'm not criticising. Gee whiz, I don't go out much either or I wouldn't have noticed.'

She softened like a sponge. 'Do you ever *want* to?' Perhaps it was a waste that somebody who looked like Jerome preferred to keep to himself.

He hesitated in his characteristic way. 'Not really. But then there's always a part of me that thinks maybe I should want to.'

Nicola never knew what made her say it. A daring voice in her head prompted, *Ask him quickly!*

'How would you like to come along to my Gratitude Group next Wednesday evening?'

Jerome paused again but not in his reflective manner. He wore a huge beam as if he was going to laugh. 'What sort of people go there?' He had the grace to blush. 'Sorry, that sounded rude. I only meant is it mostly girls? I wouldn't want to stand out.'

'No, no! Men go along too.' She didn't tell him that the only man who attended regularly was Mr Giles, who would surely be fifty years older than Jerome. Vicki was always urging them to invite others along to the Gratitude Group.

'Vicki runs it. You know Vicki. She's your mother's friend.'

'Yeah, I'd know two people then; you and Vicki.'

'Gareth Edgley would probably approve of a group like this,' she added slyly.

'I reckon you might be right. OK, I'll give it a go.'

'That's great.' Nicola found herself looking forward to something for the first time in over a month. 'Would you like to come with me, then? How about next Wednesday? We'll head off after tea.'

'OK. I'll do you a favour in return,' Jerome told her.

'What is it?'

He pushed *Distributing Heaven* back across the table to her. 'Why don't you read it? Don't just listen to my rambling about it.'

'Sure. I'd be honoured. But your summary leaves a lot to live up to.'

Jerome was on his feet. 'You won't believe what you're in for. Read it quickly and tell me what you think of it.'

'I will.' Nicola would read a dictionary if Jerome asked her to, just for the pleasure of talking it over with him. Not that she would ever tell him so. She packed the book into her portfolio with her sketches and pencils and floated upstairs to the Loft. Sitting on her bed, she flicked through the pages, reading random paragraphs here and there. It seemed to her that Gareth Edgley's writing style was more ponderous than Jerome would have her believe, but she'd committed herself.

In the book's centre were a few glossy pages of black and white photos that she studied with more interest. Gareth Edgley did not look like Nicola's idea of a hero. He had been the sort of plain and colourless young man Nicola saw hundreds of each day in the shop, with no arresting features that would make her consider sketching him. Not a fraction as attractive as Jerome. Yet Gareth Edgley had the power to fascinate people with the colourful life he'd lived and the stories he'd spun.

'I guess you never can tell,' Nicola mumbled to herself with a wry smile.

*   *   *

'Jerome, each week we go around the circle and share something positive that's happened,' Vicki explained. 'It doesn't even have to be something that's happened to you. It can be anything you've heard about or read that might help to lift the spirits of the rest of us. No matter how hard your week has been, it's impossible not to find *one* positive thing to say.' She'd done her spiel and drew a breath. 'So you can wait until everyone else has shared or you can start us off this week if you're game.'

Jerome looked bashfully at his knees but accepted the challenge. 'I don't mind having a go.' He flexed his knuckles and shuffled his feet as he thought. 'OK, I've got something. I'm glad we live in a country where we have free access to the Bible. We take the privilege for granted and it makes a life-or-death difference to your life.'

Nicola's stomach gyrated like a carousel in the stunned silence that followed. Nobody ever said anything like that. *I should have warned him!* It hadn't occurred to her to tip him off that this was not a group of Christian people. She had assumed that he wouldn't go on with this Gareth Edgley style of talk with strangers.

But Chris and Shirley appeared more astonished than offended. The elderly Giles couple were even smiling at him. Vicki appeared slightly awkward but Vicki had known the Bowman family for years. She could take Jerome as he was.

The teenager, Bianca, who would've snorted contempt if Nicola had been the one to make that comment, studied Jerome with a furrowed brow as if he were a puzzle she was trying to work out. 'It hasn't made a life-or-death difference to *my* life,' she declared flatly.

'Maybe you don't read it very often.' Jerome was polite and completely unfazed.

Bianca's mother, Shirley, placed a hand over her mouth and guffawed.

Bianca's lips twisted into their normal, cynical shape. 'I don't but that's not to say I've *never* read the Bible. I went to a private school. We were bored to tears with all those *thees* and *thous* and lists of who-begat-who. They used to have such weird names, too.' Bianca had worked on her teenage drawl to perfection. She pushed a stiffly gelled shaft of blonde hair out of her eyes. 'I mean, it all happened two thousand years ago so who cares?'

'Ssssh, it sounds as if I've brought you up to be a heathen.' Shirley's face began to shine more pink and embarrassed than Nicola's.

'I'm interested to hear more from Jerome,' Ron Giles spoke up. 'It's not often that I hear such a statement from the younger generation. I'd like to know why you're glad we have access to the Bible.'

'Well, it's partly because of something my Dad has been telling me all my life. He said that having a Bible is like having a whole list of fantastic contracts to draw on but so many people don't even know what they are. It's like leaving a fortune sitting in the bank while you're living on bread and water.'

Jerome didn't need Nicola to be anxious for him. He moistened his lips. 'I've heard what people in China do, and other countries where the Bible is illegal. They treasure every word from it they ever manage to get hold of. Give them a few verses on a scrap of paper and they'll pass it around and memorise it and guard it with their lives. I've been reading an excellent book by a fellow who knows all about that, but I won't get started on that.' Jerome caught Nicola's eye and smiled at her.

She nodded back. Right in the spot that had twisted with embarrassment moments earlier, something warm began to swell.

Bianca muttered, 'Sounds like they're better off than we are, not to have it crammed down their throats day after day.'

Nicola watched the collective eyes of the Gratitude Group turn reproach upon Bianca instead of Jerome. Nicola had never seen Bianca falter and blush before. It was a refreshing sight.

'I used to read my Bible,' Shirley remarked to nobody in particular, 'but it was so hard getting the kids interested. Not that I thought we shouldn't bother. I just...' she trailed off. Shirley was making excuses. Jerome's mention of the Bible brought waves of embarrassment out of other people, not himself. Shirley raised bright eyes to him. 'Your father must be an amazing man to have got you interested. That's all I can say.'

Vicki cut in, 'Shall we agree to be grateful that Bibles are readily available for anybody who cares to read them? Let's move on to Bianca's gratitude point.'

The girl's lashes, heavy with mascara, flickered at Jerome. The jet-black droplets always contrasted vividly with her dyed fair hair. 'I'm really grateful that if there's anything worth reading in the Bible, I've met someone who can tell me where to find it.'

Nicola found herself wincing like a huge tooth that had been set on edge. *Oh, come on! What's she playing at?* She joined in the general laugh with the group. Although amusement was not what Nicola felt, she could come up with no name for whatever it was. Bianca smiled a tight little smirk. It seemed her features were forced to move against their well-worn scowl grooves. And Jerome grinned back at Bianca. He had no idea that he was being treated to a sight that was probably even rarer than Bibles in China.

10

Michael had the better of the two electric sanders but Jerome could tell from the angle of his eyebrows that the tedious job was wearing on his nerves.

'This will take forever.' Michael was frustrated to have cleared only a few square inches of garish red paint from the old dressing table after half an hour of work on it.

'It's not as slow as it used to be years ago when Dad would make me do this sort of thing with just a sheet of sandpaper.' The memory of those days made Jerome's knuckles feel raw.

'I thought your dad mainly *built* furniture.'

'He used to but now he thinks restoring old pieces is even more fun.'

They were sanding down an Edwardian lady's dressing table that Piers had picked up at a junk yard. He was spending his Saturday morning with Laura, searching garage sales for more. Laura loved to go and hunt for old furniture with their dad. Before he left, Piers had asked Michael Quinlan to begin sanding the old dressing table back to its original condition, thinking it would be a pleasant and straightforward task to start him off with. Jerome had offered to help too because he was filling in time. It was easy to keep an eye on the house while he was kneeling outside in the fresh air.

Nicola had gone to buy a few groceries but now she was back. He had seen her return and go inside. Jerome had wanted to follow her straight away but forced himself to keep sanding instead. It would be a mistake to appear too eager to talk to her. His mother was inside working on the computer. She might comment that Jerome was always quick to drop whatever he was doing when Nicola was around. He wouldn't risk appearing too obvious. Another ten or twenty minutes should do it.

Michael switched off his sander to rub the small of his back. 'The things I do for money.'

'Hey, talking about money, do you have that hundred bucks you owe me yet?' It was time for a quick reminder.

Michael heaved a great sigh. 'Yeah, just a sec.' He sat on the grass and fumbled through his backpack. 'Will twenty do for a start?'

Jerome hesitated before taking the note. 'Do you need it for something else?'

'Well, I'll tell you what happened. My brother lent me a hundred to pay you back but I met Jamie, one of my old friends. I owed him two hundred from way back and I'd forgotten all about it. He hadn't forgotten, though. So I fobbed him off with that hundred that was meant for you.' Michael hadn't drawn his eyes away from the twenty dollar note. 'And Blake expected me to pay him back by now.'

Jerome passed the money back again. 'You take it, then.'

Michael's eyes brightened. 'Are you sure? I've been feeling guilty about putting you out of pocket. I *could* try to borrow it from Claire again but I don't really want to do that. It'd set me right back where I started.'

'Yeah, don't do that. I sort of made it worse for you by lending it to you, didn't I? Now you have two people to pay back.'

Michael's brow furrowed as he thought. 'I don't know how the math works but you're right. I actually owe *three* people a hundred dollars now. You, Blake and Jamie. What's that, fractions?'

Jerome couldn't help laughing at Michael's dilemma. 'Sounds more like multiplication. Look, I'm not that hard-up yet. Just pay me when you can.'

Michael crammed the money back into his backpack. 'Thanks, man. It'll be soon, I promise. Probably before the end of next week.'

Jerome found himself doubting that. 'No worries.'

His thoughts returned to Nicola. He hoped she would set up her easel outside again. Last Saturday afternoon she'd started a water colour of the house from the old wire fence. He could discuss Gareth Edgley's book with her there. She'd given it back to him at breakfast that morning but Sam had been there pestering them with riddles from a very lame joke book.

'Why are elephants grey? So you can tell them apart from canaries.'

'What do you call an elephant in a telephone booth? Stuck.'

Jerome told him to find someone else who might listen to him but Nicola had made the fatal mistake of laughing. Sam took it as a cue to perch on the arm of the couch beside her and keep them flowing.

'What is grey with sixteen wheels? An elephant on roller skates. What do you get when you cross an elephant with a sparrow? Broken telephone poles.'

'This work is pretty boring,' Michael remarked after awhile.

'Yeah, I warned you it would be.'

'My elbows are killing me. Hope this'll be worth it.'

Jerome had a sudden idea. 'How'd you like to borrow an excellent book?'

'What sort of book?'

'It's called *Distributing Heaven.*'

'Is that the same book Sam was telling me about?' Michael's eyes twinkled behind his safety goggles. 'I'm not much of a reader but I'll have a look to see if what he said is true.'

'But I'm not lending it to you to make fun of. It's a great book.'

Michael sniggered. 'Whatever you say.'

The front door opened and Jerome whipped up his head. Nicola was coming down the verandah steps but his mother was right behind her.

'It's looking good, boys,' Casey called. 'I'm going to take Nicola to the city shops for some retail therapy.'

Michael raised a cheerful hand. 'OK, see you, Mrs B. See you, Nicola.'

'Bye,' Jerome called. He looked down again glumly and gave the left corner of the dressing table an extra hard sanding. Another opportunity had gone begging.

Sam leaped down the steps and stretched out flat on the ground beside them.

'You'll get covered with paint shavings if you stay there,' Jerome told him shortly.

'I don't care. I wanted to go to the city too. I don't know why Mum wouldn't take me.'

'Maybe it's because you won't belt up with those annoying elephant jokes.'

Sam's eyes narrowed. 'Look who's talking! The one who bores people out of their brains by raving on about Gareth Edgley every chance he can?'

Although the sun beat down hot on the back of Jerome's neck, he turned ice cold inside. What if Nicola was actually trying to avoid him because she didn't want to be blunt and ask him to shut up? Michael's cackling laughter didn't help.

'Hey, Michael, why are elephants wrinkled all over?' Sam shouted over the noise of the sanders.

'I give in, mate.'

'Because they can't fit on an ironing board.'

'Sounds like my old man,' Michael told him. 'I haven't seen him for awhile but he's a bit wrinkly too. How about a few overs of cricket?'

Sam was up on his feet. 'OK!'

Michael pulled off his goggles and looked across at Jerome. 'Your dad won't mind if I take a break, will he?'

'Not at all.'

'Do you want to play too?'

'I think I'll give it a miss.'

Jerome kept sanding the dressing table. He wasn't in the mood for playing cricket. *Maybe I'd better wait until she mentions the book herself.*

* * *

'Go on, try it on,' Casey urged. 'It'll look fantastic on you.'

So Nicola stepped behind a changing screen in the small boutique and scrambled into the musk coloured dress that shimmered like a sunset cloud. It was the sort of garment she'd always loved but never wore because she thought they were designed for thin girls. The creator of this one, however, definitely had the fuller figure in mind.

She turned, surveying herself in the mirror from all angles. The soft fabric flowed around her midriff giving her the illusion of having a waist. Nicola stepped out to show Casey, who beamed and gave her a thumbs-up signal. Nicola put her own clothes back on and waited in line to pay for it. It was the first time since she was ten years old that she'd been excited about buying clothes.

Casey squeezed her arm. 'I'm glad you bought it. It looked ravishing. I was hoping one of us would find something good and today's your day.'

'Thank you.' Nicola couldn't keep her own eyes from the glimpse of musk felt in the bag. She wondered what Jerome would think if he saw her in it and her cheeks instantly radiated heat as she glanced sideways at Casey. Whenever Jerome's family were around, she thought it prudent to avoid him altogether.

When they were seated at a café table with frozen yoghurt drinks, Casey remarked, 'You remind me of myself when I was your age.'

'I'll bet you weren't so fat.' Nicola thought she might as well be frank. Casey had been the one who first noticed the XL tag on the dress, after all. Nicola felt her own muffin top pouring over the band of her jeans concealed beneath her pullover. That blubber never budged, no matter what she did.

'I never thought I was a fairy ballerina either. You don't think you're too big, do you?'

'Sometimes I feel like an elephant.'

'That's enough of that sort of talk. I've heard enough about elephants from Sam's joke book this morning to last me a lifetime.'

Nicola grinned and said, 'A hippo, then.'

'Utter nonsense.' Casey scoffed. 'Do you want my honest opinion? That day I met you in Vicki's shop, I thought, "Here's a girl after my own heart. She can show the world how stunning larger girls are." You have one of the prettiest faces I've seen. If you're not happy with your size there are only two options. You can either lose the weight you want or change your thoughts and think of yourself as a gorgeous, voluptuous woman. And I hope you choose the second. There are already enough poor skinny girls starving themselves to match some media ideal.'

'It's kind of you to say that. I think your second option is all that's left for me. I've already tried the first.' She didn't begin telling Casey about the many weight loss programmes she'd tried since she was twelve years old; the diet shakes she'd concocted, the kilometres she'd run on a treadmill, the calorie counting, the careful rationing of her own servings of dinner. Yet whenever Nicola relaxed slightly and ate the same as Karen and Laura, her excess pounds seemed to pile back on. Then somebody had told her that dieting was counter-productive because her body believed it was being starved and clung to every morsel she gave it. It was then that Nicola gave up in despair. It seemed that God had designed her to be always eight or ten kilograms overweight.

'I know where you're coming from,' Casey sympathised. 'I've been there too. I used to think Piers' sister had a figure to die for. Do you remember meeting Suzanne that night at dinner?'

'Yes, the lady with the photography studio?'

'That's her. She turned forty not all that long ago and she's still got the trademark flair she always had. And a different metabolism to mine.'

'But you look pretty good for somebody who's had three children.' It always irritated Nicola to hear trim people call themselves fat.

Casey's eyelids flew open. 'No, only two! Goodness, it didn't occur to me that you didn't know. Piers already had Jerome before I married him.'

Surprise surged so swiftly through Nicola she found herself gaping at Casey. Then she snapped her mouth shut.

'I'm sorry we didn't think to tell you. We've been a family for so long, it's easy to forget that not everybody knows our set-up. I even surprise myself sometimes when I remember that I'm a stepmother.' Casey laughed merrily to put Nicola at ease.

'I had no idea.' Even as she spoke, pieces began to click together in Nicola's mind. It explained why he was several years older than the other two. And why his frame was leaner and more lithe than Sam's and

Laura's, without their freckles and tawny hair.

'Jerome's birth mother died of drug overdose,' Casey was saying. 'He was little more than a newborn at the time. I never met her but she sure left her reputation behind. She was Piers' girlfriend at Uni. They never got married. It happened during his rebellious stage. Her name was Anna and she really wanted to make the world a better place. But she had depression and that drug habit. She didn't even want to look at Jerome when he was born. He was going to be put up for adoption but Piers fought for his right to keep him. Thank God he did. Life without Jerome doesn't even bear thinking about.' Casey sighed deeply. 'We have photos of Anna at home. There's one on the lounge room shelf. She was a dream.'

Well, that *figures!* Pieces kept sliding into place. Casey and Suzanne had been talking about Anna that night after dinner. Then there was Jerome's own passion for the plight of those less fortunate. Nicola wondered if such things could be inherited.

She thought about the photos on Casey's shelf and took a guess. 'Was she that gorgeous girl in the tight, black dress with all the dark hair flowing down her back?'

'Yeah, that was her. Stunning, wasn't she?' Casey lowered her voice. 'And from everything I've heard about her, I'm sure she knew it. I don't really like thinking about poor Anna.'

Neither did Nicola. Anna had possessed natural refinement and the type of exquisite beauty that made Nicola feel like a crude, amateur artist. She baulked at the thought of attempting portraits of people like Anna. There was no way she could do them justice.

Casey had started another story. 'Piers and I got married when we were both twenty-four and Jerome was four. I thought we'd have one year getting used to being a family before I started trying to have babies. I never knew how difficult it would turn out to be.'

'Did you have hard pregnancies?'

'No, trouble *falling* pregnant.' Casey pushed a strand of sunny coloured hair behind her ear. 'It took three years of really hard trying and I got myself tied in knots. All that time, Suzanne was always reminding me, "It's obviously nothing to do with Piers."' She gave a rueful giggle.

'Suzanne always says exactly what she thinks the moment she thinks it.'

'I'm glad it worked out for you in the end.'

'Do you know what did it? Giving up. It's true. As soon as I resigned myself to having just one sweet little stepson, I fell pregnant. I felt just like Hannah in the Bible. Do you remember how she prayed for a son?'

Nicola nodded.

'That's how Sam got his name. Piers used to have a dog called Sam and Suzanne asked us how on earth we could bring ourselves to name our baby after a dog. But we didn't. We named him after Samuel in the Bible. We both thought Samuel Bowman had a strong, manly ring to it.'

'It does,' Nicola said. 'And so does Sam Bowman.'

Casey sucked up her last inch of frozen yoghurt drink. 'Jerome was already eight years old before we had Sam but that baby boy was worth the wait. He had such a funny, squashy little face when he was born, like a baby cabbage. And his head was covered with the most feathery hair. I thought he looked like an angel from heaven.'

'That's a wonderful story, Casey.'

'And then to have Laura two years later was like the cream on top. I thought God was smiling and telling me, "I *told* you I love to bless you." I didn't even presume to ask for her. She was a bonus on the prayer for Sam. Our little jewel.'

Nicola watched Casey's expression, trying to remember every detail so she could grab a pencil at home and try a quick sketch. Maternal joy seemed to pour across the table. 'I think you appreciate your family all the more because of all that.'

'You're absolutely right. When Suzanne turned thirty-five she decided she might like to have a baby at last. And she fell pregnant as soon as they started trying.' Casey shrugged and raised her hands in a there-you-have-it gesture. 'I'm not saying Suzanne doesn't love Olivia. She's a beautiful little girl. We all adore her. It's just that many things always seemed to come so much easier to Suzanne than they ever did to me. But I wouldn't exchange my life for hers for any amount of money.'

Nicola basked in the joy. Vicarious joy was far better than no joy at all.

* * *

Jerome was alone with his parents when somebody knocked at the door. Nicola was working late and Sam and Laura had just gone to bed. Casey answered the knock and brought a stranger through to meet them; a neat, dark-haired man who inclined his head with a bashful manner.

'Hello, I'm Blake Quinlan, Michael's brother.'

Jerome tried to conceal his surprise as they shook hands all round and introduced themselves. In his mind, he'd pictured Blake as an older version of Michael with the same fair-haired, scruffy exuberance. When he'd seated himself and accepted a cup of coffee from Casey, Blake explained why he'd come.

'Michael's told us a lot of good things about you all. I wanted to thank you personally for giving him a bit of work to do, Piers. It's just what he needs.'

'It's a pleasure. Been great to have him.'

Blake pulled a wallet out of his hip pocket and extracted a hundred dollar note. 'Here's the other reason I came. This is for you, Jerome. I know Michael's owed it to you for some time.'

'That's OK.' Jerome felt embarrassed about accepting it. 'It doesn't seem fair to make *you* pay.'

'Don't worry about that. I like it better this way. You were a good friend to him and deserve to be paid back. And I thought he'd already done it until I asked him last night.' Blake rolled his eyes and shook his head. 'Thanks for lending it to him but in future, maybe you'd better not. I know you were helping him out. But it might not be so much of a help. You know what I mean, don't you?'

Jerome nodded.

Casey took the opportunity to put in a word for Michael. 'It's been fun for us to have him around. There's never a dull moment when Michael's here.'

Blake's smile flashed. 'I'll bet there isn't. People usually work that out pretty quickly.'

'He's a great friend to our younger children. Sam and Laura keep singing his praises.'

'Yeah, Mike was the youngest kid himself. He knows how they tick.'

'We heard you have a little one yourself,' Piers said.

Blake's boyish nod was the first thing that remotely resembled Michael's. 'We have almost two now. My wife is expecting a baby in six weeks. She says she's sure it'll be more like eight because she went way overdue with our first one.' He shook his head comically at the memory. 'That drove us both crazy. People were calling us at all hours to check if anything had happened. And we had to keep saying, "Not yet." Claire was in tears the day she went two weeks over. Ethan was pretty special, you see. He was the first baby for both sides of the family.'

'Michael thinks the world of him. He was telling us he'd be a willing baby-sitter for Ethan,' Casey said.

Blake's guarded, weary expression returned. 'I know he would. I wish we could let him. It'd come in handy at times, having a live-in baby-sitter.'

'You don't think you can?'

He shook his head. 'The thing is we can hardly trust him to look after himself. This business with the hundred dollars proves what I mean. Not to mention getting drunk and needing to be driven home in the first place. He's had health issues since our mother died a few years ago. He's come a long way in that time but he still has a way to go. I know he can be great fun, just like you said, but he can also be a hassle. Believe me.'

Casey said no more.

Piers offered to take Blake out to show him through the work-shed, leaving Jerome and his mother looking at each other.

'I reckon I can see both sides,' Jerome mused.

Casey nodded her agreement and leaned closer to whisper, 'Was one of those Quinlan boys a cuckoo? They're even less alike than you and Sam.'

'And they're not even half brothers,' Jerome added.

'Blake's pretty handsome,' she mumbled.

'If you say so, Mum.'

'It's a pity he's married or he might be nice for Nicola.'

Jerome tried to conceal his chagrin. 'I wish you wouldn't say that sort of thing.'

Apparently he wasn't successful at hiding it because she raised her eyebrows. '*What* sort of thing?'

He had to find a reasonable answer quickly. 'Wishing things were different to how they are.'

She was still staring at him. 'I'm wondering if *you're* wishing things were different to how they are.'

To his horror, he found himself blushing. 'What are you talking about?'

She merely laughed. 'You can't hide things from me. I know Nicola's very pretty.'

'Mum, will you just keep your...'

'Don't worry. I won't tell her what you're thinking.'

'You wouldn't have a clue what I'm thinking.'

'You might be surprised. Just now you're thinking you wish I'd go to bed and stop embarrassing you. So I'm going. Good night.'

'That's not all I'm thinking,' he muttered. Long after Casey went to bed, Jerome sat scowling out the window at the stars. He finally gave up and played Solitaire on the computer. The Quinlan brothers were on his mind too. Maybe it was something to do with being the eldest child of a family but it always frustrated him to perceive any need with no clear solution.

11

Nicola stood face to face with her own Personal Adonis. He was splashed in oil paint over a four foot canvas; one of her favourite pieces. How he looked like Jerome! So much so that taking the painting home to the Bowman's house was out of the question. Her cheeks began to ignite just to imagine Sam's and Laura's reactions, not to mention Casey's and Piers'. But telling them it wasn't Jerome might prove to be even *more* embarrassing.

'I think I'll leave that one here.'

'How about the one of Shane?' her mother asked quietly.

It was the pencil sketch for *First Impressions*. Nicola remembered how carefully she'd worked to get his amiable quirk of the left eyebrow spot on. Looking at it was like the twist of a knife.

'Wouldn't Mrs Turnbull or Karen like to keep it?'

She didn't miss the glance her mother and sister exchanged.

'They have other photos to remember him by,' Laura said.

Their mother added, 'This one hurts them a bit. It's such an exact likeness and he looked so happy. Maybe it represents their hopes that were lost.' She clutched Nicola's hand with her own cold one.

The phone rang and Laura stretched her arm across the coffee table to answer it.

'Oh, hi, Mrs Turnbull.' Her eyes gaped at Nicola, wide and alarmed. 'Er, yes, she's still here. She and Mum have got a lot of catching up to do.' Although Laura hustled out to talk in the kitchen, Nicola could hear her still. 'We'll give you a call when she…' Laura's voice became hushed and whispered the last few sentences. 'Bye, Mrs Turnbull.'

Nicola stepped towards the door. 'I think I'd better go. There's no need for her to stay out waiting until I've left.'

Her mother and Laura each grasped one of her arms on either side, pulling her down onto the couch.

'She said she could find things to do for another few hours,' Laura declared. 'If you leave now, you're mean and heartless!'

Nicola stared at her. How could Laura try a guilt trip on her now of all times?

'Mum has been hanging out to see you all this time. You have no idea how sad she's been. Can't you show some compassion?' Laura's hands were on her hips, her blue eyes boring into Nicola's. Nicola let herself sink back into the cushion.

'You might not believe this, Sweetie, but Pam's phone call might be a good sign.'

Home no longer felt like home. Her mother didn't look her normal self either. Ruth Price seemed to have shrunk into herself. They had been the same height, yet now Ruth's eyes were a good two inches lower than Nicola's, as they sat side by side on the couch. Nicola could see how sad her mother had become. All of Ruth's good spirits had bleached out of her, leaving her grey.

'Don't you see, it's her way of being kind and giving us our time together? She's doing it for you as well as for us. So please stay longer. If you go it'd be like flinging the gesture right back in Pam's face. And that'd make things even worse than they are. I mean *were,*' she corrected herself. 'I think we're all slowly coming to terms with Shane's death here. Now, tell us how you're getting along with your new family.'

My new family? Nicola knew Ruth didn't mean that the way it sounded. She moistened her lips and began to think of what she could say to make her mother's mind easier about her. She was telling snippets about life with Casey, Piers and their three children when Laura gasped and pointed to the window. 'Look who's here!'

Their mother's jaw turned slack. 'It's James and Karen! I'm certain I warned them that Nicky was coming today.' She groaned and sank her face into her hands. 'I didn't mean *warned.* I meant told! I thought I'd told them she'd be here.'

'You probably did. You know how Karen switches off whenever Nicky's name is mentioned.'

The next moment, Nicola's brother gave his usual brisk volley of raps on the door before swinging it open. Then James strode to the couch, sat beside her and wrapped an arm around her shoulder, which was certainly *not* usual. But she leaned against him and hugged him back. Nicola peered through the front window. Karen sat in the car with a scowl.

'I've missed you,' James said. 'I didn't know you'd be here.'

'I've missed you too. Is Karen coming in?'

'I don't think so.'

'Maybe Nicky should go out and say hello,' Ruth suggested nervously.

James' jerk of the shoulders warned Nicola what was coming. 'No, Mum, that's not a good idea.' He leaned back to look at his sister. 'Sorry, Nic. Maybe it'll work one day but not today. It'd just hurt both of you. Nothing's really changed yet.' She noticed that James' eyes were streaked with pink lines. 'You do understand, don't you? Shane was her brother.'

'Of course I understand.'

'I'll go and sit in the car with Karen,' Laura offered. 'I know how to make her feel better.'

Laura's voice, sugary sweet enough to soothe a tiger, was like a red flag to Nicola. She wanted to shout. She wanted to shake the smugness out of her sister until Laura's teeth rattled. But she had never tried that sort of thing since they were children. It had never worked back then anyway. In fact, it used to have quite the opposite effect and stir more of Laura's self-righteousness up whenever Nicola got into trouble.

'I'm just about to go, anyway. I'm glad I got to see you, James.'

This time, their mother did not protest. 'Are you sure you don't want to take your lovely sketch?'

Nicola looked down at the calm image of Shane's face and suddenly did want him after all. She wanted to shield his soothing influence from the charged atmosphere she found it in. 'Yes, I will.'

With the framed sketch tucked beneath her arm she edged past James' parked car. Nicola glanced fleetingly at Karen's icy profile in the passenger's seat but took James' advice and kept walking to her own car, parked on the kerb. If this was the coward's way out it felt like one of the bravest walks she'd ever taken.

Before she closed her own door a shrill name pierced the air. The foulness of it made Nicola's stomach churn. She'd never heard Karen use such language before. When she swung around, her sister-in-law remained frozen in the same disdainful pose, as if she'd never said a word.

Nicola closed her door and started her engine with a trembling hand. She'd placed the sketch on the passenger's seat beside her. Shane looked as if he were ready to wink at her. Nicola's tears began to stream down her cheeks. They stung her eyes, forcing her to blink every few seconds so she could see to drive. By the time she arrived home, she was master of herself again. With one last dab of the eyes she tried to slip past Casey, who was cooking in the kitchen, but Casey swung around to greet her.

'Hi, how'd you go with your family?'

'It was good to see them.' Nicola held out the sketch to draw Casey's attention away from her own face. 'This is Shane, a friend of mine who died recently. He volunteered to sit for one of my art projects, once.'

Casey's sounds of sympathy and admiration washed over her and Nicola hurried up to her loft as soon as she could. She had no idea that Casey stood gazing after her.

'She's been crying,' Casey mumbled to herself. 'She must've really loved him. That poor girl hasn't breathed a word to a soul. I must warn Jerome not to bother her or get any silly ideas. That'd be the last thing she needs.'

*　　*　　*

Nicola was putting some finishing touches to her painting of the Bowman's house. She'd started it a few weeks earlier, intending to give it to Casey and Piers for a surprise when Christmas came. They were both out so she so took the opportunity to spread her canvas across the kitchen table. Nicola sucked her bottom lip as she surveyed her work, wondering whether the house's whimsical character had come through. The window to the Loft was supposed to resemble a little peeping eye; not unlike those of Laura, who sat close to Nicola's elbow, watching her.

'That's so excellent, Nicola. I wish I could paint like you. Even though I know painting is really a waste of time.'

Laura Bowman was blunt, like other little girls Nicola had known.

'Why do you think it's a waste of time?'

'It's just that you spent so many hours doing all that work, but it looks just like a photograph that someone could snap in two seconds.'

'I know what you mean. My own sister, Laura, used to say the same thing.'

'But you didn't believe her, did you?' It was Jerome's voice. Nicola thought he'd been reading a magazine on the couch but it seemed he'd been listening to their conversation. 'Paintings are far better than photos.'

'They look exactly the same,' Laura protested.

Jerome was up at the table with them. 'No, this is totally different. See how Nicola left out some ugly bits, like Dad's broken bandsaw that's been rusting on the verandah for weeks. And she's highlighted the way the sunshine lights up the Loft window. I think she's improved the look of the place, without seeming to change much. It's all in what she chooses to emphasise. Mum and Dad will love this.'

'I hope they will but I can see Laura's point. Sometimes I wish I was a different sort of artist. I've never invented anything from my own head. I just copy things.'

'But your way of copying things is as good as inventing them from your own head. You bring out beauty in scenes that normal people would walk straight past. And that makes us see the beauty too. It's a gift you've got.'

'I can't see any beauty,' Laura said flatly. 'It just looks like our normal old house to me.'

Nicola overlooked Laura's opinion because her senses were still reeling over what Jerome had said. No comment from her teacher had ever pleased her so much. 'I've never thought of it like that, before,' she told him.

'Is the Gratitude Group on this Wednesday?' he asked.

'Yes.'

'I wouldn't mind coming with you again.'

'That'd be great. I wasn't sure you'd want to.'

'I've got a good idea,' he said. 'What if I drive this time?'

'In my car?'

He reddened. 'Not if you don't want me to. I'm going to take the test for my driver's licence soon and I like the practise.'

'OK.' Nicola settled back to bask beneath his smile.

'Are you crazy?' Laura cried.

'Why? Isn't he a good driver?'

'It'll be the scariest ride of your life,' the nine-year-old predicted.

Jerome appeared too euphoric to respond to Laura's teasing but he tugged her tawny pony-tail. 'You don't know how good I am. Mum doesn't let you come out when I'm driving.' His laughing eyes met Nicola's. 'She values Laura's life too much.'

Nicola felt an unforced smile creep across her face; one of only a handful of spontaneous ones since Shane had died. When she thought about it, it seemed Jerome had something to do with all of them.

*   *   *

He sat through another tedious session of the Gratitude Group. If it was what he had to do to spend time with Nicola without members of his family breathing down their necks, Jerome was prepared to do it. Now that he knew what the group was all about, he'd even come prepared with a less controversial gratitude point. He told them he was glad he'd made it home from work on his bike before the Friday night downpour. They seemed happy with that.

But he still hadn't got to spend time with Nicola. The other girl, Bianca, had pulled her chair beside his and said, 'I hoped we'd see you back.' Then she hadn't left his side all night. Jerome wouldn't have minded chatting with Bianca except that he was missing out on time with Nicola. Bianca reminded him of several other girls he'd been on friendly terms with at school and work. In fact, talking with her reinforced why he wanted to spend time with Nicola.

As he followed Nicola outside after the group, Jerome said, 'I don't feel like going straight home. How'd you like to stop at a café for another drink?'

She seemed surprised but nodded. 'That sounds good.'

Jerome silently congratulated himself as they walked past her car and further down the street, although he was doing exactly what his mother had warned him not to do. Casey had beckoned Jerome aside one night to whisper that he ought to give Nicola breathing space to deal with her grief over a friend's death. 'I think that must be why she's come to us. And I think he might have been more than just a good friend.'

It seemed, 'giving Nicola breathing space,' meant that Jerome was supposed to hang back like a phantom and never pass the time of day with her.

'I hear what you're saying but I reckon she appreciates friendship just as much as space.'

'I'm not saying not to be friendly. Please do! She needs all the support we can give her. I'm only asking you to show a bit of tact and don't try to monopolise all her time.'

Jerome had felt annoyance prickling under his skin. He thought she ought to be warning Sam and Laura rather than him. He hadn't managed to get close enough to Nicola all week to ask her what she thought of his book because they were either reading jokes or playing games with her. He had even said as much.

'It's different with you, though,' Casey replied.

'Why is it different with me?'

'Think about it. It doesn't take a rocket scientist to work that one out.'

He caught himself grinning, but Jerome was careful to make sure Casey would never find out how often he thought of Nicola. She was different enough from any other girl he'd ever met to intrigue him. It was more than just her gentle manner and warm smile. Most girls he'd known were like Bianca Henderson, with her canary yellow hair and bright pink T-shirt announcing, *REBEL WITH A CAUSE!*

Bianca had leaned across to whisper in his ear, 'This isn't really my scene. I like to stand out from the crowd.' Jerome had heard the same comment too often from other girls to believe her.

'I have a confession to make,' Nicola was telling him. 'Before last Saturday, I never knew Casey wasn't your birth mother.'

'Didn't you?' Although he'd wanted to forget about his mother, she would do for a conversation starter. 'Sometimes I forget myself, she's been bossing me around for so long.'

'How brave it was of Casey, to take on a little stepson.'

'Yeah, I suppose you could call it brave. But the thing is, she wanted Dad and I was part of the package.'

When they walked into the café and settled themselves into a booth by the window, Nicola asked, 'How much do remember of those early times?'

'Quite a lot. Not long before their wedding, she told me, "Now that I'm marrying your dad, you can call me 'Mum' if you like." I wasn't even four years old but I could sense how nervous she felt about saying it. For some reason, that made me laugh.'

'*Did* you start calling her "Mum" right away?'

'I don't remember when it caught on. She'd look really pleased whenever I said it, so I started saying it more often to make her happy, and then she'd give me treats from the kitchen. But it didn't take long for her to get used to it and stop rewarding me. Then I felt hard-done-by.'

Nicola's dimples flashed. 'You know, it only takes twenty-one days to set a new habit. That's what Vicki told us on the first Gratitude Group. She said it should only take us three weeks to become genuine appreciators if we worked hard at it.'

'Well, it hasn't worked on that Bianca girl yet. Or on some of the others.'

'What makes you say that?'

'Because we start by sharing all our gratitude points, but by the end of the evening we're complaining about our bad colds and high fuel prices and how hard it's been at work. What's the point of trying to think more positive thoughts about some things if we come out whining the same as usual about other things? If we're serious about it, I reckon we've really got to keep on until it sticks for *everything*.'

She'd stopped smiling. Her silence warned him to stop talking. It was poor taste on his part, to disparage the group she'd invited him to. 'The opposite of what I'm doing right now,' he added, trying to bring the smile back to her face.

She cupped her chin in her hands. 'You're on to something though. Gratitude surely can't help change our lives unless we're consistent about it. The bad thoughts make us feel miserable again and cancel the good ones out. But you've got to understand how hard weeding out the old habits can be.'

He felt chastised. 'I didn't mean you.'

'I know you didn't. But it still applies to me. I haven't been practising gratitude during the week. I haven't been guarding my thoughts at all. I've got some pretty big hurdles.'

He wondered whether or not he ought to mention what hung between them. Jerome preferred to shy away from it, yet it was growing increasingly awkward to keep hedging the point. She probably knew that he knew. Taking the risk would get it over and done with. 'Mum told me about your friend. I was really sorry.'

His stomach pitched at the sight of her expression. It was the wrong thing to say. Instead of speaking, she clamped her jaw and looked at the table top. Jerome's fingernails dug hard into the palms of his hands as his mind whirled for the best way to apologise, when he saw that she wasn't angry at all. She was squeezing her eyelids tight, trying not to cry. Then sympathy flooded him but he was too panicky to know how to express it.

His first instinct was to reach for her hand but he couldn't bring himself to do it. That might be inappropriate. Was there any protocol for such situations? Nicola was wearing a silky green blouse that matched her eyes. He could see the soft, round outlines of her arms through it. Jerome surprised himself how much that stirred him. He wanted to be a missionary and help hurting people all the time, yet found himself floundering when he got an opportunity to try. And noticing things he didn't mean to notice.

He could suggest that they go home. That might be best. But when he began to rise, Nicola's hand shot out and motioned him to sit back down. Her eyes were dry and her smile back in place.

'Sorry, I didn't want to make a scene. It's just that Shane's death was so recent, sometimes I still get…' instead of trying to find a word, she fanned her face with both hands and forced a little laugh. 'I think you would've liked him. He was a terrific guy. He'd always been my next-door-neighbour but he was more like another brother to me.'

How should he respond to that? His mother told him she thought Shane had been Nicola's boyfriend. Then why did Nicola say he was like a brother?

'Hey, you haven't asked me what I thought of your Gareth Edgley book.'

Those were the words he'd hoped to hear from her, but now he was conscious that she was using them to provide him with an escape route from the mess he'd created.

'I never really got a chance.'

'That's true. It's always pretty lively at your place. Well, do you want to know what I thought of it?'

'Of course I do.' Yet something had gone incredibly haywire. She was trying to make *him* feel better instead of vice versa. And he had to force his racing thoughts to settle down and listen to what she had to say. He hadn't given Gareth Edgley as much thought as usual for the last couple of days.

He'd had somebody else on his mind.

12

All the house lights were off when Jerome and Nicola arrived home.

'Well, goodnight,' she whispered at the foot of her small flight of stairs.

Jerome didn't want to let her go without leaving a more favourable impression of himself, or at least something to boost her spirits. 'Hey, have you ever drawn a self-portrait?' he asked.

Nicola pulled a face and shook her head.

'Why not?'

She blushed and laughed his question off. 'I don't think I could find a big enough sheet of paper.'

Jerome could think of a few different responses to that. As she was being flippant herself, he decided to risk the humorous approach.

'That's just an excuse. I saw you draw an elephant for Sam on a very small piece.'

She gaped at him for a moment. Nicola's lips twitched then she laughed. 'I need to think of a way to pay you back for that one.'

'But seriously,' he whispered, 'why don't you? I'd like to see it. I would've thought every artist would like to try a self-portrait.'

'Why would you think that? Michelangelo thought himself hideous.'

'Maybe Michelangelo *was* hideous. I'm sure he probably wasn't, though. I've never met any hideous people.'

'Well, I'm really just a student. I haven't got to the stage of considering myself a real artist. And I wasn't trying to compare my skill to Michelangelo's.'

'But you're a great artist. If you don't think you are, you're criticising my judgment.'

'I wouldn't want to do that, but maybe you'd change your mind if you were given some really great pieces to compare mine with.'

'I wouldn't change my mind. Remember what I told you the other night? You're the sort of artist who finds beauty in unexpected places.' Jerome thought he wasn't going too badly and wondered why Nicola's eyes began to gleam.

'OK, now I get it. *That's* why you think I ought to try a self-portrait.'

He took a few seconds to consider what she was getting at.

'Beauty in *very* unexpected places,' she teased, and watched her implication dawn on him.

Jerome shook his head hard. 'I didn't mean that! Hey Nicola, you don't really think...'

She had to cover her mouth to smother the peals of laughter that rolled up. He looked so appalled by what she'd read into his innocent comment, she couldn't help it. And she welcomed the opportunity to tease him. 'Didn't take me long to get you back. You'd better go to bed before you stick your foot in it even deeper.'

At her door she took one last glance at him standing on the landing at the bottom of her stairs with his face buried into his hands. As Jerome rested his forehead on the banister with a thump, Nicola closed her door with a grin. She felt a little sorry for him but he didn't know how good he'd been for her. She found it incredible that she could possibly manage such a genuine belly laugh so soon after Shane's death.

*   *   *

'I've got one for you, Sammy-boy.' Michael heaved a box of tools into the back of Piers' old station wagon. 'What did Tarzan say when he saw the elephants coming over the hill?'

'I give in.'

'*Here come the elephants.* Now, what did Tarzan say when he saw the elephants coming over the hill wearing sunglasses?'

Sam began to giggle from his perch on the car bonnet. 'What?'

'Nothing, because he didn't recognise them.'

Sam was off into convulsions and even Jerome chuckled. 'Hey, that one's not bad.'

'We're all ready to go,' Piers announced. 'Off you get, Sam.' He was taking Michael and Jerome to help him erect a sun porch for an elderly couple in the city.

'I really wanna come too.'

'You didn't when I offered you the chance last night.'

'But that was before I knew Michael would be coming.'

Piers ruffled his hair. 'Tough luck. Now, you're going out with Mum and Laura.'

'That's boring.' Sam's face was screwed into the scowl he'd perfected as a toddler.

'I'll kick the footy with you when we get back,' Michael promised.

Sam's face brightened slightly. 'OK.'

Piers and the older boys were off. Jerome let Michael have the front passenger's seat and stretched his legs out in the back.

'Michael, do you have any plans for your future?' Piers was trying to make conversation.

'Nope, I'm pretty useless at everything,' Michael replied cheerfully.

'I've already known you long enough to tell you that's not true,' Piers declared.

'You don't need to try to make me feel better, Mr B. I've worked out that I'm happier just facing the truth. That's better than trying to do all sorts of different things that I'm no good at.' Michael craned his head to look back at Jerome. 'Hey J, I forgot to bring back that book you lent me. Maybe you'd better come to my place and pick it up or I'll keep forgetting.'

'OK. Did you like it?'

There was a moment of silence from the front seat. 'I couldn't really get into it. I'm not much of a reader. I have trouble concentrating on anything for long. But Blake and Claire read it together.'

'What did they think of it?'

'I think they enjoyed it.'

Jerome decided he'd have to ask Blake and Claire himself when he went to collect the book.

'I read enough to know what that guy was on about,' Michael was peering back at Jerome again. 'Is that the sort of thing you want to do? Bum around like that Edgley bloke doing odd jobs and telling people that God's looking out for 'em?'

Jerome hesitated. Michael's description was not exactly flattering and he was waiting with the trace of a smirk.

'Well, there's nothing wrong with that.' He could have added, 'At least I have a goal,' but decided to spare Michael's feelings.

Michael wasn't going to spare his. 'I hate to tell you, but I wouldn't ever listen to a guy like you.'

'Why not?'

'I never had much in common with your type. I know you can't help it but you're the sort my mates and I used to call a square or a pansy. We had other names too, but I won't repeat them. You're just way different from us. Stable family, cool clothes and the sort of looks chicks go for. And you read books! I'll bet you got good grades at school too.'

'He did very well in his exams.'

Although Jerome could see only the back of his father's head, he could tell from the sound of his voice that Piers found the conversation amusing.

'I knew it!' Michael almost bounced in his seat. 'You see! What could you possibly understand about the way the rest of us tick?'

Jerome tried to ignore the cold feeling seeping through his spirit. He didn't like the sound of the person Michael was describing. It didn't match the way he wanted to think of himself. It sounded like Arthur Pratt, the priggish anti-hero in Gareth Edgley's book. Jerome didn't want to be Arthur. He wanted to be Gareth.

'I've had hard times too.'

A snorting sound came from Michael. 'Yeah, I've heard about 'em. You can't find the second Gareth Edgley book.' He struck his forehead with a dramatic gesture. 'Like whoa, man! That's heavy stuff!'

Jerome fought the urge to aim a swift kick at the back of Michael's seat. Instead, he laughed to prove that he could take a joke. He thought of all he'd learned about Michael Quinlan since he'd met him. Michael had discovered his mother lying dead on the floor. His oldest brother was a paraplegic and his father was a drunken renegade. Michael had been through a rehabilitation clinic to conquer a drug problem before he even turned eighteen. What did Jerome have to offer people like Michael? Or people like Nicola, who was coping with a tragedy of her own? No wonder he had floundered so dismally with her the night at the café.

'Jerome did have a very rough start in life,' Piers put in.

'But I can't remember any of that, Dad.' Jerome wished Piers wouldn't stick up for him. Having a supportive father proved Michael's point. He felt guilty for his stable family and easy lifestyle. If Jerome managed to earn enough to get him to Europe, it might lose him more credibility with the people he wanted to help. The thought pierced him like an arrow in the heart.

'He had a rough start, did he? It doesn't show,' Michael said.

'Who would you listen to, then?' Jerome challenged him.

Michael's shoulders shrugged above the arm rest. 'I dunno. Someone more like me, I suppose.'

'But nobody like you would ever do it. You said yourself, you're pretty well useless at everything,' Jerome reminded him.

Michael's face registered a moment of surprise. He laughed and sank down a few inches in his seat. But after that he looked out at the road and left Jerome alone.

* * *

Piers enjoyed the company of his two helpers. He never tired of being with Jerome, who was more than just a son to him. Jerome was a milestone. He was the marker that stood between Piers' dejected youth and his more stable manhood.

Disguised as Piers' biggest mistake, the newborn Jerome was the catalyst who had caused his father to turn to God for guidance and protection. Piers was convinced that the shower of blessings he received, including Casey and their two younger children, would never have caught up with him if Jerome hadn't come into his life and changed his outlook. Sometimes when he felt gloomy, a glance at Jerome was all it took to remind Piers how far God had brought them both.

Jerome was kneeling on the grass nailing together some planks. Michael Quinlan tapped his shoulder. Piers watched Jerome twist his head to look up. The enquiring gesture with his eyebrows reminded Piers of Anna, Jerome's mother. Years ago, Piers used to wonder if Anna practised her quirky lift of the eyebrows until she got it right, but watching Jerome proved that it was not so. Piers was always impressed by the sheer scope of all that could be passed down through heredity.

Michael rubbed a handful of sawdust into Jerome's hair. Jerome's quick smile flashed and he was on his feet, shaking dust from his hair and making a lunge at Michael, whose long legs easily straddled the rails of the sun porch they'd erected.

Michael was an interesting lad. He reminded Piers of a quality racehorse who'd spent his life walking around in a paddock. With his strapping frame, it seemed he ought to be athletic, instead of loose-jointed and round-shouldered as he was. But although the more lithely built Jerome seemed to have more energy, Michael had done a good day's work for somebody who wasn't used to the type of labour Piers had served up to him.

At the end of the day, Michael stretched himself out on the grass beside the car and arched his arms over his head with a groan. 'I'm exhausted.'

Piers took out his wallet. 'Would you like to be paid?'

Michael sat up like a bolt. 'You bet!' He flicked through the bank notes with satisfaction glowing from every grubby pore. 'I'll tell you what, Mr B, I'll use this first hundred to pay back a debt I owe. Here you go, J. I promised I would.'

Jerome handed the money back to him. 'You can keep it. Blake already paid me back.'

Michael's jaw dropped. 'Did he?'

'Yeah. Didn't he tell you?'

Michael pounded a fist into his opposite palm. 'No. I hate that sneaking idiot. Why did he have to stick his beak in?'

'He was just trying to help. Now you can keep your money. That's good, isn't it?'

But Michael's eyes were shiny with unshed tears. 'You don't get it. He still doesn't trust me!'

Jerome turned red and mumbled, 'He gave you plenty of time. You borrowed that money from me weeks ago.'

'And I told you I'd pay it back! Couldn't you have waited?'

'Are you mad at *me* now?'

'What d' you reckon, Einstein?'

Jerome looked at Piers with a what-am-I-supposed-to-do shrug. 'All I did was lend you money. I'll take that hundred bucks if it'll make you feel better. Hand it over.'

Michael was in no mood to be jollied into a smile. He scowled out of the window on the way home. Jerome stared down at his knees. Piers could think of nothing to say. It was a sombre end to an enjoyable day.

13

Nicola and Jerome agreed to try another café after the Gratitude Group. This time, she suggested one that she liked near her art school. They settled down at their table but soon after their hot drinks arrived, her eyes widened at the sight of something behind Jerome's shoulder. He turned his head and saw two young women making their orders at the counter.

'It's Laura and Karen,' Nicola whispered to him. Her face was ashen.

'Laura, your sister?' he questioned.

She nodded. 'And Karen is Shane's sister.'

Laura spotted them. Jerome guessed she must be Laura because she had a similar oval shaped face to Nicola's, though not as graceful and pretty. Laura's jutting cheekbones appear gaunt beneath her bright make-up. And her legs were twig-like, in her tight jeans. She looked from him to Nicola and mumbled something to her companion. Both girls moved across to their table, although the one called Karen shot Nicola a dirty look. Jerome found his eyes smarting in aroma of their perfumes.

Nicola avoided Karen's gaze as she made introductions. 'This is Jerome Bowman. I'm staying with his family. Jerome, this is my sister, Laura, and our sister-in-law, Karen. She's married to our brother, James.'

Laura was gaping at Jerome as if he was some freakish apparition. 'Nicky, he looks like…' She gave a giggle and snapped her mouth shut.

Nicola flamed red and stared down at her cup.

'Well, it's nice to meet you.' For a few awkward moments Laura stood making small talk. They had been out to see a movie. It was the first time Laura had been able to convince Karen to have a night out since… you know. The movie was OK. They were all proud of Karen for making the effort.

'How old are you, Jerome?' Karen asked suddenly, with a sweetness that did not match the way she'd been scowling at Nicola.

He hesitated. 'Nineteen.' A simple answer seemed more courteous than his instinctive, *Why do you want to know?*

Karen and Laura exchanged glances and Karen's freckled nose creased. 'Nicky, I can see you're suffering over poor Shane. *Pining* for him, aren't you?'

If Jerome had ever been tongue-tied in the past, it was nothing to this moment. Heat poured across his face but as he watched acute pain fill Nicola's green eyes, he knew he needed to say something fast.

'We're just having a drink. What's your problem?' His heart was thumping. That was lame and defensive but he didn't know enough about these strangers to figure out what he ought to have said. He only knew he couldn't bear to see Nicola look that way.

Laura squeezed Karen beneath her elbow. 'If you knew all that Karen's been through, you'd understand her feelings.'

'I'm not sticking around here! What a rotten end to a miserable night. At least *some people* are happy without Shane.' With a toss of her head, Karen strode to the door. Laura gave a helpless shrug and hurried after her. Nicola and Jerome sat blinking at each other. Sipping his hot drink seemed out of the question now, even though he needed something to hide his embarrassment.

'Maybe you'd prefer to go too?'

She instantly pushed back her chair. 'That might be best. You must be wondering what she was talking about.'

'It's OK. You don't have to tell me.'

They were out in the street. Although the night was mild, Nicola pulled her denim jacket collar around her neck and shivered. 'I don't mind talking about it now. Maybe I've kept it all to myself for long enough. But only if you don't mind listening?' Her eyes, always clear reflectors of her feelings, radiated anxiety to him.

'Of course I don't mind.' Yet as they walked, he wondered if she'd still want to tell him if she had any idea how his stomach was squirming, trying to prepare him for whatever it might be, in case he didn't know what to say.

*   *   *

The car was parked directly beneath a street light which flooded in on them. Nicola might have preferred her face to be shielded by darkness but it didn't really matter. She just wanted to talk about Shane. And to her own surprise, the person she wanted to tell was this gorgeous young guy with his liquid-grey eyes fixed on her.

She repeated the conversation she'd had with Shane on the bus and went on to describe the night they'd sat around the Turnbull family's lounge room with the police officer. When Nicola got to the part about what had happened to Shane, the grief that had kept her chest knotted for weeks moved to her throat so she couldn't speak on. There was a moment of silence.

'It wasn't your fault,' Jerome said at last. 'It was terrible but you weren't responsible for his choice. You didn't send him to the pub or tell him to go swimming afterwards.'

'I know all that in my head. But it doesn't change the fact that he did those things because of me. I caused the death of somebody I really loved.'

Jerome sat quietly thinking things through in his characteristic way. 'If you think that way, we could all reason that we caused something bad.' He rumpled his hair and bowed his head. 'You could just as easily say that I was the cause of my mother's death.'

'You mean your birth mother?' She thought her question ridiculous as soon as she asked it. He obviously didn't mean Casey.

'Yeah. I don't know if you heard the story. Her name was Anna. Soon after Dad broke up with her, she found out she was pregnant. She didn't want me but didn't do anything about it because she was antiabortion. And soon after I was born, she overdosed on drugs.' He spoke in the unemotional tone of a news reader. 'They think it might have been suicide because of post-natal depression. If that's true, I guess you could argue that I was the cause. Or that Dad was the cause.' He raised his eyes to look at her. 'Would that be right?'

Nicola was already shaking her head before he finished. 'It was her own decision to overdose.'

'Well then…' Jerome waited for her to make the connection.

Nicola's eyes brimmed with tears. The only way to hold them back would be to squeeze her eyes shut and hold her face rigid. But when she tried her face twisted. Her defences had crumbled. She leaned her forehead against the steering wheel and sobbed. Nicola looked at the blurry image of Jerome. 'Sorry. It's just that I really miss him.'

'That's OK.' He was twisting his long fingers together, and his eyes appeared shiny. Nicola shook her hair to cover her face.

'So maybe it wasn't my fault. It was just a horrible accident,' she gulped.

'And if it wasn't his asking you out, it might've been anything that made him upset. A bad day at work or his football team losing. I don't know if he was the sort of bloke who'd care about things like that.'

Nicola was smiling through her tears. 'He did love his footy.'

'He would've been my sort of guy, then.'

She pressed her eyes into her denim sleeve and cleared her throat. 'We're not responsible for anyone else's actions,' she repeated. It brought lightness to her spirit to hear herself say it. 'So if Karen never forgives me… well, that's her choice. But I hope she will.'

Jerome nodded sadly. 'I'm sure her brother would want her to.'

'I'm sorry about what she said to you,' Nicola told him.

'Hey, I can handle it. By the way, who does your sister think I look like?'

'What do you mean?' She needed a second to think of a reply.

'She was staring at me and then she said, "He looks like …" and didn't finish. But I guess you knew who she was talking about.'

'Yeah, I reckon she thinks you look like a work of art we've both seen. It's at home… in a book.' Nicola wanted to sink through the floor of her car. She might have been wiser to have pretended not to know.

'A work of art, hey? Well, I hope it wasn't anything by Picasso.'

Mirth bubbled up in Nicola's chest. She found herself laughing as if his remark was the wittiest thing she'd ever heard. Then she couldn't stop, even though it wasn't all that funny. Perhaps it was what she needed after all her crying.

* * *

Cruising up the long driveway, Nicola saw that the inside lights were on; a welcoming beacon in the pitch black night. When she parked in her usual spot, Jerome made no move to get out but folded his arms and spread out his feet across the floor beneath her glove box. His long legs made the interior of her car appear small.

'That story has stuck inside my mind,' he told her. 'I feel terrible too, and I didn't even know the guy. I think you've been amazing.'

Flattery swept through her, bringing shame in its wake, because she shouldn't feel pleased over such a compliment. Nicola had never noticed that grief and flattery could mix up with each other in some sort of crazy recipe for guilt. If Karen knew, Nicola thought she'd have a right to be shocked. 'I don't know where it'll all end or if Karen will ever talk to me again.'

'I guess you must've been pretty close before it happened,' he said.

'We were close when we were children. Karen and I are the same age. We used to call each other best friends. But she's been closer to Laura for a long time. We started drifting apart even before Shane's death. Last time we all went out together was the night before Laura's twenty-first. That was just a few months ago. Laura's only a year younger than we are.'

Jerome quickly figured out the math. Nicola was three years older than he was. It didn't sound like much but when she was his age, he would have been only fifteen. Back when Jerome was fifteen, he had still enjoyed inventing make-believe games to play with Sam and Laura, much as he hated to admit it. And when he'd slipped over and sprained his wrist, he'd cried for half an hour. She was already grown-up while he'd still been such a kid. Now that she was twenty-two, he wondered if nineteen seemed incredibly young to her.

'Laura and Karen were trying to set me up with men that night, too,' she remembered with a laugh. 'I was trying to chat with some fellows who Laura works with, but after a few hours I struggled for things to say. They weren't coming up with anything themselves. I felt as if the onus was on me. And at the end of the night, one of them whispered to Laura, *Your sister is such a phony.*'

'Why did she repeat that to you?'

'She thought she was trying to help me out.'

Jerome let out a short laugh. 'Doesn't sound very helpful.'

'Maybe I was a phony. There I was, smiling away when I felt like groaning with boredom. But I thought they would've preferred a phony to a grouch.'

'Do you know what I reckon?'

'What do you reckon?'

He hoped she wasn't trying to humour him, as if he was a youngster like Sam. 'Even if you were being phony, so what? There's nothing wrong with trying. We're all doing the best we can.' He could have added that he was a phony too, for persisting in going to the Gratitude Group with her. 'Maybe that's why most of the time I prefer to stay home and read rather than go out. People say such harsh things about others and I can't see the point.'

Nicola turned on her seat to face him easier. 'Sounds as if you're speaking from experience. Tell me, have you ever had a girlfriend?'

He blushed. 'Not really.'

'That's no sort of answer,' she crowed. 'Come on, tell me her name?'

His left shoulder slid further down the window. 'OK, it was Mel. Short for Melody. But she wasn't really my girlfriend. Not for long, anyway. She was in some of my classes at school.'

'Did you end it? Or vice versa?'

He never would have gone on with the story if he'd been talking to anybody else but he rather liked Nicola's interest.

'Both, really. Whenever I told her things, all of her friends would end up knowing about them too.'

'So you were that popular, hey?'

He laughed. 'Those girls were so weird, more like it. Once I'd been telling her how it wasn't fair that guys were always expected to give girls flowers when we're meant to be living in times of equal opportunity. I forget why we were talking about that. We were just mucking around. But the next morning when I walked into home group, my desk was covered with heaps of weeds tied up with string. Five or six girls were waiting for me, saying, *We heard you like getting flowers, Jerome*. Then they almost suffocated themselves laughing.'

Nicola covered a wide beam with her hand. 'You probably made their day. Don't let their silly behaviour put you off. Some girls are sensible.'

'Yeah, I've been told they're out there. Hey what the...?'

Somebody was pounding on his window with the palms of their hands. Laura stood there in her flannel pyjamas with her russety hair flowing around her grinning face. Jerome wound down his window.

'What do you want? And why aren't you in bed?'

'It's school holidays, you dope! Mum wants to know why you're sitting out here and not coming inside.'

'You weren't supposed to say that.' Sam had come up behind Laura and shoved her shoulder. 'Mum said not to say that. But she did say to ask if anyone would like a game of Scrabble.'

'That sounds a bit fishy to me.' Jerome knew Casey didn't indulge in long games at ten thirty on a week night.

'Well, she said we could sit up and play, anyway. Anyone want to join?'

'I'll have a game,' Nicola said.

Jerome was in a quandary. He knew Sam and Laura would probably expect him to refuse because he usually did. If he joined in the game they might think it was just so he could be near Nicola. But the fact was he did want to be near Nicola.

'I'll play too.' He decided to let them think whatever they liked.

14

Jerome politely pretended not to notice the panic-stricken expression on the face of the elderly lady who rummaged through her purse for a coin.

'I *thought* I had it. I counted it out before we came. Ah, here it is. I knew I had it.' She was almost panting as she placed the last twenty cent coin on the counter before him.

'Thank you, ma'am. I was sure you'd find it.' He grinned and gave her what she'd ordered; one hot coffee along with a single cheeseburger for the wispy boy who stood beside her. Although his wrists and collarbone protruded, the boy dragged his feet to their table with the lethargy of a much heavier person.

'Look at that poor little runt,' Michael mumbled in Jerome's ear. It was late. Nobody else was waiting to be served and the restaurant was almost empty. 'Why won't she buy him more than a lousy cheeseburger? I mean, come on!'

'She couldn't afford more,' Jerome whispered. 'She thought she was twenty cents short as it was.'

Michael was staring at the scrawny youngster. 'He's just skin and bone.'

'I know.' Jerome had also noticed smudgy shadows beneath the child's eyes.

'I'm gonna treat him to a chocolate sundae.'

'No, you can't do that. Rick would kill you.'

'I meant with my own money,' Michael scoffed. 'Payday was yesterday so I got a bit of cash. That kid looks as if he's never seen a decent dessert in his life.'

'Maybe you still shouldn't.' Jerome tried to explain his reluctance. 'They might think you're sticking your nose in. People can be funny that way.'

'To hell with that! If I weighed the same as a plucked chook and someone offered me a sundae I'd be stupid to take offence. I think I'll offer them both one.'

Michael fixed the sundaes. Jerome watched him breeze over to the table where the woman and boy sat. He heard him say, 'These are for you. On the house,' but didn't see the strangers' reactions because Michael's back masked them. Jerome served another customer and when he raised his eyes, he saw the waif-like boy's face transformed by a wide beam. There were traces of a chocolate fudge moustache on his top lip.

Michael was back behind the counter with him. 'It worked,' he whispered. 'They were pleased.'

'Yeah, I saw.'

'I might've made their night.'

'Maybe you did.'

A few moments later Michael asked, 'Hey J, would you like a lift home when we finish here?'

'Yeah, thanks. I'll pick up my bike tomorrow.'

Michael rolled his eyes. 'You passed the driver's test, didn't you? The way you hoard money, you could surely afford a cheap car by now.'

'Yeah, but you know I'm saving for something else. I don't need a car.'

'Of course, the missionary thing. How could I forget? Well, I have way different priorities to you, man.'

'Excuse me.' The elderly lady was back at the counter, smiling at Michael. 'I want to tell you how much your kind gesture meant to us. My grandson has just lost his mother. And I've been finding it hard to manage on my pension. Just this morning, I prayed to God that if He really cared for us, He'd give us some sort of sign today. I didn't want to wait for one more sleep. I was desperate. And it looked as if it wasn't going to happen. But as soon as you brought us those ice-creams, my grandson reminded me. And then I knew you were the sign.'

Jerome had never seen Michael at a complete loss for words before. He opened his mouth and shut it again, settling on a sheepish smile. 'That's OK,' he croaked at last.

'Bless you, young man. Bless you for your thoughtfulness and your kind heart.'

'It was nothing, really.' Michael avoided the woman's appreciative glance and looked down at the young boy. 'Hey mate, I lost my mother too. Things get easier. But I didn't think so at the time.'

The boy managed to give Michael a weak smile.

When he and the woman left the restaurant, Michael let out a long sigh. 'Whoa, that was pretty freaky, wasn't it?'

Jerome wanted to get home, sit in his bedroom and do some thinking. 'It was cool. It was just like a Gareth Edgley moment.'

Michael's eyes kindled with light. 'Hey, there's a thought. I beat you at your own game. You were too gutless to offer 'em sundaes.'

'I didn't even think of it.' It was no use pretending otherwise.

'Hey, J?' Michael's cheeks were turning brighter. 'Do you reckon it's true what she said?'

'Which part?'

Now his face was aflame. 'That God *did* use me? As a sign?'

'Absolutely.'

Michael's face screwed up. 'No way! I have nothing to do with Him. If He was real, He'd know that. He'd choose someone else!'

'Not if there was nobody else around who'd listen.' It hurt Jerome to say that but Michael didn't notice.

'I'm pretty dense for asking you. I should've asked someone else.' Michael sauntered off to the store room to collect his bag and keys.

*   *   *

As soon as he'd eaten the meal his mother had kept warm for him, Jerome slipped outside to sit on the verandah steps. Now that he was alone to think things through, he felt even worse than he had before.

'Hey, are you OK?' Nicola had come to stand behind him. She was close enough that he noticed her sweet fragrance, far too subtle to be called perfume. It was more like sunshine, fresh earth and flowers, probably the sorts of mediums artists played around with all day. Her proximity was enough to start his pulse racing. If anyone had to come out to check on him he was glad it was her, although he had nothing to say.

'Yeah, I'm OK.'

She slowly shook her head. 'I don't buy it. You're sad about something.'

'Just trying to figure out what to do with my life,' he admitted. 'Maybe I should've accepted one of those university offers.'

'But you already know what you want to do.'

'I'm going off that idea of being a missionary.'

She could hardly have looked more stunned and distressed when she heard the terrible news about her friend Shane. Nicola sank down onto the step beside him. 'Will you tell me why?'

'It's no big deal.' He was too embarrassed to look at her face. Instead he tapped a quick tattoo on the bottom step with his feet while he spoke, trying to sound off-hand. 'I've found out I don't have a knack for it after all. I don't notice what's right under my nose. And I play it too safe.'

'What do you mean? Why do you think that?'

He described what had happened at McDonald's as briefly as he could.

'Well, good on Michael!' Nicola cried.

'Yeah, you should've seen him. He was really something.'

'But I don't see why Michael's generosity should make you want to ditch your ambition.'

Jerome almost groaned. She hadn't understood. 'The thing is I didn't think of buying sundaes for them myself. And if I had, I probably would've piked out. I'm not the impulsive type.' He sighed heavily. 'I wish I was.'

'But there's more than one way to be kind. Why should people like Michael, who think first and act later, have all the monopoly on good deeds?'

He managed a laugh. 'I think they're the sort of people God can use. Risk-takers make themselves more available.'

Nicola glanced away from him before she spoke again. 'You know the other night when I told you about Shane? What you said helped me more than you might think. And I'd never have told anyone like Michael Quinlan in a million years.'

Although he was flattered, Jerome shook his head. 'That was different.'

'In what way?'

He found himself trapped in one of his tongue-tied moments. The honest reply would be that he had an ulterior motive in helping her because he was so attracted to her. Of course he would never tell her that but what would he say?

'You asked me if I'd mind listening. I didn't think to offer. So it wasn't the same.' That was lame but she seemed to accept it.

'It amazed me that Michael's idea worked so well,' Jerome went on. 'I would have thought, *If these people have problems, a couple of free desserts won't make much difference.* But you should've seen that boy's face. He was so happy over such a little thing as that.'

'But Gareth Edgley only ever did little things,' Nicola pointed out. 'You ought to know. You lent me the book. Think about it. He repaired broken fences. He bought apples and loaves of bread for the poor. He offered people directions. He did mostly the sort of thing Michael did today. Little things for isolated individuals. But he just kept doing them over and over. Things that *anyone* can do.'

The familiar stimulant of a new idea began to course through Jerome's blood. 'I reckon you're onto something!' He felt as if he'd been slapped in the face with a fact he should have known all along. His parents had often told him similar things but he hadn't listened to them. 'I've been letting myself think I have to do big things to make a difference, but who says the size of the deed has any bearing on the size of the impact it makes.'

Nicola's face reflected his enthusiasm. 'Pretty amazing to think that small people like us can make any sort of difference. So don't give up.'

Jerome grinned at her. 'You know, you're just the same as Gareth and Michael, except that you're not small. You're huge!'

Her dimples popped out. 'There's no need to mention *that.*'

He wanted to kick himself hard. 'Hey, I didn't mean...' He trailed off. What else could he say? He could tell her that he thought about her one thousand times each day; that seeing her laugh at something he said was one of his favourite things; that her sparkly green eyes always drew him in; that he didn't think she was all that big, anyway. But not even a natural risk-taker like Michael would say any of that. It only left the cringing, pathetic, speechless option.

She was still smiling as she scrambled to her feet. 'I'm sorry. I knew what you meant. I was only trying to make you laugh.'

Then he did laugh but it fell flat between them. He should've laughed in the first place instead of apologising like an idiot but it was too late. Another talk with Nicola had ended in disaster. Once again, it was his fault.

Jerome returned inside, shut his door behind him and flipped through his Gareth Edgley book, reading a few phrases here and there. He wanted to read it all over again in the light of what Nicola had said about Gareth's focus on the little things. The problem was he'd already read the book so often, he knew entire passages off by heart.

The little things! Little things *did* make a difference. He remembered a story Casey often told, about his dead birth mother's parents. She'd said, 'On their last visit to see Jerome, Sam had been interested in collecting stamps. And a few months later they posted him a whole envelope full of foreign stamps. All those years I thought they were really only interested in Jerome. When they made such a kind gesture on Sam's behalf it really touched my heart.'

The door creaked open and Sam's face looked as downcast as Jerome had felt almost all evening.

'Are you reading that *again?* Gee whiz, there are other books in the world, you know.'

'Yeah, I think twenty-four times is probably enough.' Jerome dropped *Distributing Heaven* onto his bedside table. 'How about a game of something?'

Sam gaped at him. 'What did you say?'

'I've got nothing to do. I'll give you a game. What'll it be?'

Then Sam's face began to glow like the boy's in McDonald's. Jerome felt chastened by the happy disbelief in his brother's expression. Was it really that mind-blowing that he'd offered to play a game?

'OK, how about a few rounds of computer Tetris and then maybe a board game?'

'Hold on, I didn't say anything about *two* games.' He felt obligated to show some consistency.

'I've gotta make the most of this while you're in the mood.'

Jerome swept a pile of clothes off the second bedroom chair and drew it up to the computer beside Sam's.

Perhaps that was where he always went wrong with Nicola. He over-thought every word he said. *I really want to be more of a risk-taker. I've got to be, if I want to get anywhere at all in this world!*

15

Nicola was shocked to see who was phoning her. She had just parked her car and there was Karen's name flashing on her phone screen. Nicola's fingers shook and she drew a deep breath before answering.

'Hello?'

'Hello.' Karen's voice was icy. It was obviously not going to be a friendly call.

'How are you going?' Nicola looked longingly at the red *end call* button.

'I didn't call to tell you how I'm going. I've called to find out how you're going.'

'I'm OK, Karen.' Nicola waited for whatever was coming.

'Do the people you're living with know that you're trying to seduce their nineteen-year-old son?'

So *that* was it? Nicola felt a swooping sensation in her heart. 'We're just friends. That's all.'

'Don't give me that. I know you well enough not to believe it. You'd never go to a café with somebody you aren't attracted to. Take Shane for example. If you'd only once gone out with him when he asked you, he might still be alive today.'

Nicola took her chance. 'Karen, now that you're talking to me, I've been grieving over Shane too. I've always loved him like a brother. If I made a mistake in the way I responded to him that night, I didn't intend to. I thought I was acting for the best. I'll never forget him ever. But the way he died–that was not my fault.'

'It just hurts me that you'd go out with some stranger you haven't known for long but you wouldn't go out even once with my brother, who loved you with all his heart.'

The phone felt slippery in Nicola's perspiring hand. 'Well, just for the record, nothing's happening anyway.'

'You mean the young guy doesn't fancy you?' Karen's voice was sharp.

'Not in the slightest.' That was an admission about her own feelings but Nicola said it anyway. She didn't want to pretend with Karen.

Karen was silent for a moment. Perhaps she hadn't expected to hear that. 'So now you know how Shane must've felt.'

Nicola managed to ask, 'Are you happy about that?'

'Not really. I thought I would've been but I'm not. I still think you could've given Shane a chance.'

Nicola was parked outside Laura Bowman's dancing class. It was almost time for her to walk in and pick Laura up for Casey and Piers, who were both busy. Her throat was tight but she was not going to break down. 'I know you do. But we both know Shane well enough to know that he'd hate the way things are between you and me now.' Nicola stopped to swallow and it hurt. 'If I could ask his advice, I know he'd say not to give up hoping that some day you'd understand it wasn't my fault and that you'd talk to me and be my sister-in-law again.'

'No, Nicola. Not yet. I'm not ready for this. I still hurt too much. That's what I phoned to tell you. I gotta go now. Goodbye.' She hung up.

The call left Nicola feeling raw inside. However, now the memory of Shane's gentle face no longer caused as much pain as the image of Jerome's animated one. Now that Karen knew her secret, Nicola hoped she'd have the tact not to tell anybody.

Jerome would always be the boy who'd given her Adonis a warm character that she could never add to any painting. His eyes always reflected thought ticking-over, even when his demeanour was quiet. And such thought about all sorts of altruistic ideas. Yet Jerome was also fun to tease because his sense of humour was as large as his heart. All of that was just part of why her heart skipped a beat whenever she knew he was anywhere near.

Nicola wouldn't always be living with the Bowmans. When she left, she'd be so much lonelier for having known Jerome. Even though he was younger and would never give her a second glance, she would not choose to stop caring for him if some genie should ever offer her the chance.

Shane, did you ever really feel this way about me? And Jerome, it's true that you helped me but I wonder how you'd feel to know that you've also completely messed me up? Although she was alone, Nicola forced a mirthless laugh at herself. *But I don't blame you! Even if I broke my heart over you, I know it wouldn't be your fault. And maybe that's given me the biggest help of all. But I can't tell you that.'*

It was time to walk into the dancing studio to collect Laura. Several girls were already straggling out to the cloakroom to collect their clothes and bags while others loitered in the mirror-lined studio with the teacher. As Nicola waited by the cloakroom door, she noticed a little plump girl humming to herself. The child bent with a grunt to untie the ribbons of her dancing slippers and Nicola couldn't help smiling. She reminded her of herself twelve years earlier when she and Karen used to attend dancing lessons together.

A freckled girl jeered, 'Look at Katherine's leotard. I didn't know they made leotards so enormous!'

A very familiar voice remarked, 'She must shop at a tent shop. Do you, Katherine?' It was Laura, who hadn't spotted Nicola. She was enjoying the giggles of Miss Freckles and another friend.

Furrows appeared above Katherine's brows and she placed her arms across her stomach, looking as if she longed to find a spot to shrink into.

The third girl teased, 'Katherine, do you really think you'll get the part of Cinderella? In case you didn't know, Cinderella probably didn't weigh a tonne. We think you'd be perfect as the coach.'

All three girls gave bursts of smothered laughter but Katherine raised her head high. 'Miss Thorpe says I'm a good dancer.'

'Yeah, but when you joined the class, she needed my dad to come and make the stage stronger.' Before she finished her sentence, Laura saw

Nicola. Her mouth fell open. When Laura took in Nicola's expression, she looked down at the ground. 'We were just having a joke.'

'That sort of joke hurts. Doesn't it, Katherine?'

The chubby girl looked at Nicola in wonderment and nodded.

'I think you look very pretty,' Nicola went on. 'I'm sure you are a good dancer, too. And I'm going to take this one away.' She jerked her chin at Laura. 'At least that'll be one less giving you a hard time.'

'What's going on?' The dancing teacher stood in the cloakroom doorway with her hands on her hips.

Nicola cleared her throat. 'I don't know if you're already aware but there's some nasty teasing going on.'

'I *was* aware once.' The teacher glared down at her three wayward pupils. Two of the culprits were trying to hide smirks but Laura's face was pale, her lips tightly pursed.

'I warned you girls to quit teasing Katherine or I'd tell your parents. Now I'm going to have to do it.'

'Well, I can tell the Bowmans,' Nicola said.

The teacher touched her arm and lowered her voice. 'I can tell you one thing. Laura is not the ringleader of all this. That's Melissa there. But Laura and Kelly need to learn to stop following her example. Thank you for drawing this to my attention.'

On their way out Nicola noticed Laura's face. The eyes that scowled at Nicola were smouldering. Nicola knew she might regret upsetting Laura later but for now, she did not care one ounce.

Laura flounced on the passenger's seat and pouted. 'It's not fair. That's the first time I've teased Katherine in ages.'

Nicola glanced sideways at her. Laura hadn't got around to changing from her dancing clothes. She was a rumpled, cross little figure in bright pink from her headband to her slippers.

'You don't have any idea how serious the effects of your teasing can be. Your words could scar Katherine for life. Criticism like that, which attacks the very person you are, can be impossible to forget.'

'But Katherine teases us too.'

'Whether or not that's true, keeping it going is a horrible thing to do.'

Laura's eyes widened. 'Are you saying I'm horrible?'

'No, I'm not saying that. But I think what I saw was horrible.'

Laura's chin began to wobble. 'You didn't have to embarrass me in front of everyone. You didn't have to tell Miss Thorpe. I think that was horrible.'

'I reacted that way because I've been in Katherine's place.'

'Well, I can't help it if you and Katherine are fat!' Laura's eyes were filling.

Nicola had turned onto their road. The whole thing had flared from a simple rebuke to something fiery and hot. She made an effort to answer calmly. 'You might not be able to help that but you can help poking fun at people for it.'

'But Melissa's even worse!' Laura wailed.

Nicola began cruising up the Bowman's long driveway. 'But I don't know Melissa. I don't live with her.'

A silver tear streaked down Laura's freckled cheek. 'I wish you didn't live with me. Now I'll be in trouble with Mum and Dad.'

Nicola parked in her usual spot. 'I won't tell them. I just said I would in the heat of the moment.'

'But Miss Thorpe will tell them!' Laura slammed her door and bounded up the verandah steps. Nicola followed her, glad to see neither Casey's car nor Piers' van there. Laura needed a chance to calm down. However, the boys were both home. Sam looked up from his homework and Jerome from his book.

'What's happened?' Jerome asked Laura.

Her face crumpled completely. 'Nicola's being mean to me!'

Jerome looked up at Nicola with surprise. 'What's this all about?'

'Laura will tell you.' Nicola went up to her bedroom. She was trembling too. Her chest felt tight but it was important that somebody kept their feelings bottled. For a person who didn't want her family to find out what had happened, Laura was sabotaging herself as well as Nicola.

*   *   *

After awhile, Nicola heard a knock on her door. She couldn't imagine Laura coming up to see her already and cringed because she guessed who it must be. When she opened her door, there he stood.

'Are you OK?' Jerome asked.

Nicola nodded. 'How about Laura?'

'She's OK.'

'I suppose I shouldn't have paid her out.'

'Who says you shouldn't? I reckon she'll think twice before she picks on Katherine again.'

'That was the only reason I snapped at her. Because I could understand so well how Katherine felt. I used to be just like her.' Nicola stopped, amazed to feel her eyes prickling with tears. She hadn't been so emotional about it in the heat of the moment with Laura.

Jerome bowed his head. 'I reckon Laura needs to come and apologise to you.'

'Don't you dare try and make her!'

'But she should. She was in the wrong.'

'Laura might not see it that way. As far as she's concerned, she was just telling it like it is. I am a fat slob.'

'Don't you dare say that about yourself!'

'Why not? It makes more sense to just acknowledge it. You must admit you've had a few awkward moments over it yourself. It's easier to be open about it than pretend you've never thought it.'

'But I've never thought it!' His chin jutted out exactly as Laura's had. Nicola guessed it must be a thing from Piers, although she'd never seen Piers angry around her. She'd never seen Jerome cross either, until now.

'There's no way you could help thinking it.' She was trying to understand why he was so indignant.

'I've never thought it *ever*!' he repeated. 'Do you want me to prove it?'

Nicola glanced up. 'How?'

He didn't answer with words but stepped closer and kissed her forehead. Nicola almost forgot to breathe.

He gently raised her chin so she would look at him. His eyes gazed into hers, smoky and warm. Nicola read a vulnerable question in their depths but couldn't think how to respond. She could feel his breath on her cheek and wondered why he couldn't hear her heart thumping.

Jerome already stood so close to her, it barely took any extra movement for him to brush her lips swiftly with his. Nicola thought her heart would burst. Jerome gave a lopsided smile that made her insides turn to water.

'Now do you believe me?' he breathed.

*   *   *

No sooner had Casey stepped inside the door than she was winded by something resembling a flying missile with spikes of rust-coloured hair poking from its headband in all directions.

'Mum, I've got to tell you something but before you hear it, I didn't mean to be nasty. Honest I didn't.' The rest was incoherent.

'Honey, it's OK.' Casey lowered her two grocery bags onto an armchair, careful to keep the eggs upright. She cupped Laura's face and smoothed back her hair. 'What's happened?'

Laura moaned again and buried her face in Casey's shoulder.

Casey looked across at Sam's sober face. 'Do you know what happened?'

'Yeah, I'll tell you.' Sam liked having an audience, even for somebody else's story. 'Laura an' some others were teasing a fat girl after dancing and Nicola walked in and heard 'em. Then she ticked Laura off.' He kept talking, embellishing the story he and Jerome had heard from Laura.

Casey wanted to groan when she'd heard it all but held it in when she looked at Laura's wretched expression. She kept stroking her daughter's hair. 'I know you were just going along with the others. But it backfired on you, didn't it? We all make big mistakes sometimes. I guess poor Nicola must be feeling terrible, too.'

'Jerome's already gone up to see if he can make her feel better,' Sam told her.

'You're kidding me!' This time, Casey really did groan. 'I've warned him not to do that sort of thing. That'll be the last thing she needs. I'd better go and see her too.' She gave Laura's head a quick kiss. 'I'll be back in a moment.'

16

Claire Quinlan sipped herbal tea in the kitchen and rubbed her stomach. She'd experienced more twinges than usual although her baby was still not due for two weeks. She was particularly tired and her swollen ankles ached. Claire's son, Ethan, was playing a noisy game with pots and pans up the passage and she was happy to let him. It meant that the toddler was oblivious to the raging argument between his father and uncle in the front room. Blake rarely got heated enough to snap back at Michael but whenever he did, he was sorry later.

Michael was bellowing, 'How can I help it if thirty bucks got nicked from my pocket?' It had all started when he asked Blake for a loan of money and Blake had refused.

'That sort of thing happens to you all the time! If you're too drunk to know when you're being robbed, that's your problem!'

'But I'd pay it straight back!'

Although Claire was not in the room with them, she could imagine Blake's eyes rolling in disbelief.

'Yeah, right!' Blake said.

'You don't believe me, do you? Do you think I enjoy asking? How do you think it makes me feel to be coming to you for money?'

'If you hate it that much, you wouldn't do it so often.'

'But I *need* it!' Michael managed to draw the word *need* out for several seconds.

'Then you should've looked after it. You haven't paid me back the last two times I loaned you money. The fact is you ought to be richer than we are. You don't pay a cent to keep this roof over our heads and we don't even charge you board.'

Claire saw Blake stride into her field of vision through the open door. He'd rumpled up the left side of his hair.

'You must've been pretty smashed not to feel someone slip their hand into your pocket and slide out your wallet,' he added.

'It wasn't in my wallet. I left my wallet home. The money was loose.'

Blake stopped mid-stride. This time, Claire saw his horrified expression.

'If you think I'll lend you anything if you're that careless, you can think again!'

'How about *you?* 'Michael's voice had risen by decibels. 'I never did what *you* did the time *you* were drunk!'

Blake's utter silence was more terrible than any sound he could have made.

'Michael, think what you're saying!' Claire shouted from the kitchen. 'That has nothing to do with any of this!' She forced herself to stand up and walk in with them.

When Blake did speak again he was quieter but still furious. 'And have you noticed that I've never got drunk since? I learned a lesson.'

Michael stood with his fists cocked, hazel eyes blazing. 'Yeah, you're so perfect! I'll tell you what you are. A tight-fisted hypocrite! Thirty bucks is all I'm asking for. As if that's gonna break you.'

'Keep it coming. You really make me feel like lending it to you now. You're such a nice guy.'

Michael was almost weeping. 'If it wasn't that Mum's dead and Dad's a basket-case, I wouldn't even be here! I only drink a bit because my life is so rotten!'

'You've had some very tough breaks. We all know that. And we've been trying to help. But ultimately, it's your responsibility to get over them. Nobody else can do it for you.'

Michael kicked Claire's tapestry foot stool against the wall. 'I'll tell you where you can stick your help! You wouldn't help me out of a wet paper bag! The only help I get from you are these stupid lectures! I'm not staying here. I'm leaving for good! Why don't you find someone else to live here? Someone you might be able to squeeze some board out of?'

'Don't even think of imposing on Jerome's family and expecting them to have sympathy! Don't spin that hard-done-by-everyone-else-is-to-blame trick on them!'

Claire caught Blake's arm and shook her head at him. He was going too far and he'd blame himself later.

'Mind your business. At least he's a good mate!'

'Michael, wait 'til you calm down,' Claire cried. She loved her passionate young brother-in-law. 'Don't go like this!'

'I'll never get calm around him!' Michael slammed the screen door shut behind him and they heard the squeal of his car tyres.

Claire looked at her husband with a sigh. His contrite face was already appearing.

'Was that my fault for trying to reason with him? Maybe I shouldn't have let him get under my skin like that.'

She reached up and caressed his dark hair on the right side, messing it evenly all over. 'I guess you wouldn't be human if you didn't lash back sometimes. Our problem is Michael thinks all that stuff he says is true. About none of us caring for him.'

'I know he does. How can we convince him it's rubbish? I wish he'd just stop to think. But I reckon that's asking the impossible.' Blake rested his cheek on her head and pulled her closer. He stopped to grin wryly at the huge bulge beneath her maternity pants. 'This gets between us, doesn't it?'

'Only a little bit.' She directed his hand to rub the side of her stomach. 'It's been really sore today.'

'And still two weeks to go,' he reminded her.

'Maybe even longer now. What baby in their right mind would want to come out into that sort of atmosphere?'

* * *

When he leaned close to kiss her again, Nicola's whirling mind screamed, *'Why is he doing this?'* She knew Jerome liked her but not *that* way. How could he possibly like her the way she wanted him to? She had to muster enough sense to keep her wildest fantasy separate from reality. His sympathetic heart was getting the better of his judgment. *Should I warn him to stop before he's sorry?*

This time, he pulled her closer for a hug. His fingers were dangerously near her most despised area above the band of her jeans. Nicola instinctively pushed him away. 'What are you doing?'

Jerome let his arms drop by his sides. 'Sorry! I just wanted you to see...' Dismay spread across his face even worse than she'd expected. Jerome flipped up his palms in an apologetic gesture. 'Can you just forget I ever did that? I won't repeat it.'

The door was flung open and Casey stood gaping at them. It was obvious she had heard the last thing Jerome said.

'Before you say anything, I'm sorry.' Nicola desperately wanted to put off hearing whatever Casey had to say. 'I'm sorry about Laura, too.'

When she spoke, Casey's voice sounded kind but more troubled than Nicola had ever heard it. 'I'm not cross about Laura. I know exactly how it must have been. She told me all about it.' Then she turned to her son. 'It's you I'm cross with! Haven't I warned you not to bother Nicola with...?'

'Yes, you have!' he cut her off. 'No need for you to butt in.'

'You warned him?' The heady implications of Casey's words fizzed through Nicola. Only Casey Bowman's clouded face helped her keep her joy bottled. It still couldn't be the way Casey made it sound.

'Nicola, I'm sorry. I've suspected the way he's been thinking for some time. Maybe I should've spoken up before.'

'You shouldn't be interfering now! I was handling this OK until you came crashing in!' Jerome's hands were jammed into his pockets but his shoulders were shuddering.

'You don't understand I'm interfering for your sake, too. Because I don't want to see you hurt.'

'Too late, then!' he blurted. 'And you're making it ten times worse! Stop doing things for me!' Panic set in and his shoulders began shuddering even more violently. 'This is none of your business,' he shouted. 'You aren't even my real mother!' Even as the words poured out of his mouth, Jerome was horrified at what he'd said. His heart lurched as he watched every trace of colour flee from Casey's face. 'Mum, I'm sorry!' His own face crumpled in confusion and humiliation. 'I didn't mean that! It came out wrong. I only meant that you don't have to mother me so much. It's not as if I'm Sam or Laura.'

This made it worse. Casey's chin hung slack. Jerome let out a groan as his gaze flickered wildly from her to Nicola and back again.

Casey's face was chalky-white. 'Jerome, how long have you felt I'm not your real mother?'

'I'm just being a jerk. It's nothing. I'm sorry. Forget it.' The shuddering, if possible, became even more acute. 'I'm sorry, Nicola.'

Casey's chin had begun to quiver. 'Forget…?'

'I ought to move out of here,' Nicola said quietly.

Jerome spun around to stare at her. 'No, you can't leave! Not you too!' He snapped his mouth shut.

She flinched beneath his anguished gaze. 'I'm just trying to do the right thing. Look what I've caused.'

'No, this was my fault! Not yours.' Jerome was used to slipping into the role of peace-keeper. He felt marginally calmer as he adopted the long-practised part. 'Can't you both forget what I said? What I did? I promise… it won't happen again.' A panic-stricken glance from one heartsick face to the next showed him he was asking the impossible. 'Ever.' He lowered his gaze and cursed himself. His head was spinning. He couldn't bear the way they were looking at him. He had to get away for awhile to figure out how to fix things.

Nicola saw tears spring to his eyes before he turned on his heels and left. She heard him descend the steps in two thumps and swing the front door shut behind him. Casey's face was in her hands and she was sobbing. 'How long has he felt that way?'

'I'm sure he didn't mean what he said. You saw him. He shocked himself as much as he shocked you.' Every fibre of Nicola's nerves tingled to dash out after Jerome but she knew she'd never catch up with him. And she was aware that Casey was in no frame of mind to be left alone, even though Nicola was certain nothing she could say would help. How could it? Jerome might not have meant to say what he did, but he had still said it.

Nicola was not surprised that Casey had not realised Jerome did not think of her as his mother: she was sure that until the words came out of his mouth, Jerome had not realised it either.

* * *

'Hey, where are you going?' Sam had raced outside after Jerome and struggled to keep up with him.

'I don't know yet. You go back.' Jerome sprinted down his driveway and heard his eardrums pounding. Moving fast was the only way to ward off thoughts of humiliation and despair. They were almost at the end when a car turned at breakneck speed onto the narrow driveway, forcing both boys to leap into the blackberry bushes along the steep embankment. It was Michael Quinlan's beat-up, brown Holden sedan and Michael's face behind the steering wheel was pop-eyed and shocked. He slammed on his brakes and wound down his window. 'Hey, why the big hurry?'

Jerome jumped back down and gingerly plucked a few prickles from his palm. After the ordeal he'd just suffered, it hardly made him wince. 'I could ask you the same question.'

'I was coming to see you.'

'Well, I'm out of here.'

'Where are you going?'

Jerome shrugged. 'As far away as possible.'

'Hop in then. I wanna get away too. Where shall we go?

Jerome needed to be moving or better still, hitting something. 'I dunno. Just drive. Somewhere there's a punching bag I can pound.'

'I know a pub.'

Jerome rolled his eyes. He was in enough trouble without the prospect of having to bail Michael out of a mess. 'How about ten pin bowling?'

Michael's eyes lit up. 'OK, your treat. I'm broke. Let's head to the bowling alley at Murray Bridge.'

'Yeah, that'll be great fun.' Sam started to climb into the back of Michael's car but Jerome jerked him back out by the collar of his school shirt.

'Not you. You go and tell 'em where I'm going.' He was in no mood for Sam's resentful pout. 'You heard me. Push off!'

'You're a rotten, mean...'

Jerome didn't wait to hear the rest. He slammed the front passenger's door behind him and watched Sam's eyes pool up. Jerome heaved a sigh. He'd already driven two people to tears, and now he'd made it three. 'Let's go, then.'

As Michael backed the car onto the road, he took a sympathetic glance at Sam's woebegone face. 'I would've taken him.'

'Yeah, well you don't have to look after him and make sure he gets home in time for bed.' Jerome's tone was sneering.

Michael glanced sideways at him. 'What's eating you?'

'You don't want to know,' Jerome declared flatly.

Michael looked as if he did want to know, but he decided not to pursue the subject. 'I have a bit of a problem. I might need petrol later and I can't afford it.'

'Don't worry. I've got money.' Jerome was ready to abandon his missionary plan. He'd just proven that he was too pathetic. He folded his arms across his chest and glowered at his feet, hoping Michael's company would distract him from his darker thoughts.

'Well then, can I tell you why I'm mad?'

'Sure, go ahead.'

It wasn't as distracting as Jerome had hoped. Just another rambling story about how stingy and unreasonable Michael's brother was. Blake refused to loan Michael a measly amount of money to last him through to the end of the week. Apparently he only ever remembered the times when Michael didn't pay him back but never the times when he did! Jerome had heard it all before. His mind wandered but he tried making appropriate sympathy noises in the right spots.

After several kilometres, Michael's car began shaking violently, rattling their heads against the backs of their seats.

'What the heck's that?'

'How should I know?'

'Well, it's your car!'

'But it's never done this before!'

A loud crack sounded beneath the bonnet.

'For crying out loud, pull over!' Jerome shouted.

Michael just managed to do so before the car shuddered to a stop. 'This isn't my lucky day,' he groaned.

'Yeah, tell me about it,' Jerome muttered.

17

'OK fellers, it's the fan belt,' the mechanic told them. 'They can go sudden like that. I'll fix it as soon as I finish this other job I'm working on.'

'How long will that take?' Michael didn't mean to sound impatient but it had been a long hour. They'd had to flag down a passing motorist on the Freeway who was willing to help them tow their car to the nearest garage. That happened to be in Callington; a dry country town which probably never had much happening at any time, let alone an early week-day evening.

The man fixed his small black eyes on Michael. 'Maybe an hour but you shouldn't complain. Fact is your job will take me well past closing time.' He leaned on their bonnet and ran a hand through his lank, greasy hair. 'If I really wanted to be a pain I'd tell you I couldn't start on your car until tomorrow. But because I'm such a nice bloke, I'll work late for you.'

'Thanks mate. You see, we have somewhere we really need to be.'

'Is that so?' The mechanic squinted through the pale, early evening sunshine at what lay beyond his garage door on the outskirts of town. There was nothing but brittle-dry land with straggly gum trees and tufts of mallee grass. He grinned, displaying chipped and crooked teeth. 'I'm not used to folk in a hurry.'

'I think what my mate meant is that we've got somewhere we really don't need to be, and that's here.' Jerome thought how his parents often said, *You'll laugh at this some day so why not start now?* He was tempted to take their advice, until he thought fleetingly of Nicola and his mother and the mess he'd left behind him at home. *Mum,* he thought, *what on earth possessed me to say THAT?* As he recalled it, he doubted if he'd ever manage to laugh again.

'Where are you off to tonight, anyway?' the man asked.

'Ten pin bowling at Murray Bridge,' Michael admitted. 'We wanted enough time to get a few good games in.'

The mechanic's teeth flashed again behind his prickly moustache. 'If you were going tomorrow, you might've seen me there. Thursday is my bowling night. But then I wouldn't have been able to fix your car. Lucky for you it's only Wednesday. Give me an hour. I reckon I'll have it finished by then.' He turned back to his other job and switched on a strong floodlight on his wall.

Michael and Jerome began to wander along a dirt road that was the same faded tan colour as the rest of the countryside.

'Do you reckon we should find the pub?' Michael suggested.

Jerome shook his head and kept striding. 'You have no money, anyway.'

'But you do.'

'Not for that. You want to be fit to drive once the car's ready. We might as well just have a walk.' The dirt road seemed to taper off beyond the edge of the town, so he climbed over a barbed wire fence and kept heading west, toward the sunset. Jerome quite liked the crunch of brittle grass beneath the soles of his shoes. There was something about it that soothed his shattered nerves. Something too about the fiery flash of sky lighting up the quiet, arid land–the scene was almost shrine-like and he wondered how Nicola would set about painting it. *Nicola!* The thought of her made his stomach churn again. *Is everything going to remind me of her? Or Mum?* Jerome set his jaw and increased his speed.

Michael kept pace with him. 'I can't stand this. Do you reckon I should call Blake to come and get us?' He pulled his mobile phone out of his pocket but paused before pressing the buttons. 'I really didn't want to ask that rotten nerd for any more favours so soon.'

'Don't worry about it. By the time he gets here, the car might be nearly fixed anyway.' They'd come across a narrow, sandy trail that Jerome guessed had probably been made by sheep or other animals. He moved into it and watched red, dusty clouds swirl around his ankles.

Michael grumbled, 'This isn't what I had in mind for tonight.'

'Me either. But we'll still fit in some bowling.' There were a few benefits of being stranded. It meant that he could postpone facing Nicola and his family for even longer.

'Will you slow down?' Michael grumbled. 'We're miles away from town and we'll have to walk back in the...'

His words snapped off as they both plunged into what felt like nothing. One moment there had been firm ground beneath their feet but it unexpectedly disappeared. A voice in Jerome's head screamed, *What's happening?* But that question had to take second place to *What should we do?* He automatically ducked his head and stretched his arms to break his fall. His hands scraped down some sort of steep wall and he managed to grasp hold of something poking out of it. It was knobbly and woody, like a tree root. He clutched it hard and pressed his feet against the side of the wall. No sooner had Jerome caught his breath than the root snapped. He was falling again, backwards this time.

THUMP! His left hip and shoulder landed with a jolt that knocked the wind out of him. A surge of pain rippled through the rest of his body, then settled back with a searing intensity in his hip and shoulder. He turned his head and flexed his limbs. Nothing seemed broken but the palms of his hands were raw and moist. He wiped one palm down the front of his shirt and guessed he was smearing blood all over his T-shirt.

'Hey, Mike!' Jerome's voice sounded like a deep echo as he began groping about. He was sitting in several inches of something cold as mud but dry as powder. Jerome filtered some between his fingers and the dank, musty odour almost made him gag. His fingers touched something warm and hairy. Jerome choked back his yell when he felt the shoulder it was attached to and realised it was Michael's tousled head. At the same moment, the tousled thing made a low moan. Jerome's skin crawled. 'Hey man, are you right?'

Michael whimpered as he sat up. 'I hit the bottom of this hole feet first. My left ankle's killing me.' As he tried to scramble up, he let out a scream.

'Hey, sit down again! Try not to move it too much.' Jerome's heart was pounding hard.

'What the hell is this hole?' Michael was trying hard not to cry.

'Stuffed if I know.' Jerome groaned as he twisted around and tried to feel for handholds. There were none. Pain shot through his hip as he pulled himself up. The hole was narrow enough for him to almost stretch his fingertips from one side to the other. There was just enough room for him and Michael to huddle at the bottom. And the dim patch of twilit sky seemed a good four metres above their heads. 'Someone must've dug it.'

'They're idiots, then. They could've put up a warning sign!'

The musty aroma was making Jerome feel queasier by the moment. 'It might be an old mineshaft, or something.'

'Who'd dig a mine right out here?'

'I reckon Callington used to be a copper area.' Jerome was sifting through his memory of school excursions.

'Well, thanks for the history lesson,' Michael grumbled, 'but let's get out of here.' He choked on a sob as he tried to stand again. 'This ankle hurts like you wouldn't believe.'

'Do you reckon you'll be able to hold me up for just a few minutes while I try climbing on your shoulders?'

'I'll try. Hurry up!'

Jerome pulled off his shoes and, ignoring his hip pain, stepped in his socks onto Michael's broad shoulders. Michael gritted his teeth and panted as he used every reserve of energy to stretch to his full height. He held his breath and kept his muscles tense while Jerome slapped the smooth sides of their trap. But Jerome's knees kept buckling as Michael's shoulders gradually caved in beneath his weight. They tried again and again.

'You're all wet,' Jerome cried. Michael's shirt was growing damp beneath his socks.

'Yeah, I'm sweating bucket loads. Isn't there *anything* to grab hold of?'

'It's impossible.' Jerome's words echoed through the hole as he stepped back down. 'Even when I feel as high as I can, there's still about a metre of wall above me. And it's all 180 degrees.'

Michael sank his face into his hands. 'Now he's giving me a flaming *Maths* lesson!'

'180 degrees means straight up and down!' Jerome snapped.

'You could've just said straight up and down!'

'It doesn't take a genius to work it out.'

The patch of sky above their heads had deepened to navy blue. Jerome rubbed his sore hands up and down his cold arms in a vain attempt to warm them.

Michael was digging around in his pocket. 'I should have thought of it straight away. I'm definitely calling Blake *now.*'

'Yeah, call Blake! Just get us out of here.'

But Michael stopped with the phone half way to his ear as a horrible thought occurred to him. 'I haven't got any credit on the phone. I've run out!'

'Then call Emergency Rescue. That's free. Doesn't take a genius to figure that one out, either.'

'Good thinking. It's 911, right?'

'No, that's America, you moron! You watch too much TV. It's triple zero.'

He waited for sickeningly longer than it should have taken for the call to go through. When Michael let out a whimpered swear word, Jerome repeated it himself to see if it would help him to let off steam. But it made him feel even worse.

'Damn phone's not picking up any signal!' Michael cried. 'Why is everything I own a lemon?'

'It might not be the phone. Maybe it just won't pick up signals from four metres underground in the middle of nowhere.'

Michael's response was to smash his mobile phone against the rocky wall. Jerome caught hold of his elbow.

'Stop it! You want to be able to use it when we get out of here, don't you?'

'If we get out!' Michael was clearly crying. 'This is all thanks to you!'

'Why?'

'We could've been sitting in a cosy pub. Or better still, back on the road on our way to the bowling alley. But who wanted to take a walk? Out in the bloody sticks? This is totally your fault. And do you know what? It doesn't take a genius to figure *that* out!'

Jerome slouched back against the wall without a word to say in his own defence. *I shouldn't have even got out of bed this morning.*

*   *   *

Piers Bowman came home to find Casey and Nicola sitting at the table with red eyes. He thought for a moment that Sam and Laura were in trouble but when Casey left her chair to seize his hand, he realised by her trembling that she'd suffered a much greater shock than any childish prank. Only the sight of Sam's faint grin showed Piers that nothing truly terrible had happened.

'What's up?' he asked.

It was Sam who answered. 'Jerome had an argument with Mum *and* Nicola!'

That didn't seem world-shattering to Piers. It was unlike Jerome certainly, but it wasn't sufficient to cause this wild, teary-eyed distress. 'Has he apologised?'

'He's gone off with Michael,' Sam said. 'They're going ten pin bowling and he was too stingy to let me go with them. Michael wouldn't have minded.'

Ten-pin bowling? It didn't make sense. Piers glanced at Nicola before scrutinising his wife's face more carefully. 'Bad argument?' He could not quite credit that Jerome the peacemaker had stormed off without an apology to have a good time with his friends.

'Piers, he hates me,' Casey wept.

Piers shook his head, unable to believe that such a huge misunderstanding could have blown up in his absence. 'What happened, sweetheart?'

'He told me to butt out because I'm not even his real mother!'

Casey's face crumpled as she spoke.

'What?' If the world had suddenly tilted further on its axis, Piers could hardly have been more astounded. Whatever he had expected to hear, that would be bottom of the list. *No, he thought in astonishment, it wouldn't even make the list!* Only the sick swoop of his stomach felt real. That felt terribly real. 'Why would he ever say that? That's not Jerome. What did you argue about?'

Frenzied talking poured forth from everyone. Piers tried to concentrate on Casey's words but she could not speak coherently. Nicola wasn't much clearer. He had to piece together most of the story from the two children.

'Jerome kissed Nicola!' Laura's eyes were wide like saucers.

Sam's eyes were even wider. 'He never even kissed Mel.'

'I told him to be sensitive to your feelings, Nicola,' Casey sniffed. 'We know you loved Shane, but...' Casey sniffed.

Nicola interrupted before anyone else could talk over her. 'No! I wasn't in love with Shane. He was a wonderful friend who was like a brother to me. If you were warning Jerome to keep away from me because of that...' Her face burned red in a flash. 'You didn't need to.'

'What's this got to do with you not being his real mother?' Piers asked Casey.

She clutched his wrist hard, staring at Nicola. 'What do you mean I didn't need to?'

Nicola flushed brighter still, if possible. 'It was different with Jerome.'

'But I heard what you said to him!' Casey's eyes were popping. 'You told him to stop! I thought I was helping. Why did you push him away?'

She thought the reason ought to be obvious. 'Because he was just trying to be kind! He let his sympathy carry him away.'

'Sympathy's never led him to kiss a girl before,' Piers said, in wonder.

Nicola stared at him, not quite in disbelief. *Would his father know everything Jerome did or didn't do?* 'Maybe not,' she said. 'But I'm sure he'd never do it in his right mind. Why would he? Look at him! He's so gorgeous and smart. And I'm a lot older.' Her eyes pooled with tears. She couldn't bring herself to mention her size. That part was plain to everybody, anyway.

'Not all that much older,' Piers said compassionately, trying to come to grips with the thought that this was the first girl–no, *woman*–in whom Jerome had ever shown real interest. 'How old are you? Twenty-two?'

Nicola nodded and sniffed.

'Then when you're eighty, Jerome will be seventy-seven. That's not such a big difference, is it?' He leaned across to squeeze Casey's hand. 'He's such an intense, serious boy. You know that. He'd take first love so hard. He must've been really torn up inside to say what he said to you. Have you tried to phone him?'

Casey drew a shuddering breath and nodded. 'But he ran out without his phone. Sam found it ringing on the couch.'

'Well, we know he's gone ten pin bowling with Michael,' Sam put in. 'They'll have to be back some time.'

Piers nodded. 'We'll be waiting right here when he comes. However long it takes.'

*   *   *

The mechanic stamped around his garage and looked at his watch for one last time.

'That's it! I don't reckon they're coming.' He muttered obscenities as he switched off the lights and locked his door behind him. 'They must've got sick of waiting and called someone to come and pick 'em up. While I'm here slaving my guts out for them after closing time. Would've been nice if they'd let me know!'

He kept swearing as he climbed the slope to his own car. 'I'll be giving those ungrateful young wretches a piece of my mind when they front up tomorrow.'

18

Michael and Jerome had stopped yelling for help when their voices became croaky. Jerome's throat felt as scratched as the palms of his hands.

'We'll keep trying when we have enough voice back,' he rasped. 'In the morning someone will have to hear.' The prospect of spending all night trapped in the pit had become a chilling reality. The patch of sky above them was now the same inky black as the inside of the pit.

'Nobody will hear us then, either!' Michael predicted with a groan.

'What are you saying? Of course they will!'

'No, they won't. Nobody has ever found this stinking hole before us. So why would anybody find it now?'

Jerome hadn't thought of that and he didn't appreciate Michael's drawing it to his attention. 'They'll have to find us now. Our families will come looking for us when we don't turn up at home.'

'I'm not sure how long my family will take to start looking,' Michael told him. 'I told 'em I'm leaving home. Blake and Claire might not expect to see me back for a long time. But at least your folks will be getting worried.'

'Well, maybe they will. But they might not start searching for a fairly long time.'

'Why? What happened? Why did you leave in such a hurry?'

The hip, which had not bothered Jerome for a while, suddenly started to ache ferociously. 'Don't even ask,' he said with a shrug. 'I wouldn't know where to start.'

'But I don't get it. Your family is great. I'll tell you what I reckon. The reason you won't tell me what happened is because it's totally stupid, whatever it was, and even you know it.'

'If you must know, I kissed Nicola.' There was no telling how long they'd be there and Jerome knew Michael would wear him down eventually. It was horrid enough being trapped in a cold hole without being disparaged every time he opened his mouth.

'What the....'

Jerome was glad he could not see the expression on Michael's face in the darkness. And even gladder that Michael could not see the heat spread across his own.

'What on earth made you go and do a crazy thing like that?'

Jerome felt a sudden urge to smash his own head against the rocky wall and put himself out of his misery. 'She was upset about something and I was trying to make her feel better.'

'Sounds like that didn't work!' Michael hooted.

'Of course it didn't. What did I expect? And then Mum barged in and ordered me to keep my hands off her, but I'd already apologised to Nicola. So I told Mum to mind her own business. She kept raving on and I said something... well, dumb. Insulting, even.'

'You mean you've never insulted your parents in your life before?' Michael was incredulous.

'Not like this,' Jerome admitted. 'I still can't work out why I even said it. And they both got all upset so I told them I was going out for awhile.' He was silent for several seconds. 'Now you have it. Satisfied?'

Jerome could feel Michael's nod, not see it. It was suddenly followed by a shake. 'OK, out of all the girls you could choose, why pick Nicola?'

'Will you drop the subject?'

'I prefer girls who look more like models.'

'Yeah, well that doesn't surprise me.' Jerome knew Michael was blind about many things.

After a moment of silence, Michael grumbled, 'What the heck is Nicola looking for, anyway?'

Although Jerome couldn't see Michael's face, he turned his head in the general direction of his voice.

'If she could've just let you kiss her, maybe we wouldn't even be in this mess. We'd be sitting at your kitchen table having a good card game with Sam and Laura. And we'd be drinking hot chocolate or coffee. And my ankle wouldn't be throbbing like torture.'

'So it's her fault?'

Michael didn't answer.

'My fault then, is that it?' Jerome persisted.

Michael didn't answer that either. 'I can't understand sheilas,' he went on. 'You've got to be flamin' Brad Pitt to impress 'em. What gives 'em the right to be so choosy?'

'It's no different to you saying you only like girls who look like models.'

'I suppose so, but here's where I'm different. If a reasonably good looking girl decided to come and start kissing me, I tell you, I wouldn't complain. If she doesn't fancy you, what hope would the average guy have?'

Jerome sighed and rested his forehead on his knees. He'd said far too much already. He wouldn't bother explaining to Michael that he was the last guy any girl would want. *I've driven Nicola away. That's what I've done. Why couldn't I just cool it, like Mum said?* Jerome had always been a jittery wreck around females. He knew that no one suspected it and he'd taken care to hide it. But to him it was no wonder at all that Nicola had pushed him away. A wave of despair larger than the pit engulfed him as he thought of what he'd said. *'Not you, too,'* he'd blurted, when she said she'd better leave. Jerome let his burning face slide further between his knees. What a deplorable, needy thing to come out with. *'You can't leave!'* How pathetically childish. What must she be thinking? She was undoubtedly packing her bags. He was sure he'd never see her again.

Michael would never understand, he thought. *I'm a hopeless case.*

He'd known it a long time. He'd never been completely at ease around his school friend, Melody, even when she admitted that she had a crush on him. She'd chased him and he'd let himself be caught for a while until it was obvious, even to her, that it wouldn't work. And later, whenever he met Claire Quinlan, the inevitable mute feeling tangled itself around his brain, even though she was Michael's married sister-in-law. Why had he imagined–for even one second–that things might be different with Nicola? Just because she was beautiful and sensitive, he, Jerome, was still the same inept goofball.

'You can't leave! Not you, too!' What sort of weak, manipulative thing is that to say? he asked himself. *No girl has ever left me.*

Why would any girl even be interested enough in me in the first place? To leave, first of all, you've got to love. Even my mother never loved...

Jerome captured the thought, allowing it to remain unfinished. He back-tracked it. *Even my mother...*

Touched the raw, wounded pain: *mother.*

Not Casey, he thought. *I've just hurt her so badly. Not Casey. She loves me.* He felt his mouth quivering and heat flowing around his eyes. *I love her: so why did I say what I did?*

An image of the self-assured Anna Carter came to his mind. It sat on the cabinet shelf gazing disdainfully out of the photo-frame, her tumbling waves of long, dark hair spilling across her shoulders like a super-model. His parents always kept her photo among others in the family album. *For my sake,* Jerome thought to himself. *Because they say I need a special token of my biological mother to honour.*

He had never told them that he could barely stand the sight of it. He couldn't even begin to contemplate flinging their thoughtful gesture back in their faces. They'd be appalled if they found out that, in mastering a desire to want to smash it, he now only looked at it with icy detachment. It was a perpetual nibbling reminder whenever he passed that shelf that Casey was Sam and Laura's mother, but his was a haughty mannequin who hadn't ever wanted him.

Maybe that was why he'd never found the bold, showy type of girl appealing.

If his own mother hadn't wanted him enough to even look at him, why should anybody else? He'd been living with the thought for almost twenty years and the hollowness and pain didn't ever go completely away. It would disappear for long, long periods but then it would return, more savagely than ever.

My mother left me, he thought. Jerome squirmed in the dust and rotated his shoulders a couple of times to shake the stiffness from them. His feelings about that were something he'd been able to hide well so he felt it was no great problem. Well, not a *new* problem. Nicola's feelings were now the problem. He'd allowed himself to yearn for Nicola with a passion he'd never felt for anyone else.

Well, maybe that was a problem, actually. A big problem. But at least it had only been his problem until he made it hers too, by forcing himself on her. And it didn't matter how often he turned it over in his mind, he couldn't figure out how to solve it.

*   *   *

Nicola snapped her head up when she heard the knock at the door. *Jerome!* she thought, before realising that Jerome wouldn't knock.

She could see Casey's nerves were on edge as she jumped up and hurried to answer it.

Blake Quinlan stepped inside and gave them a friendly smile. 'I'm glad you're all still up. I came to find out if Michael's here with Jerome.'

'They aren't here,' Piers told him.

'Oh,' Blake said. 'He left in a bad mood and I need to catch up with him. I know if I tried to phone him he'd hang up on me.' He gave a hollow laugh. 'He ran out without telling us where he was going and said he's leaving home.'

'They drove off hours ago,' Piers said. 'Sam says they said they're going ten pin bowling.'

'Jerome was fairly upset too!' Casey told Blake. 'He wanted to get away from us for awhile.'

Blake gave a rueful sigh. 'Is that so? Hey, are your ears burning too?'

Piers forced a dry chuckle. 'Put it this way, I wouldn't care to be a fly on the wall at that bowling alley.'

'I'm glad Mike's with Jerome, anyway,' Blake told them. 'Let's hope Jerome will be able to calm him down. I suppose we'd do best to just let them hang out together and get it out of their systems.'

'Maybe that's wise,' Piers agreed. 'After all, they're not kids anymore. They're nineteen-year-old men.'

'That's what Michael's always reminding us, but sometimes it's easy to forget when he acts just like Ethan. OK, I'll respect his feelings and trust him to be responsible. But that's much easier to say knowing he's with Jerome.'

When Blake left, Nicola went up to her bedroom. She did not intend to sleep. Instead she curled up in her window seat to keep her eyes focused on the front yard, intending to hurry downstairs as soon as she saw Jerome arrive home. She had to know he was OK. *At least we know he and Michael are bowling. He must be waiting until he thinks everyone will be in bed so he can creep in without facing any of us.* She smiled to herself. *Little does he know, but I can wait him out any day. Or night, for that matter.* She had no idea what she'd say when she saw him, but she couldn't rest without seeing his face.

Every minute ticked past like an hour. Waiting was far harder than Nicola expected. When her muscles grew stiff she paced the room and then returned to the window seat with her chin resting on her knees. Eventually she set out her work clothes for the following morning and brushed her hair with five hundred strokes just to pass time.

At two o'clock he still hadn't come. Her stomach churned sicker by the second. Bowling alleys didn't stay open all night. Either he was very angry and upset or something had happened to him.

She took her purse and keys and tiptoed downstairs. *I can't stand waiting like this.* She would fill in time going for a drive. He'd surely be back by the time she returned.

The question was where would she go? At that hour the South Eastern Freeway was almost clear of other traffic. The boys would no longer be bowling. That much was certain. Anxiety pumped from Nicola's heart, swirled in her stomach and spread through her limbs, making her fingers clamp stiffly around the steering wheel.

It finally occurred to her that it might have been a terrible mistake for Jerome, in such an overwrought frame of mind, to have gone off with Michael.

What if they had gone to a pub to share a few drinks? Nicola had never seen Jerome drink but Michael could be persuasive. And it wouldn't have taken much arm-twisting with Jerome in such a vulnerable state.

He might even slip Jerome some alcohol without him knowing. Michael was in a foul mood himself and had reason enough to urge Jerome to drink with him. His gripe against his own family had become so huge, he'd told them he was leaving home.

Blake Quinlan had expressed relief that his brother was with Jerome but the more Nicola mulled it over, the more her heart fluttered for the opposite reason.

She drove down from the hills and through the quiet city with no fixed destination in mind. At last she found herself moving slowly along the Brighton beach foreshore, peering from her wound-down window out to sea. Beneath the moonlight the sand shone the same luminous silver as the water. It was all one flat, never-ending sheet that could swallow a person whole. Nicola felt her throat tightening.

A dark, angular patch stood out in the sand. She slammed down her brake foot to study it closer. Trembling, she parked the car by the kerb and climbed out on rubbery legs. A few steps revealed that it was nothing but a long chunk of driftwood covered with seaweed. Nicola's knees collapsed beneath her and she sat down in the sand.

What did I think it was? Why did I even come to the beach? She couldn't deny the fleeting dread that she'd discovered a body washed up to shore.

I've got to pull myself together. That happened to Shane. It won't happen to Jerome!

She pulled off her sandals and paddled a little until her ankles itched and tingled like ice. Then she sat down again and covered her feet with sand. Nicola began to rehearse what she would say to Jerome when she saw him again.

Why did you do that? What came over you? Perhaps she wouldn't be quite so blunt but she longed to know what he'd been thinking. Boys not half as handsome as Jerome had always spurned her like bubble gum stuck beneath their shoes. Boys like Jerome never kissed girls like her. That was a simple fact, like gravity or taxes.

Bianca Henderson understood the unspoken law. She had made

a beeline for Jerome whenever he stepped into the Gratitude Group with Nicola. Bianca knew the natural order of such things. It had never crossed her mind that Jerome and Nicola might be a couple. Actually, it had never crossed Nicola's mind either. She recognised her place. Although Bianca had been quite right, it still festered deep in Nicola's soul. But she accepted it as the way things always had to be.

How could he really be attracted to me? Nicola could not convince herself it was possible. Perhaps he was deluding himself, obsessed with doing a dumpy, quiet girl a favour with some sort of misguided Gareth Edgley zeal. That had to be it.

That is it, she thought. *Jerome to Nicola's rescue, 'distributing heaven' just like Gareth Edgley!* She felt abruptly miserable. He was probably keeping clear of home because he'd come to his senses and couldn't decide the easiest way to let her down.

Why has he never had a steady girlfriend, anyway? Nicola's sister, Laura, often used to joke, 'Stop poring over those art posters, Nic. If you ever find a man that stunning who's single, I can tell you he's probably gay.'

Could that be it? That he's gay and it's not a Gareth Edgley thing after all? That he was kissing me because he doesn't care for girls and I'm so dumpy and fat that I'm emotionally safe? Was it something as twisted and perverted that Jerome himself hadn't even realised? Perhaps he has no idea how a boy like him is supposed to feel and behave. If he had any rational sense, why would he choose to kiss someone like me over a girl like Bianca Henderson?

This is ridiculous. Now my brain has completely malfunctioned. I'm thinking utter rubbish! I know he's straight! I'm sure he was just feeling sorry for me. Nicola shook the sand off her feet, stood up and brushed down her jeans. A sunrise appeared over the horizon like a heavy heart bleeding red streaks into the sky.

Whatever happened, she would always have the soft, shy brush of his lips to store deep in her memory. Nicola closed her eyes to cherish the full impact of the melting heat in her stomach. Her thoughts lingered over his fresh, intoxicating scent and the nervous pressure of his hands around her arms. Her supreme moment had been over in a flash but one thing was certain. She was ruined for anyone else.

Jerome, when I get home you'd better be there!

*   *   *

Piers and Casey had gone through the motions of going to bed but it was pointless. After an hour of tossing and turning, Casey was up again. Piers found her at the kitchen table with the lamp shining on her bright hair and red satin nightgown. Casey's head was bowed as she sat hunched over a book.

Her drained face revealed the news but she spoke it anyway. 'He still hasn't come home.'

'I guessed.' They were two of the hardest words Piers had ever said. He sat beside her to see what she was reading. He had expected to find her Bible but the book was *Distributing Heaven* by Gareth Edgley.

'I never really had a decent look at this,' Casey said, placing her hand over Piers'. 'Maybe he resented that. I can't stop thinking about what he said to me. I tried to ignore it on the grounds that he was highly emotional when he said it. I can live with being a scapegoat. But I just can't put it out of my mind. You should have seen the way he blurted it out without any thought at all. And he looked stunned too. Who knows how long that might have been building up inside of him?'

Piers saw her eyes turn moist in the dim light. He moved his chair closer to Casey's and kissed her hair. She leaned her head back on his shoulder in the usual way. At least something still belonged to the world Piers thought he knew.

'I'm having trouble believing this at all. If we've failed him, how could we have known? He's always been such an obliging and well-adjusted kid. Far more stable than I was at his age. He's never given us a moment of trouble.' Piers stopped trying to make excuses. Instead of congratulating himself for bringing up a bright, responsible young man, he should have realised that something was not quite right. His eyes fell on the black and red cover of *Distributing Heaven*, and for some reason, he shuddered.

'I know what Suzanne would say. She'd tell us it's Anna's blood coursing through him and there was nothing we could do about it.'

Piers shook his head. 'No. We can't let ourselves off that easily. There were warning signs that he was troubled. We just chose to ignore them and hoped they'd work themselves out.' He opened Gareth Edgley's book and whistled under his breath, stunned by what he saw. A myriad of cross-references and pencilled comments in Jerome's neatly rounded script filled the margins of every page. With unsteady fingers, Piers continued turning pages. Wherever he looked there was more. He wouldn't have been surprised if Jerome had jotted enough notes to fill a thicker book than Gareth Edgley's.

'We saw the warning signs.' His voice was husky and he cleared his throat. 'This obsession with Gareth Edgley is just so...' Piers tried to come up with a suitable word but his overwhelmed brain wouldn't oblige him. 'Obsessive,' he finished lamely.

'But we thought it was a passing phase. It didn't seem harmful.' Casey was making excuses for them too and they both knew it. 'It's just a positive story written by a good man who was trying to make a difference in the world. It was nothing like Anna and her drug problem.'

Piers nodded. 'That's right. No drugs. No alcohol. No porn.' He sighed heavily. 'But still an addiction just the same. What I'd like to know is *why?*'

'It's my fault that he ran off. I laid a guilt trip on him. When he said what he said to me, I didn't think how he must be hurting.' Casey sank her face into her hands. 'He tried to apologise but I was caught up in self pity. I'm a terrible mother. I should have raced after him. I wish I had. But do you know what? When he said that to me... I wanted to slap his face! Hard.' She let out a quivering sigh. Piers pulled her closer and stroked her hair.

Casey wrapped her arms around him but held herself rigid. She was completely baffled by Jerome's resentment. 'How could he mention his real mother?' she asked. 'He's never mentioned her before. His real mother didn't kiss him goodnight for ten years until he told her he was too old. She didn't clean him up when he got carsick or answer his same questions over and over, a thousand times. She didn't help him with his homework or watch him play football. And she didn't sit there, proud as punch, when he graduated Dux of his class.'

'I know.' Somehow, Piers had grievously failed his son. He wouldn't fail his wife too. He'd let her vent her feelings. But he was stuck for the right words to say. 'I know you were hurt. I was hurt too, just to hear about it. But when he said that to you, I'll bet he wasn't giving her a single thought. How could he? He never even knew her.'

Casey pulled herself out of his embrace and faced him with flashing eyes. 'Piers, I never liked having that photo there.'

'Which photo?' He was baffled.

Instead of answering, she marched to the cabinet shelf in the next room and returned with the framed photograph of Anna. She thrust it at his chest. '*This* one! I've held my peace for years for your sake and Jerome's. But after what he said I don't want to anymore. I don't want to look at her.' She eased herself back into his arms. 'I suppose you think I'm terrible.'

He shook his head, even though she wouldn't see him with her face pressed into his pyjama shirt. Piers was worried to distraction about Jerome but managed to force a grim laugh. 'I've never been particularly fond of that photo. And I was the only one who really knew her. It reminds me so much of the mess I used to be in. You don't know how often I've thought I'd rather stick it in an album and move on with my life. But you know what we talked about. We thought we owed it to Jerome to keep it there.'

'Well, if he wants it, he can keep it in his own bedroom from now on.' She caught her breath in a sob. 'That is, if he ever comes back. I thought he was only going out for a little while. Piers, where on earth is he?'

'Hey, read this.' Piers' caught sight of something Jerome had written in the open book before them. The sentence was jerky and heavily underscored.

This has been right under my nose! I hate being so thick. I'll never be like Gareth! I might as well just give up.

Piers' tired eyes were stuck reading it over and over. *Is he serious?*

Something bitter bubbled in his chest. It rose to his throat and prickled behind his eyes. Then he wept, as he held Casey close. 'Did I do anything to make him think he has to prove himself like this? I've always been so proud of him. Maybe all this time, I should've been making that even clearer to him.'

He traced his finger around the looping shapes of his son's writing. 'But I really thought he knew.'

* * *

Nicola hadn't expected to find anybody else awake when she got home but Piers and Casey were sitting out on the steps, sipping tea.

'Isn't he home yet?' The verandah posts seemed to spin around her.

Casey's haggard face appeared ten years older. 'We've phoned the Quinlans. Michael didn't go home either. They're concerned too.' The strand of hair she tucked behind her ear was limp.

'But we haven't heard any bad news,' Piers added. 'If they were in an accident overnight, surely we'd know by now.' He tried to sound confident but his grey eyes were hollow and smudged. 'I'm certain they'll be back today.'

Casey got up to pour Nicola a cup of tea and Nicola only accepted because her swirling stomach needed something to help it settle.

'I was thinking I might not go in to work today. I'm feeling a bit sick.'

'Maybe it would help pass time if you did,' Casey suggested. 'You know I'll phone you as soon as we hear anything from Jerome. I'm sure when you get home he's bound to be here.'

Nicola could see the sense in that plan. Waiting for him at home would tear her nerves to shreds, so she got ready and went to work. It was a brisk Thursday morning trade and she was kept busy serving customers. All the time, her silent mobile phone sat like a rock in her pocket. Nicola flipped it open several times to see if she'd accidentally missed a call but there was nothing. The churning, sick feeling returned in full force but she knew food or drink was the last thing she needed.

Something must have happened to them for sure. Jerome would never let this much time pass without letting his family know where he is. Some guys might, but not him. And no matter how he feels about me, he knows all about Shane. He has too much compassion. He'd never stay away overnight and put me through this again.

An elderly man eased an armload of at least a dozen books on the counter before her. 'Whew, that's a relief.' He gave a cheerful, toothy smile. 'I'll still have to carry them all the way through the mall back to the car. Sometimes I just don't know when to stop.'

Nicola forced a polite smile, even though her mouth was so dry, her lips stuck to her teeth. 'At least you'll be able to carry them in a bag.' Coming to work had been a mistake. Her broken heart was sapping her energy. She had none left for small talk with customers.

'Can I pay for them with my credit card?'

'Of course.' She scanned the barcodes of each book while the old man jerked his chin at his largest purchase; a heavy volume full of glossy European photos.

'I reckon this one's the find of the day. I'm flying back to England the day after tomorrow and it'll weigh heavy in my luggage. But I couldn't resist. It brings back good memories. I used to be a missionary in that same part of the world many, many years ago.'

'That's good. I'm glad you found something that suits you.' Nicola longed to get away from people. She picked up his credit card. 'Would you like to sign or use your PIN number, sir?'

'I'll sign for them, thanks.'

When he scrawled his signature she went through the protocol of matching it with the back of his card. G. M. Edgley.

'Thanks, love. Have a great day.' He heaved the heavy bag off the counter with a grunt.

Nicola's glance settled on the merchant's copy of his receipt. Something had struck a chord in her memory. The man's name was Edgley. Her mind began to forge quick connections. He was a missionary from England. Nicola's hands turned clammy. He must be around the right age. When she peered at his initials her heart swooped. She raised her arm to grab his attention.

'Excuse me, sir, will you come back?'

He turned with an inquiring smile. 'Forgot something, did I?'

'No, it's just... Pardon me, I'm probably wrong but is your name

Gareth Edgley?'

Wonderment filled his faded blue eyes. 'That's me alright.'

Nicola clutched the edge of the counter and stared at the pattern of his tweed coat. She raised her eyes to the strands of grey hair combed across the top of his shiny head.

'Are you the man who wrote *Distributing Heaven?*'

His breath burst out in a rush. 'Well, I'll be jiggered! Don't tell me you've heard of *that?*'

Her head was spinning. 'I sure have. I've read it. I enjoyed it a lot. And I know your biggest fan ever!' She was jabbering too fast. Nicola swallowed and made an effort to slow down. 'He's spent months trying to find you. He wanted to tell you how much he loved your book, and to find out how he could get your second one. He was searching library catalogues and the internet and even telephone directories. It made him so frustrated when he couldn't find you. I can't even begin to tell you how upset he was. Because you're his hero.'

'I don't know what to say.' Gareth's head slowly shook from side to side. 'This sort of thing never happens to me much anymore. And it used to all the time. It was over forty years ago when I wrote those books.' He began searching with a trembling hand through his pocket and produced a notebook and stumpy pencil. 'I'd be happy to meet your friend. I'll tell you what, why don't we all meet at a good café near where I'm staying? Here's the address. You come along with him. I'm only in Adelaide until tomorrow. So would tonight suit you?'

The largest surge of nausea engulfed her, as if she had a proper stomach virus.

'It'd be wonderful, but I'm not sure if we can. I don't know where he is.'

Her anxiety must have shown because Gareth Edgley reached out and gave her shoulder a bracing squeeze.

'Don't worry, you'll find him. He'd have to be mad to leave a lovely young woman like you, who cares so much about him. I'll tell you what, here's my email address. Your friend can get in touch with me back in England.'

Nicola couldn't stay at work after that. She obtained Vicki's permission to leave and walked dazedly through the mall. Tears streaked down her cheeks.

I can't believe this has happened, she thought, distraught. *Gee, thanks a lot, God! You couldn't have picked a worse time for a miracle if you'd tried! If only this had happened a day or two earlier, Jerome would never have gone away! What an awesome surprise this would have been. I can't even imagine the look on his face. But instead he'll be so disappointed.*

The tears became a torrent. *That is, if I ever see him again to tell him.* Her greatest fear seized her mind once again. *He might be dead. Shane did something completely unexpected and unthinking. What if Jerome does too? What if he's already dead? Oh God, then I'll die too! I might be able to live without Shane but you can't expect me to live without Jerome.*

Why did this have to happen? He would have been overjoyed to meet Gareth Edgley. I can't understand your rotten timing. Nicola choked back a sob. *Rotten?* she thought. *It almost seems malicious. I don't know why I'm even talking to You because You didn't save Shane. I've been praying to You for all these years but now I'm sure it's pointless. You never do anything for anybody. At least not for anybody like me.*

19

Jerome forced himself to close his eyes and draw several deep breaths but his shaking continued. His body was reacting to his confinement in ways he had never expected. His muscles were twitching and his arms and legs going into spasms because they so desperately needed to be stretched. He scrunched up tight, wrapped his arms around his knees, leaned his head on top and tried to imagine plenty of wide open space around him.

Michael hadn't spoken for a long time and Jerome wondered if he'd been able to catch some sleep. No sooner had the thought crossed his mind than Michael's voice croaked, 'Hey J, what if they don't find us before we starve to death?'

'We'd probably die of thirst first.' Jerome's throat was parched and his tongue almost dry enough to cleave to the roof of his mouth. Yet his clothes seemed slightly moist after a night in the pit. His jeans chafed against his legs. If his mouth was damp and his clothes dry, it would have made all the difference.

'Which of us do you reckon will croak it first?' Michael's speculations were growing steadily more morbid, reminding Jerome that they were already buried deeper than the dead.

'I reckon I'll croak it first, because I can't stand listening to you.'

'No, seriously man, I can't take much more of this pain. It's throbbing right up my leg. Feel this ankle.'

'OK.' Jerome caught his breath at the massive, balloon-like swelling beneath his fingers. 'Gee, that must hurt! But at least you have something to take your mind off not being able to move.'

'I'd swap with you if I could,' Michael said sourly. 'I'm sure it's broken. Probably should be in a cast.'

'Well, if we ever get out of here, you can get me to sign it.'

Michael stopped leaning against the rock wall and sat bolt upright. 'What do you mean *if*? You're supposed to say when! You're the one who was certain we'd be found. And now you're saying *if!*' He was almost weeping.

'Take it easy. Saying if we get out of here isn't as bad as asking which one of us will croak it first. So you're allowed to be negative and I'm not, hey?'

'Yes! Because you can't stop being positive! You've got to believe we'll get out of here. Because you're the Christian. That's our only chance. God might listen to you but He'd never listen to me.'

'Well, I reckon He would. Why don't you ask Him to rescue us? And you start by saying when. Might shock Him into doing something for us.'

The light was not too dim to show that Michael's face was twisting like rubber. 'Do you think I've never tried? When I was little, I used to pray until my voice was hoarse. I prayed when my brother Sean had his accident that crippled him. Do you think God ever did a thing to help? All He did was make Mum die.'

Jerome forgot about his fidgety limbs. His skin crawled with the familiar, hopeless feeling of being trapped with nothing to say. This time, he was trapped both verbally *and* physically.

'He didn't make her die,' he said at last. 'It was an accident.'

Michael's response was swift and savage. He kicked the wall with his good foot. 'Will you stop talking that pathetic Blake-drivel? God didn't bother to stop her dying, then! Same thing! Religious prat!'

'Sorry.' Jerome didn't miss Michael's obscene hand gesture between sobs. 'I shouldn't have mentioned your mother. What can you expect from me? I've totally screwed things up with mine. I'd be no help to anybody.'

Michael grunted. Then both boys lapsed into silence. Jerome found himself mulling over what he'd said to Casey before he left.

Where did I pull that from? If we die, that'll be her last memory of me. And I didn't even mean it! She'll think I hated her but I never did. What made me go and say something so mental?

The whole thing baffled him. He'd never thought any such thing before. Not about Casey. It was Anna he resented. Anna who made him feel as if he were in a black pit with unscaleable walls. *Ironic,* he thought. *I run away because I've said something stupid about my real mother and I find myself in a real black pit with unscaleable walls.*

It was Casey who'd helped him more than she'd realised. Sometimes he thought he might have committed suicide but for her. She had always made him feel worthy when he was feeling useless, hopeless, unworthy. Casey was his mother – his *real* mother – and that was that. She'd always been one of his favourite people. He'd been delighted to find out she was going to marry his father. At first she had been shy about calling herself Jerome's mother but he'd never had a problem with the concept himself. He'd grown used to it far sooner than she had. As far as he had been concerned, he had never had a mother before and now he did. It had been a deliriously, intensely wonderful feeling.

If anyone had been miserable during those early years, it was Casey herself. He remembered a drawn-out phase of thermometers, temperature charts and visits to the doctor. Jerome hadn't understood most of it but he knew that it was all to do with his parents wanting another baby. He remembered the morning he'd climbed out of bed, started his usual dash to their bedroom and heard his mother crying. Jerome had stopped short near their door while an instant lump knotted itself deep in the pit of his stomach.

His dad's muffled voice had soothed, 'At least we have Jerome.'

He had flinched to hear his own name spoken in such a grave, heartbroken tone.

His mother's reply wasn't muffled. It was loud and distorted with tears. 'I know, but I really wanted a baby of my own too.'

Jerome hadn't given that morning a thought for years but now he could clearly remember the blue and white striped flannel pyjamas he'd been wearing, and even the round, smiley face tattoo on the back of his hand.

'Piers, it's not fair!' she'd gone on. 'People like me who'd love a baby try and try, yet others have them when they don't even want them.'

Jerome sensed that it was not a good time to leap giggling onto their bed, hoping to be tickled. Instead, he'd tiptoed back to his bedroom to tidy up his toys. He'd felt guilty for overhearing something that was not meant for his ears, but even when his mother opened his door and lavishly praised his neat room, the murky shame still stuck. He knew it was something to do with what she had said and that he could do nothing to fix it. He wanted to belong to Casey in the way she wanted. For the first time, he realised he was not enough. Not good enough, not special enough, not worthy enough. He had always known those things were true about himself and Anna, but the first pinprick of doubt needled him that day that it might also be true about himself and Casey.

Michael started talking again. 'My mum believed in God. She was the most faithful Christian you'd find anywhere. I miss her heaps.' His shoulders were jerking.

'Then maybe you'd feel better if you did what she'd want you to do. And I'm sure she wouldn't want you getting bitter at God and being depressed all the time.' Jerome figured that if Michael could speak his mind freely, he'd do the same. *Hang the consequences,* he thought. He tensed his muscles, expecting Michael to lash out at him, but Michael didn't.

'How am I supposed to do that?' he asked bitterly. 'How can I help being depressed all the time, after the horrible life I've had? I don't see how I can ever be happy.'

'That's what I don't understand about you. Because sometimes you're the happiest person I know. I've seen you at your place with little Ethan. Or round at mine, hanging out with our two brats. You seem really happy then. Anyway, if your life is so bad, why are you so anxious to get out of here and have another crack at it?'

Michael wiped his eyes with his sleeve. 'Because I don't want to see Ethan or the new baby, or even Sam or Laura, have such a rotten life as I did.'

'Are you saying you want to help make their lives better?' Jerome felt a sense that he'd tapped a vein of gold.

'I dunno. Well, yeah. They all have fun with me. I might be able to do a little bit of good.'

'Sure you could. It's not only them, either. There are scores of kids who are sick or sad and they could *all* use your help, if you could figure out some way to give it.' Jerome realised that he was unconsciously using what Gareth Edgley called *Limitless Thinking*. Gareth had written, *Find a need or passion and don't limit yourself to what the world would have you believe you are capable of, because your potential impact is only restricted to the dream God plants in your imagination.*

'Are you practising your missionary thing on me?' Michael sounded almost hopeful.

Then Jerome remembered. Although he was several feet underground, his spirits sank even deeper, if possible. 'No, I've given up on that.'

'But why, man? It was such a big deal to you.'

Jerome was tired of people trying to convince him to stick to the thing he'd decided he could never pull off. It would be much easier for him if they'd just accept his word. 'I've found out I'm not all that suited to it after all.'

'Why? Just because kissing Nicola didn't pay off? Well, big deal. You've found out that you shouldn't try to help girls by kissing them. And even though she didn't like it, I'm sure she'd still want to be your friend and see you out of here alive.'

Michael's words set off something inside of Jerome that made him scramble to his feet and try to shake his restlessness out. It didn't work.

Of course, you useless, self-pitying nerd! he thought. *She wouldn't want me dead! Shane was only her friend too. In fact, after Shane...* It was another thought he captured and allowed to remain momentarily unfinished.

'I know she would,' he said, suddenly throwing off all his listless despondency. 'That's why we have to make it. Listen Mike, we can't croak it. We've got to hang on for as long as it takes to get help. Because Nicola couldn't handle it if anything happened to me. She probably feels like dying now.'

'But you said she doesn't fancy you, mate.' Michael was gingerly poking his swollen ankle.

'I know that. But you don't know what happened to her before.'

'So are you gonna tell me?'

'Well, see, she had this friend called Shane who lived next door to her. One night he asked her to go out with him and Nicola told him no, because she didn't want to date him. She just wanted to stay friends. So Shane went straight off to drown his sorrows.' Jerome winced at his own unfortunate choice of words. 'Then he thought he'd go and have a swim. And he ended up being found really drowned. Washed up by the sea.'

'Whoa!' Michael breathed.

'Yeah, whoa. His family blamed Nicola for his death.'

'Not her fault,' Michael said.

'Yeah, but she blamed herself just as much. Held herself completely responsible. And she might think that I was mad at her last night after all that other business.' A chill tickled the back of his neck. 'It'll be a repeat of the whole thing for her. She'll think it's her fault. That's why we need to get out of here alive. If we don't, she'll blame herself for me and you too. Because I dragged you along with me.'

'Stop thinking about it,' Michael said quickly. 'We will hold on. I'll tell you what, I'll even pray!'

'It must be desperate if you're willing to pray.'

'I'd kick you if it wouldn't hurt so much.'

There seemed nothing further to say. Silence filled the pit again. Jerome let his thoughts wander back to the time when his mother wanted a new baby more than anything else. At last Sam had been born.

Jerome remembered sitting with his feet dangling over the seat of a plastic hospital chair while his dad proudly lowered the new bundle into the crook of his elbow. He remembered Sam's squashy pink face with its tightly closed eyes. Sam's eyelids had made the biggest impression because Jerome had wanted them to open up and look at him. He'd rubbed his finger down a velvet cheek, trying to make those incredibly tiny eyelashes flicker but they just stayed closed. He looked up to tell his parents, but the expression on his mother's face had driven every other thought from his head.

Casey's eyes were fixed on Sam's sleeping profile with a triumphant radiance Jerome had never seen before. 'How do you like him?' she'd asked.

Until that moment, Jerome had been delighted, almost drunk with the happiness hovering in the air around him. 'He's great.' It had been the truth but something inside him stung because a dark voice whispered to him that his mother had her real son now. Having a substitute had probably never come close. Even at the age of eight, he'd known that he ought to ignore that desolate ache. He'd closed the door on it but there were times when it swung open of its own accord, no matter how hard he tried to lock and bar it and nail it shut forever.

Maybe my name should've been Ishmael.

He loathed his adult self even more for letting that thought creep in. He knew his family loved him. He was thinking rubbish. He really was demented, like his grandfather, Jean-Michel Dupont. He'd taken it out on his mother but it wasn't Casey's hang-up; it was his. If he were above the ground, Jerome would have tried to jog it away. But if he were above ground those thoughts would have stayed buried where they belonged. They were part of a bitter, resentful person he couldn't stand.

All he could do was clench his teeth and try to block those thoughts out. But now that he'd let one slip through, others followed. Jerome imagined that he held a laser gun aimed at them. Whenever one of those unleashed thoughts slid into his head he shot it down in flames.

Idiot! Idiot! Idiot!

It was vaguely satisfying to imagine them sizzling to ash on the ground of the pit.

The problem was he thought he'd already done that, years ago. *I wonder,* he asked himself, *if thoughts that are buried alive actually stay alive.*

* * *

Nicola dreaded returning home to find no Jerome. Piers and Casey would surely have phoned her if they'd heard anything at all from him.

Suddenly, she yearned to see her own mother and feel her arms around her. Nicola drove to her old home and regretted it as soon as she saw James and Karen's car parked out front. She'd forgotten that it was Thursday. They often visited Ruth on Thursdays because James had a half day at work. Nicola's first instinct was to back out hastily but she noticed a twitch of the lounge room curtain. Somebody had spotted her.

The front door swung open and her mother hurried down the porch steps and opened the car door. 'Nicky, we didn't expect to see you.' She stopped short at the sight of her daughter's face. 'Something's happened, hasn't it? What's wrong, baby? You come out and tell me.'

Nicola stepped out of her car on shaking legs. James stood behind their mother and even Karen had poked her head around the screen door, curious to hear what was happening. Nicola was weeping in her mother's arms.

'My very best friend has gone missing. It's Jerome. You haven't met him but I'm sick with worry about him. He disappeared last night and should have been back long before now. I'm so scared something bad must have happened to him.' Coming to her mother's house had not eased her dread at all.

'Who's Jerome?' James sounded bewildered.

Karen stepped off the porch. 'He's the boy Laura and I met, isn't he?'

Nicola nodded and drew a ragged breath. 'It's happened just the way you said you hoped it would.' She felt wound far too tight to control what should or should not pour out of her mouth.

Karen's blue eyes shot wide open. 'What do you mean I hoped it would?'

'Don't you remember? You said you hoped I'd never find anyone else to love me and that someday I'd feel the same way I made Shane feel. Well, since you phoned me last night it's panned out like that in every way.'

James spun around to face his wife. 'You phoned Nicola last night? You didn't tell me you phoned her. What was that all about?'

Karen's face was chalky white. She said nothing.

'Was it to try and make her feel bad?' James persisted. 'Karen, I've been putting up with your attitude towards Nicola for long enough now and I'm sick and tired of all this vitriolic…'

'I didn't mean it!' Karen's voice tumbled out in a rush. 'I needed to let off some more steam.'

Still rocking Nicola, Ruth stretched a hand toward Karen. 'Listen, love, we know how you feel but it's time…'

'It's time to *stop!*' James cut in. 'Mum, she's been letting off steam for almost two months now. We know how hard it's been to deal with what happened to Shane.' When he paused to clear his throat, Nicola's spine prickled. Her brother was crying! A shiny tear streaked down James' cheek. He quickly rubbed it off but she'd seen it. 'It wasn't Nicola's fault!' he went on. 'Nicola wouldn't hurt a fly and I won't have my wife giving her nasty phone calls.'

Nicola stepped forward to touch her brother's shoulder. 'James, don't be hard on her. That won't change anything. Karen, if I had a choice I would've fallen in love with Shane. It would've been so much easier for everybody if I'd fallen for Shane. I wouldn't have even met Jerome. But it seems we can't choose who we fall in love with.' She turned to go.

'Nicola, wait!' Karen's voice shot out after her. 'Don't try to put a guilt trip on me for this. Just because I said those things, I was angry. I didn't mean them. Jerome's disappearance has nothing to do with the things I said. It wasn't my fault.'

'I know that.' Nicola turned to face her sister-in-law. 'Do you know how I know? Because I understand. Shane's death wasn't my fault, either.'

Karen's last threads of composure snapped. Her throat worked and then her face was in her hands. 'I know!'

Later, Nicola wondered which of them took the first step. She was holding Karen close, patting her shoulder while Karen trembled and wept, 'The reason I was so angry is that I would've loved to have seen you with Shane.'

'I loved Shane as if he was James,' Nicola told her. 'I couldn't think of any greater compliment than that.'

Karen turned her watery face to look at her husband and reached for his hand. 'It's just that I still miss him so much. I'm sorry, everyone.'

'Me too!' Nicola's throat was so tight she could barely speak.

'I hope Jerome comes home,' Karen said.

'I'll let you know what happens.' But Nicola had no hope. She hadn't been phoned. It was ominous enough for Jerome not to contact his family or return home when he should have, but sinister beyond words that Casey and Piers hadn't contacted her either.

* * *

She came home to exactly what she'd been praying not to find. Piers, Casey and the two children sat around the kitchen table with the phone in the centre, waiting for something to happen. Piers clutched a small photograph. This time, Sam's face was the most blotchy and miserable of all. Nicola's knees quaked with the despair of finding that what she'd expected was true.

She guessed that she'd walked into one of the long, barren moments when everything to say had been said for the time being. But when she joined the Bowman family at the table, they began a fresh round of talking.

'Jerome and Michael are still missing and even Dad thinks they should've come back or called us by now,' Laura blurted.

Casey continued pouring out the news. 'We've called everyone we could think of who they might have contacted. My parents, Piers' mother, Suzanne and Eric, my sister Abby. Piers even called Jerome's grandparents in New South Wales. Do you remember me telling you about Anna's parents, the Carters? They haven't heard from him either.'

'And now *they're* worried,' Piers added dryly.

'Dad's called the police,' Sam croaked. His eyes had been rubbed to pools of jelly.

'Now that they've been gone for over twenty-four hours, they're officially missing persons,' Piers said.

Laura gasped and Sam let out a stifled sob. Piers put on a soothing voice for their sake. 'That doesn't really mean much, though. It's only a time thing. Don't be frightened, kids. Remember, Jerome and Michael are together. They're bound to be safer together.'

Nicola found it hard to believe his platitudes while his voice wavered. It was clear Jerome had never done anything remotely like this in his life before. *Just as Shane had...* Before she had even finished the thought her heart expanded with more grief until there was barely room in her chest to breathe. Piers' comforting words and his chin, tilted with determination to take his own advice, reminded her strongly of what she might lose. Jerome and his father were alike in far more than just looks. She moved around the table to look over Piers' shoulder at the photo he was holding.

'That's you and Jerome, isn't it?' She wanted to take the old snapshot from his hands and never give it back. Jerome had been a tiny baby with a feathery mass of black hair and his eyes were squinting as they faced the sun. Piers himself appeared not much older than Jerome was now. His hair had been shaggier than Jerome's, his nose a slightly different shape and there was something shy and guarded in his stance and expression. Other than that they were remarkably similar.

'You were almost as handsome as Jerome,' Nicola breathed.

Piers managed a weak grin. 'Would you listen to her? She sounds surprised at that.'

Nicola would have blushed if she hadn't been washed-out with anxiety. 'Sorry. I've forgotten my manners.'

'That's OK,' he told her. 'I know it was a real compliment.'

Sam, who would have normally hooted some wisecrack, drew his eyebrows together and said nothing. His face was the colour of raw pastry.

The telephone shrilled, making them all jump. Piers fumbled with the receiver when he answered it. 'Hello... oh, hello Blake. No, we haven't heard any more.'

Nicola almost cried. Tears were streaming down Sam's face. They all waited while Piers repeated what they'd told Nicola. And when he hung up, his shoulders drooped.

'There's nothing more from their end, either. They've been doing the same as us and phoning everybody they could think of. Blake even tried their father's mobile phone, just in case Michael managed to talk

Jerome into tracking him down. But their dad hasn't heard a thing from the boys and he abused Blake for not looking after Michael better.'

Casey's eyes flashed. 'He has a nerve, after walking out on the whole family!'

Suddenly Nicola knew she could bear waiting there no longer. It had been gruelling enough when Shane disappeared but this time her heart would surely explode if she didn't do something. Although she had no clue where Jerome might be, she was not going to sit and watch the hands of the clock tick around. History was *not* going to repeat itself. Nicola seized her handbag and keys again. 'I'm going to look for them.'

'How could you possibly know where to start?' Casey's swollen eyes were too much like Pam Turnbull's had been and Nicola quickly looked away. She didn't want Casey's raw grief to smother her own dwindling ray of hope.

'I'll start at the bowling alley.' She was clutching at straws but had to start somewhere.

'They wouldn't be there still,' Piers cried. 'They went there last night!'

'I know but I'll ask anyone if they saw them.' Nicola tapped her handbag to feel the small, square shape of her digital camera. There was a photo of Jerome and Michael together somewhere on it. She'd taken a shot of them kneeling in the grass, varnishing a small chest of drawers. Mrs Reynolds had asked her class to come up with photos of people hard at work and that had been Nicola's contribution.

'Please phone me if you hear anything.' Her exhausted head spun as she climbed back into her car and the fingers that turned the ignition key quivered. Nicola would never rest until Jerome was found. Embarking on a wild-goose-chase would help kill time, if nothing else.

*   *   *

The atmosphere of the bowling centre bombarded her senses. The cacophony of shrill laughter and frenetic movement all around her was overpowered only by the odour of fried take-away food from the kiosk. Nicola had to stand still and wait her turn in a long queue. Desperate thoughts swooped from her head down to her stomach, which hadn't stopped twisting for twenty-four hours.

There are so many people working here. How can I be sure I'll be speaking to the right person? Nobody will be able to tell me where the boys went next, anyway. But at least I'll know they've been here. At last she was at the head of the queue. Nicola stepped up to a middle-aged lady with peppery curls and the name *Rosie* embroidered on her red T-shirt. Nicola had to speak loudly to be heard over the din.

'I'm looking for two friends of mine who were here last night. Have you seen them?' She showed Rosie the screen of her camera.

Without bothering to look, the woman replied, 'I wasn't here last night.'

Nicola wasn't going to give up. She raised her voice even louder to catch the attention of the next operator; a girl named Tegan with a bobbing, ash-blonde ponytail. 'Excuse me, were you working here last night?'

'Yeah.'

Nicola was too far back to show Tegan the camera photo. Instead, she shouted, 'I'm looking for two young men who might have been here last night. One has longish blonde hair, a similar colour to yours. The other one has dark, slightly wavy hair and a gorgeous smile.' Nicola stopped to catch her breath. She was divulging useless information. Even if Jerome had been there, he was probably in no frame of mind to be smiling. 'Anyway, he's really good looking.'

Tegan shook her head. 'Lady, do you know how many people pass through here? There's no way we can remember individuals.'

Nicola had expected no less but it still hurt. The customer beside her had moved away with his bowling shoes so she was able to edge slightly further along the counter to show Tegan her camera. 'Just in case you saw them... here they are.'

The girl took a cursory glance. 'They're both cute. Maybe I would've remembered seeing them. But sorry, I can't help.' She dismissively raised her eyes to the person behind Nicola and called, 'Next!'

Nicola slumped onto a plastic backed seat. *I'm pretty dumb. Did I expect to find Jerome and Michael back for another game or what?*

Now that she was here, she would ask as many people as possible. Nicola shrank from approaching strangers. It would almost certainly be a waste of time but the only alternative was returning to her loft bedroom to face another intolerable night without Jerome.

Before she could entertain second thoughts she approached the family at the nearest alley; a red-haired mother with four noisy children.

'Excuse me.'

Nobody heard her. Nicola tapped the mother's shoulder and raised her voice. 'Excuse me.'

The red-head jumped and spun around.

'Sorry for scaring you but have you seen these two friends of mine?'

After squinting at Nicola's camera, the lady shook her head. The four children each went through the motions of looking too. They shook their heads like their mother.

'Thanks anyway.'

She moved on to a young couple who had just finished lacing up their bowling shoes. 'Excuse me but have you seen these two friends of mine?'

They looked at her as if she must be crazy. 'No.'

Nicola sighed. Perhaps she should be catching people as they left the bowling alley. She dashed after a skinny teenager before she stepped out of the door.

'Excuse me but have you seen these friends of mine?'

'No. I wish I *had,*' the girl joked.

'Well, thanks anyway.'

Nicola let out a groan. It was going to be a long night.

*   *   *

The evening sky faded from brilliant orange to grey dusk for the second time since they'd fallen down the shaft. The boys had stopped shouting for help because singing was easier on their vocal chords. They belted out a selection of popular hits and then progressed to hymns. Curiously, Michael could recall the words of several hymns because his mother used to play them around the house. The powerful lyrics echoed up from their pit to float away into the vast night. Eventually Michael remarked that singing increased his savage thirst too much to continue. Thick silence poured back into the gap they had filled with their tuneless music.

'How long does a prayer take to work, J?'

Jerome didn't answer. He knew what Michael was thinking: another night in the pit would be unbearable and there was no chance anyone would find them now that it was after sunset. 'Dunno,' he said finally. 'Not many of my prayers get answered.' He hoped that the one he'd been praying silently for the last few hours would, though: that whatever happened, whether he and Michael got out or not, Nicola would know she was not to blame.

'Terrific,' Michael said sarcastically. Then he had a thought. When his mother had her accident, he'd been alone in the house with her. He'd prayed without the faintest clue what he was doing. His brothers and sister-in-law, who knew more about God, had been attending conferences and camps. Their father had been off somewhere, probably getting drunk as usual. He would have been no help, anyway. By the time Sean, Angela and Blake had returned, any chance their mother might have had was finished. 'Hey J, doesn't it help if more than one person prays?'

Jerome didn't need Michael to kick him. He wanted to kick himself. How come he needed Michael to remind him of these elementary things? 'Yeah, it does,' he said. 'Where two or three are gathered in My Name, I am there in the midst of them.'

'OK, then,' Michael said. 'You pray and I'll 'AMEN' 'cause I'm not really good getting the 'thees' and 'thous' right. Maybe that's been our problem.'

'You don't have to 'thee' and 'thou' at all,' Jerome said. 'God understands modern English.'

'Yeah, I s'pose He must, being God,' Michael said, sounding mildly surprised. He looked up and saw a cobweb of stars high above. 'Hey, God, I know you're probably busy running the universe but J and me are in a big fix.'

'Please help us God,' Jerome said, 'and please, *pleeeease,* in Jesus'

Name, reassure Nicola this has nothing to do with her.'

'You have got it bad, J.' Michael shook his head. 'Bad with a capital B.'

'Amen.'

A new silence fell between them but this time it was less tense, a faint sense of hope was stirring.

The night was getting colder. A faint fog seemed to swathe the pit. It took Jerome some time to realise it was his own breath misting in the chilling air.

'Hey J?' Michael began after a long while. 'Just say we get out of here and I try and get a job working with kids. Would I have to go back and study?'

Jerome was going to say, *That depends what it is,* but decided a one word answer would waste less energy. He needed it all for rubbing his icy arms. 'Probably.'

'But I hate studying. I remember how hard Claire studied when she decided she wanted to be a counsellor. I don't think I could stand it.'

'But you hate working at McDonald's too.' It seemed Jerome was in for another conversation so he might as well talk, although he was distracted by the gooseflesh on his arms which felt like tiny, prickly bubbles.

Michael thought quietly for a moment. 'Well, all that study was worth it for Claire. She always says that counselling those girls at the pregnancy crisis centre is the best thing she's ever done. I can't imagine myself as a counsellor, though. I definitely wouldn't want to teach them anything, either.'

'You wouldn't have to. There are thousands of other ways you could help kids.'

Michael winced with pain as he flexed his ankle a little more than he had intended to. 'I like fooling around better than anything else. Maybe I could go to clown school, or something.'

'Yeah, why don't you go to clown school? You'd be great.'

'But do you reckon they'd make me write essays?'

Jerome shrugged. 'Who knows? Maybe there'd be some early childhood theory or something. Your guess is as good as mine. That shouldn't be a problem, should it?'

'Well, I hate other people marking what I've written and assessing how bad it is.'

'So do I, but that'd only be for a few years.' Talking about the future gave the illusion that they would definitely get out of there.

'If I was a clown, I'd probably see different groups of kids all the time. That'd be OK, but I might be better sticking to one or two familiar kids.'

'You could be a male nanny, then. Mum met one at a friend's place. He told her there's always plenty of work.'

Michael let out something between a laugh and a whimper of pain. 'A male nanny? That'd show Blake and Claire, wouldn't it? They never trust me with Ethan unless they're in the next room or breathing down my neck. It's got to be something that'd show 'em all. Sean and Angela, too.'

'Why is it always a personal crusade to show 'em?'

'Because they don't care about me.'

'What are you talking about? I've never met Sean but it's obvious that Blake cares. He makes your friends feel welcome. Well, he makes me feel welcome. He always has time to chat with us. And Sean always keeps in touch with you. I'm sure they both care.'

'Only because they're my brothers,' Michael grumbled.

'Well, isn't that reason enough?'

'No! Not when they're just obliged to care about me.'

Jerome cringed. He knew all about obligation. He owed his life to other people's obligations. If Anna Carter hadn't honoured her obligation to protect small, defenceless creatures, he would never have seen the light of day. She'd rejected him but at least she'd stuck to her principles. *That's all I am,* he thought. *A principle. An inconvenient, unwanted principle.* Casey had been obliged to care for him too, because getting Piers meant getting Jerome. *I was part of the package that came with Dad. Inconvenient, unwanted at least. No,* he decided, giving Casey her due, *she wanted me a lot but not nearly as much as she wanted Sam and Laura.*

It wasn't only Anna and Casey. Jerome knew his father well enough to guess how heavily obligation must have weighed on his shoulders. Piers had been nineteen years old when Anna fell pregnant. The same age Jerome was now. The idea of being saddled with a brand new baby was unimaginable. It would have been no different for Piers. The older Jerome grew, the more it dawned on him what an unwelcome dilemma his father had faced.

The custody battle Piers had fought to get Jerome had been a colossal nuisance. That was family legend. The last thing Piers had needed at that stage of his life was a baby. It must have been pure obligation. Obligation that Jerome was deeply grateful for, but how different it had been for Sam and Laura, who had both been longed for and greeted with delight.

Jerome wished he didn't resent his family's pity toward him. That made no sense to him whatsoever. It wasn't their fault that Piers' biggest mistake had turned out to be him. He wished he could believe his father unreservedly when Piers told him he'd turned out to be one of the best things that had ever happened to him. But Piers always had a habit of looking on the bright side of anything.

Although Jerome knew all about obligation he had nothing but platitudes for Michael. 'Whatever you call it, it's obvious they still care. Like me with my grandparents. I mean my birth mother's folks. I have nothing in common with them and hardly ever see them but I know they care about me just the same. And I know it's because I'm their only living relative.' Jerome closed his eyes with a pang. His grandparents would suffer too, if he died down the shaft. 'But they're always pleased to see me. And it's the same with you and your brothers. Because you really only have each other.'

'I guess I want it to be even more than that with them,' Michael said. 'I want to give them some reason to care about things I do. Not just because I'm their brother.'

'Well, go and do some study, then. Give them something, if it'd make you feel better.' That was the best advice Jerome could offer.

'It isn't as easy for me as it would be for you. You just don't understand what it's like for the rest of humanity. You were born under a lucky star or something. Everything's a breeze for you. You have everything going for you and I have nothing.'

That was too much. Light flashed behind Jerome's eyes. Something fierce and electric was rising in him. In the frigid confinement of the mineshaft where he was going to die, all the rubbish gushed out.

'JUST SHUT YOUR MOUTH!' It rang through the pit, reverberating in his head. 'You say that sort of thing all the time! Can't you see *anything?* I have *nothing* going for me! I'm a total mess! And now I'm stuck down a hole with a self-pitying jerk who doesn't even know when he's well off.'

He pummelled the rock wall and yelled as pain jarred up his wrists. It took his last thread of self-control not to punch Michael too. Jerome longed to pound the whiner to pulp. Tears dripped down his chin and drenched the neck of his T-shirt. He drew a ragged breath between clenched teeth. A sane spot deep inside of him felt guilty that Michael had to deal with a basket-case but he couldn't stop now. He began kicking the wall until his ankles throbbed like his wrists.

Michael, surprisingly, seized Jerome's elbow and held on tight. 'Hey, calm down! What's eating you? You're not a mess! No way!'

Jerome released his breath in gasps. 'Do you really want to know what's eating me? To start with I shouldn't have ever been born. And I had a manic-depressive lunatic for a mother and a paranoid psychopath for a grandfather.'

Michael was surprised by the fierceness and tension in Jerome. 'But you're not like that,' he said, dropping Jerome's arm. 'Not until now.'

'Who says I'm not? Look at me! A lot of the time I honestly think I am.'

Michael, who always wore his emotions on the surface of his life, was astonished to realise that Jerome had hidden his insecurities and intense self-hatred behind an ever-smiling mask. 'What sort of garbage is that?' he asked. 'You always want to do good. The guys at work don't call you *goody-boy* for no reason.'

'You are so dense, Michael.' Jerome held his breath and listened to the tumult in his eardrums. 'I always want to do good because I want to prove it to myself.' When he could breathe more evenly he added, 'And all I've ever proven is that I'm exactly the opposite.'

'Hey, what is this? You're the sort of guy people really admire.'

'Yeah, well if they do, they're misguided.' Jerome squeezed his stinging eyes shut. 'Do you know what I said to my Mum just before I left? I told her she's not even my real mother. *That's* the sort of guy I am. You nailed it before when you said you wouldn't listen to someone like me!'

Michael, whose mouth scatter-sprayed things like that all the time, wasn't sure what to say. 'But isn't God supposed to forgive us?' His voice had turned pitchy.

'Yes, but...'

'But what?' Michael interrupted. 'I blow my fuse like that at people all the time. Just ask my brother. Blake reckons God forgives us when we're sorry. That's the only part that of the whole Christian thing that appeals to me. But what would I know? You're the expert.' He paused. 'Is there a limit on how many times God forgives people?' He threw his head back and looked at the sky. 'Or are you just too proud to ask?'

Jerome was stunned into silence. He couldn't refute Michael's words. God did forgive: that was the truth. He should have known that. He did know it. He'd studied the Bible until he knew it back to front. How had he overlooked God's forgiveness? Was the concept so familiar to him that he gazed straight past it? Had it gone in one ear and out the other? How obtuse could he possibly be?

He squirmed as he considered Michael's final jab. *Or are you just too proud to ask?*

Beneath all his self-pity and feelings of worthlessness, was it a case of wounded pride? Was it that he wanted so much to be first in Piers and Casey's lives that his tormented pride wouldn't allow him to share them with anyone else?

He felt torn between intense relief and immense shame. Yet one thing stood out: of course God had promised to forgive the tainted wilderness inside his heart. That was why Jesus had come and died on the Cross for him. It was elementary and it didn't really matter whether it was pride or stupidity: either way Jerome had missed it.

A voice deep in his heart seemed to urge him, *Lay it all down. You don't need to hold on to all this any longer.*

His taut nerves turned limp. Accumulated exhaustion from nineteen years of trying to crush his shame and guilt filled him. When he was eight, Jerome had gone through the motion of asking Jesus to forgive his sins. Yet he'd carried the oppressive load for an extra eleven years along with the loads of Anna Carter and Jean-Michel Dupont; people he didn't even know.

He'd spent all that time digging around inside himself, trying to excavate whatever goodness he could find to make up for it. And attempting to fool himself that he was making progress.

I've had enough. Jerome let out a shuddering sigh. *I'm sick and tired of it. I know your Word is rock solid, like the walls of this shaft. So I need you to take it from me. I can't get rid of it myself. You know I've tried. Will you please forgive my resentment, bitterness, unforgiveness, self-pity and all the rest?* He paused to shake his head. What a mortifying list there was. *I'm sorry for overlooking your forgiveness for so long. I wasn't thinking straight.*

He scooped mounds in the dust while his chest fluttered. *What am I supposed to do next?* Jerome was usually busy trying to figure out the proper way he ought to think and feel. At last he understood what an impossible burden that had been. Yet letting his mind relax made him strangely ill at ease. He just wasn't used to it. He shied away from accepting himself as he was, in all his brokenness.

He had always lived by trying to impress others. Perhaps he simply needed to stop trying to build himself into something admirable and let God form him into the person He wanted him to be. For the first time, Jerome wanted nothing more than to step back, accept his hopelessness and become an empty vessel that God could use however He pleased.

He gazed up at the sky. Busy stars seemed to zig-zag before his tired eyes, leaving white trails behind them. Jerome blinked and re-focussed until they settled back into their places and went on with their job of beaming the light they'd been pouring out from the beginning of time.

It's never been about me anyway, has it? It's always been about You.

The words of a song he'd sung thousands of times filled his mind. *Turn your eyes upon Jesus, look full in His wonderful face, and the things of earth will grow strangely dim in the light of His glory and grace.* Jerome hid his face in his hands, trying not to let Michael see that he was weeping. He still had such a long way to go.

All have sinned and fallen short of the glory of God. If he ever got out of the pit, he would stop the pointless drudgery of making up for his own badness. He would begin to focus on Jesus' goodness instead.

Blessed are they whose transgressions are forgiven, whose sins are covered.

After a long interval, Michael ventured, 'Hey, J, are you back to normal yet?'

Jerome found it incredible that he could smile again so soon. *Blessed is the man whose sin the Lord will never count against him.* 'I don't know if I was ever what anyone could call normal. Sorry about going off at you.'

'Well, listen, mate. I'm only gonna say this once because I don't want to start making gratitude a lifestyle, you understand. People'd get the wrong idea about me. But you've done me more good than anyone.'

Gratitude, Jerome thought. *Nicola might've gone to her Gratitude Group. When we get out of this, I gotta take Mike.* He smiled suddenly to himself. *Hey,* he realised, *I thought when then, not if.*

'How's that?' His query echoed off the walls.

'Because you have time for me.'

A laugh fizzed in Jerome's chest. 'I don't have much choice at the moment, do I?'

'Hey J, you made the choice the night you loaned me a hundred bucks.' A chuckle seemed to come from Michael. 'You know, J, I'd never ask this normally but we've been stuck down here for so long and we might never get out. I'm just curious. What made you like me?'

'What? Who says I do?'

'Come on, back when we first started talking? You lent me the hundred bucks and it wasn't because you're family or you had a gang of friends waiting to extort another hundred outta me. Why'd you like me?'

Although he was not confident at giving serious answers on demand, Jerome kept finding himself in situations where he needed to try. 'I dunno. Maybe 'cause you're fun. I can have a joke with you.'

'Is that all?' Michael sounded crestfallen.

'And you're totally genuine,' Jerome added.

'I've never known what people mean by *genuine*.'

'What you see is what you get. You don't pretend to be what you're not.'

Michael snorted. 'You're crazy, then. I'm the biggest liar of all times.'

'I didn't mean what you say. I meant your personality. You're easy to chill out with. And you're interesting. You do fun, unexpected things and keep us all wondering what you'll come out with next.'

'Anything else?'

'Come on, isn't that enough? Why did you like me, anyway?'

'I don't think I did,' Michael said honestly.

Jerome shoved him gingerly, careful not to disturb his foot. 'Well, thanks a lot! After making me say all that about you. That's great.'

'I don't mean I *didn't* like you. I just didn't think about it much. I was more interested to know if *you* liked *me*.' Michael gave a sheepish laugh. 'Hey, it's all about me. Pretty selfish, I know. But that was then. I do like you now.'

'Well, thanks. But you haven't said if you like the real me or the favoured, nerdy waste of space you thought was me.'

'You're as bad as I am,' Michael announced. 'You just want to be flattered.' He sighed. 'I dunno. Which one is my friend?'

Jerome thought for a moment. 'Both of us,' he said.

'Then maybe I like 'em both. Fact is, I can't think of anyone I'd rather be stuck here with if I had a choice.'

'I suppose I should say thanks. Don't know if I could say the same, though.'

'Don't get me wrong. I meant any other bloke. I can think of hundreds of *women* I'd trade you for.'

'No, you wouldn't,' Jerome told him. 'Not if they could smell you.'

'Well, you're not that good on the nose anymore yourself, Pretty-Boy.'

'You don't have to tell me.'

'If we die, we could alert someone by the stink.' Michael sniffed beneath his own armpit and groaned.

'I think we already could,' Jerome said.

The biting coldness turned his limbs rigid again and he couldn't stop shivering. He wrapped each of his hands around the opposite arms, hunching into as small a space as possible. *Was getting me trapped in this filthy pit the only way you could show me you've forgiven me?*

'Hey, I really need to warm up. Are you ready to sing again yet?' he asked. 'Or even pray. I think we'd better remind God we're here, don't you?'

20

It had grown so late that new customers had stopped entering the bowling centre. Nicola scanned the place and couldn't see many people she had not already asked. There was a wiry man in scruffy jeans with a shock of untidy black hair and a stubbly chin growth. She crossed the floor to him.

'Excuse me but I wondered if you've seen these two friends of mine?' Her voice had grown hoarse from shouting the same thing repeatedly.

This time, she was rewarded by a glint of recognition in his beady eyes.

'Yeah, I've seen those two. Their car broke down last night on the way to Murray Bridge and they had it towed to the nearest mechanic. That was me. Jim Jarvis is my name.'

Joy broke over Nicola like sunshine. 'Where did they go then?'

'That, I can't tell you. They never came back for the car. They were supposed to be back within the hour but they never showed up again.'

The sunshine was snuffed. Icy dread clutched her throat.

'I was expectin' them back all day today,' Jim Jarvis went on. 'I was gonna give 'em a piece o' my mind.' His wheezy laugh grated her nerves. 'I can tell you where their car is. In my garage on the outskirts o' Callington.'

'But... where are they, then?'

Jim Jarvis' quizzical expression sickened her more than any face she'd ever seen. 'Sorry, I can't help with that one, love. Maybe they called some other friends and went off with them.'

No way! Nicola thought. 'They'd never have done that,' she said.

The grubby mechanic shrugged. 'Well, perhaps you'd better call the police.'

Nicola felt like gagging. She couldn't expect this stranger to care the way she did. She mumbled her thanks and headed for the door. The chilly night air did nothing to calm her. The bedlam from the bowling alley still spun inside Nicola's head. Although hope was draining from her heart, she knew where to go next.

*   *   *

She couldn't stop trembling as she stood with her forehead pressed against the cold window pane. Shivers rose from deep inside Nicola, rattling her to the bones. She had called into a supermarket at Murray Bridge for a packet of batteries and the strongest torch they had. Finding Jim Jarvis' garage had not been difficult because Callington was a small town. Nicola had seen enough of Michael's car to recognise it instantly when she saw it in there.

This seemed far more ominous than finding nothing. Where were the boys? Hideous suggestions churned up from the same place as her shivers. *What if they'd met a serial killer? Murderers sometimes hang around quiet country towns at night.* Nicola knew she was going to be sick. She hurried away from Jim Jarvis' welcome mat as waves of nausea kept rising while she tried to purge the repulsive idea from her mind. Shaking her head, her hair had come out of its coil and stuck in rat-tails around her damp face. The spasm ended almost as suddenly as it began and she returned to her car.

Piers and Casey would be waiting for news, along with Michael's family. And the police would need to know about her discovery of the car. Nicola's parched throat burned like acid. Before flipping open her phone, she turned on her digital camera and gazed at Jerome's beaming photo.

He was achingly gorgeous. Nicola re-lived every captivating thing about him; the strong symmetry of his cheekbones and chin, his jaunty way of walking, his quick-witted way of coming up with jokes at perfect moments. Her mind caressed the memory of the shy, loving expression in his smoky grey eyes just after his lips had brushed hers. Nicola longed for Jerome more than her own life. As her eyes stung with tears, she turned off the camera and all that she had left of him disappeared. When she'd painted her Personal Adonis, Nicola had felt empty inside knowing that he was merely a figment of her imagination. Having a real Adonis and then losing him was something she knew she'd never recover from.

Lord, I'm sorry for speaking to you that way before. I need another chance and we both know you're my only hope. You know how much I love Jerome. But he went off thinking I don't. I still don't know if I could ever tell him, because I still don't know if he meant it himself. But if only you bring Jerome and Michael back to us, I'll be the happiest person in the world.

As soon as she stopped praying, heavy misgivings flooded back. Nicola feared that her prayer would not be an acceptable offering to God because there was no shred of faith to back it up. But some of Jerome's words from his first night at the Gratitude Group filtered through her mind. He'd said, 'My dad said that having a Bible is like having a whole list of fantastic contracts to draw on but so many people don't know what they are. It's like having a fortune sitting in the bank while you're living on bread and water.'

Nicola raised her head. She believed what he had said. Perhaps that meant that she *did* have a shred of faith.

You've promised to protect those who love you. And Jerome truly loves you and honours you with his whole heart. So I trust you to protect him, wherever he is. I refuse to believe that he and Michael are dead because you brought me face to face with Gareth Edgley today. And to think I almost didn't go to work. It was such a stunning, serendipitous moment! I don't believe you would have orchestrated that if you didn't mean for Jerome to meet him too one day.

What's more, you know I painted Jerome. I painted him long before I even met him. My Personal Adonis is Jerome. I didn't know it but You did.

I'll take all that as your sign that Jerome is not going to be another Shane. Please show me what I need to do!

* * *

Little Ethan Quinlan was happily guiding his Matchbox cars across the lounge room floor. Normally he would have been in bed but his parents seemed to have forgotten about him. They sat on the couch talking softly to each other while Ethan ran a car right over his father's foot and he didn't even seem to notice.

'The only people we haven't called are Sean and Angela,' Blake mumbled, 'and that's because I'm sure Michael and Jerome wouldn't have tried contacting them, in England.'

'And if they had, Angela would have phoned us.' Claire looked at the small, splayed out feet of her son and sighed. She was delaying the bedtime ritual because all she could think about was Michael. Earlier that day she'd been in to tidy his bedroom but it tortured her with memories of him. His clothes were strewn across the floor, and his distinctive, slightly musky smell filled every crevice. The thought of never seeing her mercurial, restless young brother-in-law again was too horrendous to contemplate. She broke out in perspiration at the fleeting thought.

'Now the thing we thought was good has become bad,' Blake remarked.

'Don't talk in riddles. What do you mean?' Claire had a sinking feeling that she shouldn't ask.

Blake watched Ethan guide another car across his foot. 'I mean the fact that he's with Jerome. I could've believed that Michael would go this long without calling us. But Piers and Casey are certain Jerome would've definitely called them. So that's a big worry.'

Claire's stomach swooped with the terrible dip she'd expected. 'When should we tell Sean and Angela?' she whispered.

Blake groaned and buried his face in his hands. 'I can't even bear the thought of telling Angela about this over the phone. You know she'll completely freak out. And there's absolutely nothing she and Sean can do. Let's wait a few hours longer to see if the police come up with anything.'

Ethan seemed to be building a whole parking-lot over Blake's feet.

'Daddy, stay still.'

'I *am* staying still.'

'No, you're wriggling.'

Blake realised he'd been trembling without even knowing it. 'Sorry, mate.'

'Where's Unca Mike?' Ethan sounded as if he wanted a more reliable human prop.

Blake moistened his dry lips. 'We're hoping he'll be home soon.'

Ethan accepted his words and resumed humming as he pushed his cars around. Blake wondered if Ethan would take the news that he might never see Michael again with the same equanimity. Spots started flashing before Blake's eyes at the thought of having to tell him.

Suddenly the telephone rang. Blake leaped out of his seat, scattering Matchbox cars in all directions. Claire hugged Ethan's face against her chest and soothed his protests while Blake took the call.

'Yeah, what've you heard? ... You mean they left it there, the bloke fixed it but they didn't come back? ... Well, my guess is as good as yours. You'd think they can't be far away, if they had no way to drive... Yes, sure. We've got to find something.' As he hung up, he closed his eyes and shook his head.

Claire could barely force herself to croak, 'What?'

'Nicola found his car.'

'How'd she do that? Where was it?'

'It'd broken down and they left it with a mechanic in Callington. They told him they'd be back to pick it up within a couple of hours but that was early last night and he hasn't seen a trace of them since. And Nicola came across the mechanic in the bowling alley where she was making enquiries.' Blake jammed his shaking hands into his pockets and began pacing the floor.

'What are we going to do next?'

Blake suddenly glanced at Ethan and scooped him out of her lap. 'Let's talk about it when I've put this fellow to bed.'

Tears were welling up and spilling onto Claire's cheeks. She couldn't imagine how Blake could muster the strength to talk so calmly to Ethan as he helped him into his pyjamas. *Oh Michael, Michael, what have you gone and done?*

It was not only her face that was wet. The cushion she was sitting on was saturated. Claire stood up in a hurry. The seat of her maternity pants was soaked and streams ran down her legs.

'Blake, come here! Quick!'

He came carrying Ethan in one arm and holding Ethan's toothbrush in the opposite hand.

'I think my waters have broken!'

He needed only a glance at the couch. 'I'll say they have.'

'What shall we do?' Claire took a step forward to cup Ethan's soft face in her hands. A tightening around her waist made her gasp.

'I'll phone your parents to come, and then I'll finish putting Ethan to bed. And when they get here, you and I will go off to the hospital.' Blake tickled Ethan beneath his firm knob of a chin. 'Guess what. The baby's coming soon.'

'But it wasn't supposed to happen *now!*' Claire cried. 'Not while we're waiting for news about Michael and Jerome. I'm not even supposed to be due for another two weeks. Why can't this ever happen when we want it to happen?'

She thought Blake was laughing but saw that he was almost crying. He placed the toothbrush in Ethan's hand, pulled Claire against him and held them both tight.

*   *   *

Laura had drifted into an exhausted sleep and Piers carried her to bed. She was the only one who didn't know that Nicola had found Michael Quinlan's car. Piers didn't stop gazing at the old snapshot. 'Doesn't this remind you how God has always taken the best care of Jerome?' he mumbled to Casey.

She grasped his hand. 'You're absolutely right! It's been so obvious. Think of Jerome's birth. He would have been put up for adoption if you hadn't decided you wanted him. After all those hassles you went through, when people kept urging you to change your mind, you stood your ground and got to keep him.'

'And the day I won that battle was the day this photo was taken,' Piers said. 'Those few years when it was just Jerome and me were great times because I was getting to know God at the same time. That's when I started praying for Him to always protect Jerome. And He's never let me down before.'

Piers loved his three children with all his heart. Jerome was like a rainbow to him. Long ago, Piers had promised God that if He helped him win custody of his baby son, he would never stop depending on Him for everything else. Whenever Piers looked at Jerome he remembered his own personal covenant with God. It was inconceivable that Jerome himself, the source of the covenant, had been unhappy. If Jerome never came back, Piers knew the fabric of his world would unravel.

'Do you remember when Jerome was three, and I saw him fall off the top of that high slippery dip?' Casey shuddered at the memory. 'He plummeted down, head first. I expected him to be seriously hurt.'

'Yeah, and he came through with just a few minor bumps. What did I tell you?'

'And there was the time your creepy father wanted to abduct him and take him back to France. It still gives me chills when I think about how close it was. But if God can bring Jerome through that, he can bring him through anything.'

'It's as if God's been writing a story for Jerome,' Piers mused.

But ever since Nicola's phone call, Sam had sat hunched over, breathing heavily. Suddenly a green tinge spread across his face and he bolted for the toilet. He didn't close the door behind him and his parents heard him retching over the bowl.

Piers got up and followed Sam. He found his son huddled on the floor with his cheek pressed against the cold tiles. Sam's teeth were chattering.

'Dad, I feel so sick. I wish I'd gone with them, because then I'd know where they are. It's my fault that they might be dead! What can I do?'

Piers took hold of Sam's hand and helped him scramble to his feet. 'I'll tell you what you're going to do. The best thing. You have the most important job of all. You're coming back to the table with us to help us keep praying. Because no matter how bad it looks, God has been faithfully guarding Jerome for almost twenty years and He's not going to stop.'

Sam buried his face in Piers' shirt and sobbed while Piers stroked his hair.

*   *   *

Nicola had found no businesses open that late in the quiet town. She'd knocked on some doors with her camera, but none of the householders had seen the boys. Nicola was not ready to give up. Driving home to wait for whatever the police would turn up was out of the question. She would keep on searching, even though that meant wandering out into the pitch black scrub near Jim Jarvis' garage. She had run out of other ideas. Normally the scuffles of nocturnal field rodents would have spooked her but tonight they didn't matter.

Although Nicola's torch beam was strong, the sweeping void beyond it was thick as ink. *There's nothing out here! Who am I trying to kid?* Yet as the thought came, her beam shone on something a little different than the brittle grass she'd seen too much of already. There was a dusty ribbon of a path but what made her heart jolt against her chest wall was the sight of a footprint in it.

It's probably nothing! That footprint might be old. Nicola had been disappointed too many times to let her hope rise. She raised the torch higher and discerned more footprints in the dirt ahead. Then her skin prickled and she didn't care if she was getting her hopes up. She hurried along the path. 'JEROME! MICHAEL!' Adding sound to the chilling silence made her flinch. Nicola's thin scream evaporated into the immense sky. Her breath came in ragged gulps that sliced her lungs like knives. Her ankle twisted on a small, sharp rock but not bad enough to slow her down.

'JEROME!' Now her mouth and nostrils hardly seemed wide enough to suck in the air she needed. 'JEROME! MICHAEL!' Nicola knew she might be heading straight into a murderer's hide-out. She shook her hair back from her face and began to run. If Jerome was there, even a murderer's hide-out was exactly where she wanted to be.

* * *

Darkness had set in again so deep and thick that Jerome could no longer see Michael. He heard him moaning and felt him wriggling hard.

'What are you doing?'

'Pulling my jeans down,' Michael grunted.

'Why?' Jerome was beyond the stage of caring. He simply asked because of an impression that talking was all that was keeping them alive. Once they stopped, they'd sink into a torpor which they'd never flounder their way back out of.

'Because my legs are so itchy I can't stand it anymore. And my ankle is throbbing so bad I wish I'd just die and get it over with.'

Jerome had a disquieting feeling that this sort of talk would sink them into the mire faster, and he worried slightly that he was no longer as cold as he had been before. General numbness was definitely pleasanter than freezing but he wondered if it was the beginning of death creeping over him.

'We've prayed and nothing has happened,' Michael complained. 'It's just like before when Mum died.'

'It's not like before. Maybe something's happening right now.' Jerome's words sounded as numb as his arms and legs felt, but he kept saying them because words were the only positive action he could take. He'd learned something from his father. For the first time ever, he could do nothing but admit that circumstances were entirely out of his control.

'Do you know why I've never believed in God?'

'Why?' Jerome thought he might as well ask, although Michael's new train of thought did not sound promising.

'Because I was an accident.'

'Well, so what?'

'Mum was only supposed to have Sean and Blake. Nobody wanted me. I only got conceived because Dad came onto her when he was drunk.'

'But I still don't follow why you don't believe in God.'

'Well, come on! Think about it. How am I supposed to believe that the whole world isn't a freaky accident when I was a freaky accident?'

'You're the one who called yourself freaky. Not me.'

'Yeah, very funny. Maybe that's why I've always felt like everybody in my family thinks I'm just a duty. They probably all think it'd be easier without me. This might be a blessing for them. It's a rotten feeling, knowing you were an accident.'

'Don't forget, I was an accident too.'

'Yeah, I know.' Michael must have managed to get his pants down because he sat completely still. 'But somehow, things always seem different for you.'

Jerome wasn't so numb in his emotions after all. Something was stirring and he recognised it as irritation. 'The only difference is that it was an even bigger mess when I was born. My birth mother wanted to put me up for adoption straight away, and lots of other people thought she should have had an abortion. My birth caused heaps of problems for many people and I was a total mistake. But do you know what? I've just decided that's why I believe in God.'

'What? You believe in Him because of that?'

'Yeah, you stop and think. Maybe the people who appear to be accidents are really God's best gifts to the world.'

'Yeah, right.' Michael's tone was sneering.

'Think about it, Mike. There's no way we would've ever existed if God didn't want us here. We weren't ever planned by people. Just by Him. Got it?'

'Holy smoke!' Michael breathed. 'That's freaky! I mean good freaky!'

'I could've either been aborted or adopted by some losers. Instead, I'm with my real family.' Jerome felt a sudden longing to see Sam's cheeky, freckled face. It seemed he hadn't seen his brother for years, instead of days. But it hurt to think about that. Instead, he recovered his positive train of thought. 'It was out of my control. Ever since I can remember, I've always been trying to fix things. But that's stupid. There are so many things that only God can fix. He arranged all that for me when I was still too small to know what was going on. So He can surely get us out of here.'

'Well, I wish He'd hurry.'

'And do you know what else I reckon? If we get out of here, you should stop feeling sorry for yourself. Sounds to me like you want your brothers to boost you up so you can feel better about yourself. Well, I reckon you've got it the wrong way round. You've got to feel better about yourself before anyone else will build you up.'

'Enough already,' Michael growled. 'You're wasted at Macca's. Ever thought of being a shrink?'

'And have to talk to people like us all day? No way.'

Michael gave him a languid poke. 'As if I'd pay money to talk to you, anyway.'

'Yeah, my advice is always free. Hey, here's another idea. You could start your own business.'

Michael thought silently for a moment. 'You mean like organising fancy birthday parties with themes or something?'

'Hey, now you're talking. I didn't have anything in mind but a party business sounds awesome.'

Michael moved his injured foot slightly. 'Why don't you do it with me? Let's make a deal. If we ever get out of here, we'll do it. You can handle the paperwork and stuff.'

'Sure, why not. I haven't got any other…' Jerome's words trailed off. Something was happening in the blackness above their heads. There was a shaft of light moving across the top of the pit. It was swaying back and forward far lower than the stars.

Michael gripped his arm. 'Do you see that?'

'Yeah!'

'JEROME! MICHAEL!' The voice was very familiar. It sounded like the shout of an angel.

They both filled their lungs. 'NICOLA!'

Jerome's vocal chords seemed filled with dust and Michael sounded just as congested. But the small glint of light halted.

Her far-off voice called, 'I hear you! Where are you?'

'HERE! DOWN A HOLE!' Jerome bawled.

Michael added, 'CAREFUL! DON'T YOU FALL DOWN HERE TOO!'

The frustration of being unable to call specific directions made Jerome incredibly anxious. He couldn't guide Nicola to the right or the left. He couldn't even tell if their hole was in front of her or behind her, having no idea which direction she was coming from.

'I'M COMING!' Her voice sounded slightly closer and they could tell she was sobbing. 'I'M COMING! KEEP CALLING!'

'OVER HERE! DOWN HERE!'

The light gradually turned into a strong torch beam and poured into their pit. Her outline was a blur but they could hear her crying. Now they were able to see each other's filthy, emotional faces. Tears streaked down Michael's cheeks, turning the dirt to mud. Jerome nudged him. 'You'd better pull your pants up now.' He could barely articulate the words.

Nicola was half laughing, half crying. 'What are you doing down there?'

'Waiting for you,' Michael quipped. 'What else?'

'Weren't looking where we were going,' Jerome had almost got a grip on himself.

Nicola began laughing hysterically. 'I know that sounded like a dumb question.'

'Our car broke down,' Michael grunted as he wriggled his jeans back over his hips. 'I wanted to go have a drink at the pub but the Brain here thought a walk in the middle of nowhere was a much cooler idea.'

All three laughed as if they'd never stop.

'Don't suppose you packed a folding ladder in your handbag?' Michael asked.

They laughed again.

'How did you find us?' Jerome demanded at last.

'You won't believe it. I went to the bowling alley at Murray Bridge and asked everybody I could find if they'd seen you. At last I came upon that mechanic who had your car. Then I went to his garage and found it.' Nicola, reliving the moment she thought Jerome might be dead, buried her face into the crook of her elbow while her shoulders shook.

'You're fantastic!' Jerome called up at her. 'See Mike, I told you we'd be found.'

Michael elbowed him muttering, 'When was that? I was the one who told you we'd be found.'

Nicola swiped her eyes with her sleeve. 'Well, you can argue who told who what while I go back to the town and phone for help!' She grinned down at them. 'I left my phone in the car. Wish I could stay with you, but I'll be back shortly. Thank God you're safe.'

'How long will you take?' Michael cried. 'You can't leave me down here with this know-it-all by myself for a moment longer. You don't know what he's like.'

No, Nicola thought. *I don't, but I hope to.* Suddenly, they all went from laughing to crying, but Jerome nudged Michael again, whispering, 'Stop blubbering, you dope. We're rescued. And we're going up out of here like men. Not like wimps.'

'Look who's talking!' Michael gave one last huge sniff as Nicola waved to them and set off. He brightened suddenly. 'Hey,' he said, turning his face to Jerome. 'Now you're gonna have to start a business with me.'

'Or what? You gonna blackmail me with all I've said? You wouldn't tell Nicola, would you?'

'Nah,' Michael said. 'Of course not! I'm gonna blackmail you with the fact that it's not done for a goody-goody like you to break his promise.' He grinned. 'And you promised, J. You promised.'

*   *   *

Nicola's feet seemed to fly as she headed back toward the dimly glowing lights of Callington. Her heart had already soared up past the stars. It was reasonable that her feet yearned to follow. She had to muster all her scattered senses to keep her eyes on the pebbly ground, careful for uneven terrain.

She caught her left foot on a jagged rock, pitched forward and landed heavily on her hands. It jolted the wind from her lungs, setting her heart pounding. The vigorous rhythm turned into a song of praise. *They're alive! He's alive! Jerome's alive!* Blood gushed through Nicola's ears like the addition of a joyful drum roll.

She'd ventured further into the scrub than she'd thought. Nicola's body reminded her that it was not quite as agile as her soaring spirit. A vicious stitch wound its pain from her bottom rib to the top of her right shoulder. She hunched over to try and draw slower, calmer breaths. It was no use. They kept coming hard and sharp. Yet every knife stab around her heart, every pounding twinge in her shoulder sent pure happiness coursing through her.

She raised her aching eyes to the fathomless ribbon of the Milky Way. Many of its stars appeared to be whirling, flashing, and popping out of their orbits to congratulate her.

'Thank You.' Her whispered gratitude wafted up to blend into the rest of that rapturous night. She had a tremendous gratitude point. One that would last her the rest of her life.

For now she could hardly wait to hear Piers' voice on the other end of the telephone. *How welcome are the feet of those who bring good news.* Nicola intended to relish every moment for all it was worth.

21

'She found them!' Piers' voice resounded like a jubilant bell peal through the whole house. 'She found them! She found them!'

Casey's weak legs managed to take her as far as the couch where she hunched over and mumbled a prayer of thanks. A groggy Laura stumbled out of her bedroom, smiling. Piers hadn't said *where* they found them, but the tone of his voice told her that all was well.

'Would you believe they fell down a mineshaft?' he exclaimed.

'A mineshaft?' Casey's eyes were wide. 'Are they OK?'

'Michael hurt his ankle but other than that, they seem fine. Nicola told me they're both in good spirits.' Piers' face crumpled and he buried it in Casey's hair. His shoulders were shaking. 'If we go now, we'll get there the same time as the rescue crew and ambulances.'

'Ambulances?' Laura's face clouded. 'I thought you said they're OK.'

Piers swung her up beneath her armpits as he used to when she was a small girl. 'Well, Michael hurt his ankle. And they might be dehydrated or in a bit of shock.'

Sam's moist eyes were almost hidden behind a huge grin. 'Jerome's such a dreamer, but I thought even he would notice a great, gaping hole in the ground.'

Casey drank in the sight of Sam's face. Joy radiated from him and his cheeks were shining wet. She leaned across the couch to pat his shoulder and he threw his arms around her and hugged her hard.

*   *   *

'He's hurt his ankle, but other than that, they're fine.' Blake sat on the edge of Claire's hospital bed and kissed her. Claire's parents stood at the foot with a bright-eyed Ethan jumping up and down between them. He'd woken up at home and been unable to settle again so they brought him to see his parents.

'Thank God for that,' Kate Parker said.

Claire breathed into her gas mask as another contraction gripped her hard. 'Have they got them out of there?'

'No, it'll be awhile yet because they're calling a rescue crew. But the Bowmans are almost there. I was talking to Casey on the phone just then.'

'Are Casey and Piers going to be there when the boys come out?'

'Not just Casey and Piers but Sam and Laura too. And Nicola's there already, of course.'

'But we won't be there for Michael.' An anxious knot appeared between Claire's eyebrows.

'Well, we would be, if we weren't here.'

'You should go,' she said at once. As Claire leaned across for the mask again, Blake rubbed her between her shoulder blades.

'But I wouldn't make it back in time. The midwives said the baby might be here any time.'

'You should go anyway.' She looked up at her parents. 'Mum, Dad, help me to convince him. Jerome will have his whole family waiting for him and Michael will have nobody if Blake doesn't go. Think how he'll feel, after being trapped down there for two nights. You have to go!'

'But you need me too.'

'Not as much as Michael does.'

Blake looked at his father-in-law, who lowered his gaze and shrugged. Kate mumbled something about what a difficult choice Blake faced. 'If only we could tell who'd be out first; Michael or this baby.'

'Blake, you have to go!' Claire insisted. 'If you stay, I'll be furious.'

He rose reluctantly to his feet. 'Oh, well, in that case…'

She quickly clutched his hand in both of hers. 'You know I don't mean that. I know you want to welcome this baby into the world with me. It's just that I know you love me, but Michael's never been sure about it. And if you don't prove it to him today, there might never be another opportunity.'

'But the Bowmans know what's happening. They'll tell him. Michael would understand…'

'I know he'd understand with his head. But if your face is one of the first he sees when he's rescued from that hole, he'll know it with his heart, too.'

Blake stood gazing into the precious blue eyes that seemed to penetrate the depths of his soul. The trust and affection he read there never failed to awe him. He looked at the swollen bulge beneath her white hospital gown and the small beads of perspiration on her brow. She was trying to smile at him.

'I know you know I'm right. I want you to tell Michael that if I wasn't having a baby, I'd be there too.'

Blake looked at the older couple again. 'Will you look after her?'

'We'll be right here,' Kate said. 'You might even make it back before the baby comes.'

Claire inhaled so deeply, the machine rattled. 'No, he won't! Don't wish that on me, Mum.' She tried to laugh.

'I'll take Ethan with me.' Blake took hold of his son's hand. 'Michael might prefer to see him rather than me, anyway. Especially since it was my fault that he ran out.'

Claire's beam of approval was the reward he needed. 'That'd be perfect.' She didn't seem ready to completely relinquish his hand. Instead, she pressed the back of it to her cheek. 'Cheer up. We have this beautiful boy. We're going to have a new baby at any moment and Michael's safe. What more can we ask for? I love you with all my heart.'

Blake kissed her forehead and even though he didn't trust himself to speak, he had to try. Claire's tender strength was more than a match for his.

'You mean the world to me, too. I'll be back as fast as I can.' Even those simple sentences almost choked him.

On his way down the corridor with Ethan, a voice called, 'Blake, wait!'

He turned on his heels as his heart lurched. It was his father-in-law, who rarely addressed him directly. He had never quite forgiven the terrible thing Blake had done in his youth. He had always made it clear that Blake was a person he simply tolerated. He certainly never spoke his name. Why was William Parker breaking his own rules?

The older man approached them slowly. 'You can be sure we'll look after her.'

Blake smiled. 'Yeah, I know. Thanks.'

William cleared his throat with a 'haven't finished yet' sort of rasp. 'I wouldn't be so hard on myself if I were you. You said it was your fault that he ran out, but from all I've ever noticed, you've been pretty damn good to that young brother of yours.'

The whole exchange felt like a dream. 'Well, I've tried.'

William patted Ethan's head. 'That's probably why you've found it easy to be a good father to my grandson.' He raised his hand quickly as Blake drew a breath to speak. 'Don't say anything. There's no need to thank me. I like to think I give credit where it's due. But I'm holding you up.' With that, he turned and strode swiftly back to the labour ward.

Wow, what was that? Suddenly, Blake knew it was going to be a great day. All at once he longed to be right where Michael was. He didn't need any credit for loving his brother. Volatile, funny, warm-hearted Michael was easy to love. If he arrived too late, it would be as terrible as Claire said. Blake swept Ethan off his feet and sprinted out of the hospital into the faint flush of dawn. Ethan's chuckles gurgled in his ear and he didn't stop running until he reached his car.

'Daddy, do that again.' Even Ethan was panting and he'd been carried all the way.

Blake laughed as he strapped him into his car seat. 'There's a good chance I'll do it again when we get to where we're going.'

*   *   *

The boys tried to stand up together to greet the rescue crew. Michael swayed on his good leg and leaned against Jerome's shoulder to steady himself. Jerome's knees were knocking together. He heard Michael breathe in a suspiciously heavy manner beside him and nudged him in the ribs.

'Remember our deal. Men, not wimps.'

'Yeah, yeah.' Michael wiped his face.

It seemed like no time before they were both hoisted up to the earth's surface. Blazing sunlight dazzled Jerome's eyes and he instinctively closed them. A couple of days in semi-darkness seemed to have turned him into some sort of plankton. As soon as he grew used to the brightness pouring through the backs of his eyelids, he opened them a chink. There were his parents, Sam, Laura and Blake Quinlan with little Ethan. Jerome's eyes watered even though he was not crying. He turned to explain his tears to Michael and saw that Michael's cheeks were also streaming.

Something in his mother's face arrested his attention. It was a look he'd seen from her once before and he wouldn't have remembered it unless he'd been thinking about it down the shaft. Her eyes were shining with the same radiance they'd contained when Sam was born. But this time, she was looking at him.

Jerome took a few steps and faced her. 'Mum, I'm sorry.' He felt it was best to clear it straight out of the way. 'Can you ever forgive what I said?'

Casey's face twisted but she smiled and tried to make light of it. 'Of course I do. But let me warn you, if you ever say it again after these past two nights, I'll hit you first, so I'll be the one asking forgiveness.'

'I hope so,' Jerome said. Then he flushed. 'No, no, that's not what I mean. I don't want you to ask for forgiveness. Oh God, this is turning out all wrong. I'm getting confused again.'

'What he means, Mrs B,' Michael said, shaking his head, 'is that you're welcome to knock the stupidity out of him any time.'

For a few seconds Casey could not speak. She cleared her throat and went on. 'There's more than one way of being a real mother,' she said softly.

'Yeah, I know. You've always been real in all the ways that count.' His eyes sparked. 'I've always wanted to belong to you more than to...' He choked up, unable to finish as Casey stood on the balls of her feet and wrapped him in a hug.

A cloud of dust from his hair tickled her nose, making her sniff harder. She stood back, gripping his shoulders, to drink in the sight of him. 'Do you know, I have a confession to make. I think you know I've always felt really sorry for her.' Casey couldn't open her mouth without choking up. She rested her forehead on Jerome's shoulder. 'But I've never told you that I've had to fight jealousy too. That you were hers, not totally, completely, a hundred percent mine. Look what she could have had.'

'Mum...' Jerome could hardly speak. Filthy as he was, he held her close.

'But her loss has been my gain,' Casey whispered into his tangled hair.

His father, sporting two day's growth on his chin, clutched Jerome's other shoulder.

'It's great to see you.' Piers' voice was husky. 'We haven't stopped praying.'

'Hey, J,' Michael called as he was hoisted onto a stretcher. 'Maybe it was their prayers that got us rescued, not ours.'

Jerome opened his arms wider to include both his parents. He felt his heart would burst. Sam and Laura were there too. Jerome tugged Laura's pony-tail. Then he noticed Sam's red eyes.

'Hey, why the water works?'

'Because you weren't there hogging the computer, numbskull.'

'You didn't really think we'd disappeared forever, did you?'

Sam grinned. 'Only for a moment.'

A paramedic eased Jerome back onto a stretcher and wrapped a blanket around his shoulders.

'It's OK,' Jerome told him. 'I'm not cold anymore. And Michael's the one with the crook ankle, not me.'

'This is all standard procedure. You'll both be going to hospital for observation but you should be able to go home soon.'

Jerome twisted his neck to look at Nicola, who had hung back watching his reunion with his family. Her eyes were swollen almost shut with purple pouches beneath them and the parts of her face that weren't blotchy were streaked with dried, brown tear trails. When she saw him looking at her, she flushed and spoke a few words that he couldn't hear. He smiled back and raised his hand. Then a wide beam lit up her face. His sore eyes drank in the sight of her. The painful apology would have to come later.

Nearby, Michael was lying on another stretcher as his ankle was wound in cloth. He raised his hand to grasp Ethan's little fingers. 'Hey, give me five.' Then he twisted his head to look around at Blake. 'Where's Claire?'

'In the hospital. She's having the baby.'

'You're kidding me!' Michael's face turned chalky pale. 'What are you doing here then? I've stuffed things up again, haven't I? The worst part is over now that we're out of there. You didn't need to come. I'm sorry, man.'

'Hey, I wanted to come. Claire wanted to come, too.'

Michael calmed down visibly. 'Why?'

'Why would you need to ask? For the last day and a half, we thought you might be dead. I'm going to have a whole life with this new little person but you and I already go back nineteen years. If anything had happened to you, I would've found it hard to recover.'

'Really?'

'Of course. When we found out that you were OK, I had to come. And you should have seen Claire. All doped up with gas and pethidine, but she still managed to kick me out of the hospital room.'

Michael let out a ragged laugh. 'It was rotten timing, though.'

'The timing was perfect. It would have been horrible if Claire had to deliver this baby not knowing if you were dead or alive. Now she's really happy.' Blake tousled Michael's hair. 'I reckon you even gave her ...' He was interrupted by the buzzing of his mobile phone. Blake extracted it from his pocket with fumbling fingers and flipped it open.

'Hello ... Here already? Are they both doing well? ... That's fantastic. Tell Claire I can't wait to get back and see them.... Yeah, he's here.

He's right beside me. I'm going to tell him right now. I want to talk to Claire as soon as she can. Will she be able to phone me back then? ... Thanks. It's great news.'

He snapped his phone shut. 'That was Claire's dad. The baby's arrived.'

'And?' Michael struggled to lean up on his elbow. 'Hurry up! Spit it out!'

'It's a little girl!' Blake laughed as he watched Michael's jaw turn slack.

'No! Not really!'

'It's true. A nine pound girl.'

'But Quinlan guys hardly ever have girls. We all know that.'

'I know! I don't know how I managed it, either.' Blake's eyes were sparkling.

Michael twisted on the stretcher to call back to his friend. 'Hey J, guess what? We've got a girl! I mean, he's got a girl. I'm an uncle again.'

A general cheer erupted and Jerome gave Michael and Blake a thumbs-up sign from his own stretcher.

'Hey Ethan, you have a sister. You're luckier than us. Your dad and I never had a sister. Hey, I don't need to bother going to hospital myself. These fellows have strapped my ankle up already. I want to see Claire and the baby.'

'You'll have plenty of time to see them.'

'Well, I want to be around when you phone Sean and Angela. Don't call them without me.'

'I promise I won't. We'll tell them what happened to you, too. We'll call them soon. And I'll phone Dad at the same time.'

Michael let his head collapse back onto the stretcher again. 'Mum would've loved to have a granddaughter.' He felt a tear slide into his ear.

'That crossed my mind, too.' Blake leaned down to hug his brother and Michael raised his arms to wrap them around Blake's shoulders.

'Well done, man.'

Blake beamed. 'Thanks.'

'Guess what! J and I are gonna start a business helping kids. Maybe I'll even have to do some study.'

Blake straightened up to turn to look at Jerome more carefully. 'Hey, what have you done with Michael? My brother never says things like study.'

'Actually, it was his idea,' Jerome said.

'I'm totally serious,' Michael said. 'And I'm really going to do it because I promised.'

Blake appeared baffled. 'Promised Jerome?'

'No! In fact he promised me he'd help, like I said. No, I promised someone far more important than him. I promised God.'

22

Jerome hadn't wanted to go to the hospital but the sight of a neat white bed in a dim cubicle was enough to make him yawn heavily. His exhaustion penetrated deeper than his bones, seeping through his soul and spirit. Sitting down a mineshaft turned out to be surprisingly more tiring than running a marathon. No sooner did he lie down than he was drifting miles away.

Jerome longed for a deep, restful slumber but his brain was still churning with activity, filling his dreams with desperate questions, uneasy misgivings and strange heavenly beings. An angel was waiting for him behind his eyelids. At least Jerome guessed it must have been an angel.

'I know you want to rest,' the angel told him. 'Bear with me for a moment first. What have you done to deserve rest?'

Jerome seemed to hear the question more with his heart than his ears. He instinctively responded the same way he'd done thousands of times before and scrambled for answers. They charged through his head in no particular order.

'I studied hard and finished High School. I was even Dux of my class. I've helped my dad out with his business and done lots of work around the house. I always wanted to help people. I haven't done anything as great as Gareth Edgley yet, but I'd still like to give it a go if I could work out how. Maybe this new business with Michael...'

He tried to get a proper glimpse of the angel but his eyes wouldn't focus. They still seemed strained after hours of trying to peer through the musty, dark atmosphere of the shaft. That puzzled him. He knew that as he was surely dreaming, his eyes must be closed anyway. Dream eyes shouldn't be so tired. Jerome couldn't figure it out. The dream angel shimmered like a pillar of light with a blurry shape and something about the rigid angle of that pillar told Jerome he hadn't given the proper answer. He heaved a sigh. He'd expected that all along.

It came as no surprise when the angel said, 'That's all… nice, but what else?'

Nice? Jerome wondered at the sense of hesitancy and distaste that came across with the word. 'I've tried to keep fit,' he added. 'I jog a lot and go to the gym. I played football until last year. I only stopped competitive sport because I wanted to study more. I've been over and over Gareth Edgley's book to pick up anything I might have missed.'

'That's all nice and OK too. Anything else?'

Jerome felt the gnawing dread of standing before a teacher who was waiting to hear a presentation he'd forgotten to prepare. That had never actually happened to him but he'd had the teacher dream several times over the years. Even that one didn't make him feel as ill-prepared as this angel one.

'I don't have a clue,' he admitted at last. 'I always wanted my life to count but I haven't made it.' Then he remembered in a rush. 'Wait, there is something. It came to me when I was down the shaft. It was after something Michael said.'

Trying to remember what it was made the important fact slide further away. Jerome was tired of thinking, anyway. Surely he had a right to stop thinking while he was asleep. He deliberately emptied his mind and then the answer slotted in.

'I deserve rest because Jesus died for me so that I could have rest. I'm a child of God.' He had repeated those words glibly over the years but this time he saw their immediate impact. The pillar poured out brighter light as if it was smiling at him.

'Now you've got it. Enjoy your rest.'

'Thank you.' *What a weird dream.* One more thought shot through his head. *He brought me up from a desolate pit, and set my feet on a rock, making my steps secure.*

Jerome turned over on his side to face the darkest wall and let deep, relaxing waves of slumber roll over him. He hadn't wanted to go to hospital for observation, but now that he was there, he didn't want to wake up for several hours.

*   *   *

Nicola spread her range of artist's pencils across her bed for the hardest assignment of her life. She had a few more hours to tackle it while Jerome was being retained in hospital for observation. *At least if it looks really terrible, I won't have to show him. And I do have a very big sheet of paper.*

Before starting, she gazed at the painting of her Personal Adonis that leaned against the wall of her Loft. After a quick shower, Nicola had been back to her mother's house to pick it up. She'd intended to slide it straight beneath her bed but hadn't been able to smuggle it up to her bedroom without the two children noticing.

Laura had demanded, 'When did you do this painting of Jerome? And what on earth is that bath sheet thingy he's wearing?' Her face had wrinkled up into little laughter lines.

'It's a toga.' Nicola explained that the painting was an assignment. 'Homework,' she said. She tried to make it clear that it wasn't Jerome at all but her own personal idea of what Shakespeare's Adonis must have looked like.

'Shaking spear's *what?*' Sam's comical, wide eyes made her want to laugh but Nicola held herself together.

'There's an old legend that the goddess Venus was in love with a gorgeous young human man named Adonis. He went out hunting a boar and was gored to death, and she was so heart-broken that she put a curse on love. From that time on, anybody who fell madly in love with anybody was doomed to suffer as greatly as she had. And this is my idea of how he might have looked.'

Sam and Laura stared at each other with glee. Nicola knew what was coming and when they erupted into peals of laughter, she joined in.

She was still too euphoric with relief that Jerome was safe to mind a bit of embarrassment. They knew how she felt about him, anyway. She'd made it clear that she loved Jerome to everyone but Jerome himself. She still couldn't decide if she'd ever tell him.

Casey had said, 'You'd be perfect for him.' Nicola closed her eyes and tried to stay buoyed up by Casey's words but it was difficult to believe she had really meant them. Surely she thought that her smart, handsome son could do better for himself than a shy, fat girl who worked in a book shop. But Nicola's low opinion of herself had ended up getting Jerome trapped down a mineshaft for days. She longed to figure out why he had kissed her. The notion that he was really attracted to her was still too astounding to take seriously, yet she wanted to believe it with all her heart. That was why Nicola had decided to tackle her self-portrait.

She put on the velvety, musk-coloured dress that she'd bought on her shopping day with Casey. Then she stared pensively into the mirror, resolved to push past her aversion and begin. There must be something to appreciate for Jerome to even consider kissing her. The skin beneath her cool fabric warmed at the thought of it.

Nicola decided to start simply by pretending she was somebody else. The basic shape took place beneath her 2B pencil; an oval face with quite a broad, intelligent forehead and firm chin. Thick, brown hair twisted up in a coil. She moved down to sketch the chest and paused to see how it appeared on the paper. To her surprise, the bosom she'd always called huge and dumpy turned out to be merely voluptuous and shapely.

She moved on quickly to fill in her arms. Instead of being chunky and heavy, they appeared to be solid, capable arms with large hands that could wield pencils and paintbrushes with some skill. They could also wrap attractive parcels, wash clothes, cook meals and might one day cradle babies of her own; precious and small like the Quinlan family's new baby. Warmth infused Nicola's cheeks again, making it difficult to stay objective. *This can't be what Jerome sees,* she thought. *Can it?* She quickly filled in the curve of her stomach as she watched it gently rise and fall in the mirror. Next she added the shape of a leg beneath the dress; generous and healthy like the arm. Now there was mostly just shading to be done.

She'd purposely left the eyes until last. They were long-fringed, bright green eyes that seemed to gaze back at the artist with some sort of mute appeal. Nicola studied her likeness, wondering what it was trying to tell her. It seemed to be something like, *I know you've never really liked me but I am what I am.* Her own eyes stung a little but she sensed something light waiting to begin breaking out of the sadness.

There was something else tucked in the corner of her mirror. Her mother had given her a small photograph of herself at the age of three. Nicola picked it up and placed it beside the new sketch. It showed an earnest-faced little girl with chubby folds around soft wrists that hugged a small rag doll against her chest. The symmetrical contours of the oval face were already beginning to show. Nicola discovered a few tears coursing down her cheeks; warm and sticky.

She looked at the tiny girl and mumbled, 'Whenever I said you're ugly and frumpy, I didn't mean you. I meant the older you.' Somehow, that explanation didn't cut it. 'Maybe that's the same thing. I'm sorry if I've done you more harm than anybody else. But God's given you a skill to use. You shouldn't have ever listened to me before when I said nasty things. But listen to me *now!* You deserve happiness as much as anyone else.'

23

Jerome was soaking in the bathtub. He usually had showers but now he felt that he'd been missing a treat. He'd even squirted in some bubble bath and white, warm froth lapped the sides, filling his bones and washing away his memory of cold, grimy darkness. He was thinking of what his father had said to him on the way home from the hospital. 'I just want to tell you this, Jerome. I've always been as proud of you as I possibly could, but after these past few days, you've just increased my faith stronger than it was before.'

A fresh breeze from the window carried the fruity scent of passionfruit vines from outside. Jerome would never take being warm for granted again, or being able to stretch out. Even though his hairy knees poked up over the sides of the tub, it was more spacious than the mineshaft.

Somebody rapped on the locked door.

'Who is it?'

'It's me, Nicola. Are you going to spend all day in there?'

He felt his body temperature rise hotter than the bath water. He'd expected to hear Sam's voice, or Laura's. 'I'm coming out soon. I'll just finish washing my hair.'

'I haven't had a chance to talk to you alone, yet. I'm taking you out tonight. Are you up for it?'

He screwed up his face and exhaled hard. He would have groaned except that he knew she'd hear him. She obviously planned to break his heart gently. 'Yeah, but you don't have to do that. I'm cool about...' he grimaced again. '...everything.'

'Jerome, you don't even know where I'm taking you. I have a huge surprise. Don't make me say anything else. But you'll love it.'

'Well, OK then.' He was puzzled. 'So what should I wear?'

'Something smart and casual.'

'Are you gonna shout me dinner? Is that the surprise?'

'Yeah, you guessed it. That's it.' Her merry laugh told him that wasn't it at all, and he found himself frowning in puzzlement. She was behaving very strangely. Almost as if she was looking forward to the painful process of stomping on the already broken pieces of his heart.

*   *   *

Nicola changed into an Indian skirt and a plum coloured, lacy top. She found it difficult to stop smiling for long enough to apply her make-up. *This,* she thought, *is going to be one of the supreme moments of my life.*

Downstairs, she found that the whole Quinlan family had arrived for a visit. Michael was sitting in the boys' bedroom at the computer with Sam beside him and little Ethan on his lap. In the loungeroom, Blake and Claire sat on the sofa with their new baby. They looked up to greet her.

'I was just telling Casey and Piers about Blake.' Claire patted her husband's knee and gave him a teasing smile. 'When I went into labour, he was completely stressed out but tried so hard not to show it. I'll never forget the sight of his face when he told us that Michael was safe. But he'd lost the plot by then and I had to boss him around and tell him to get over to Callington as fast as he could.'

Blake stroked his daughter's downy-soft hair. 'I know I didn't have the baby or fall down the shaft. You and Michael had been through far more than I had. But I still crashed that night.'

'We were so happy when we saw you tearing over with Ethan,' Casey said. 'Claire, he ran as if he had a pack of wolves behind him. They only just made it before the boys came up. It meant a lot to Michael to see them there.'

'I was glad to be there too, and I've got to thank Jerome if he ever comes out of the bath. Michael told us some of what they were talking about down that shaft. I don't think Jerome has any idea how good he's been for Mike.'

'I guess that's what friends are for,' Piers said.

'And Michael's good for him too,' Casey added. 'Jerome has a tendency to get a bit too introspective at times and Michael knows how to joke him out of it.'

'Yeah, we know he's fun,' Blake said, 'but over the last few years he's lost a few friends.'

Claire shifted the baby to a more comfortable position in the crook of her elbow. 'We were worried when Michael first made friends with Jerome.' She peered toward the boys' open bedroom door and lowered her voice, even though they were oblivious to any conversation. 'Blake and I both liked Jerome a lot but we wondered how long it would take him to grow tired of Michael's attitude. Michael can be careless with his friends and very demanding at times.'

'And if they stopped being friends, we were worried about the effect that might have on Michael,' Blake said. 'But they've stuck together and Mike says Jerome's the best mate he's ever had.'

'You know, you two have had such good practise with Michael, you'll be wonderful parents to your own little ones when they're teenagers,' Casey said. Then the attention turned to the baby, Faith Rowena. Claire shifted her to Laura's knees and Laura stroked her soft, sleeping face with her finger.

'I love her. I wish she was our sister,' Laura said.

'You can come and see her whenever you like,' Claire promised her.

'She is so sweet.' Nicola wanted a chance to paint a portrait of Faith's petal-smooth face. Part of her wanted to study every flicker of the baby's delicate eyelashes and part of her was acutely aware of the sound of Jerome's bath water flowing down the drain. He would be out soon and her heart started flopping in her chest.

'Any baby of Claire and Blake's couldn't help being beautiful and good,' Casey declared.

'She has her rowdy moments,' Claire told them. 'I'm glad she's putting on a good show now.'

Nicola found it hard to imagine any baby disturbing Claire's refreshing serenity.

Then Jerome came out with drips falling onto his shirt collar and the other boys followed. Michael lunged across the floor on his crutches and eased himself into an empty armchair. Nicola had sketched a caricature of him on his cast at hospital, and since then every spare inch of the cast had been smothered with black graffiti.

Blake told Jerome, 'I was just telling your folks, you're like a dose of medicine.'

'You mean I'm hard to swallow?'

Blake laughed. 'I meant you always do people good.'

'And he started with me, almost nineteen years ago,' Piers said.

Jerome wished he had another wisecrack on the tip of his tongue. All he could come up with was, 'Well, thanks.'

'You're very smart tonight,' Claire looked at Jerome's black pants and grey striped shirt and gave an admiring whistle.

He blushed. 'I'm going out with Nicola.'

'Cool,' Michael exclaimed. 'Can I come?'

Before Nicola could respond, Casey teased, 'I don't think it's a general invitation.'

Michael scratched his head as he pretended to ponder. 'Oh, I get it. It's only for good-looking intellectuals whose names begin with J.'

Sam and Laura howled with laughter while Jerome seized the corner of a cushion and swung it back into Michael's face.

Even Blake put on a crestfallen act. 'That's too bad. I was thinking it sounded good.'

Nicola giggled and looked at her watch. 'Well Jerome, you're the closest match to Michael's criteria. Are you coming?'

'Yeah, get him out of here!' Sam cried. 'I want to tell Michael about the surprise.'

'You know what the surprise is?' Jerome asked.

'Course I do,' Sam said. 'I had to help Nicola with the computer.'

'What?' Jerome asked as Nicola pulled him out the door.

Claire waited until she heard Nicola's car start, then leaned forward to enquire, 'Is there romance in the air?'

Casey laughed and confessed, 'I hope so. I've suspected he liked her for a long time and now I know she likes him too. But I poked my nose in and almost ruined it completely.'

'So now we're going to leave our noses out of it and wait for them to work it out for themselves,' Piers added with a grin.

'This place is magic when it comes to romance,' Casey said. 'Nicola is the second young woman who came here to board in that upper room and stirred romance where she didn't expect it.'

'Tell them who the first one was,' Laura chirped.

'OK, it was me.' Casey smiled sheepishly. 'I came here when I needed a place to stay and Piers needed a boarder. We were both twenty-three and Jerome was just a little three-year-old.' She took a playful swat at Sam. 'When your turn comes, we only need to look out for another young girl who needs a place to live. But that won't be for at least another eight or ten years.'

'Hey, Mr and Mrs B, would you like to go out too?' Michael asked. 'I can stay with these two jokers while you're gone.' He jerked his chin at Sam and Laura.

'Say yes!' Sam cried. 'C'mon Mum, you and Dad deserve it!'

Piers and Casey looked at each other. 'We'd be crazy not to take advantage of an offer like that,' Casey said, 'But I hope we don't end up wherever Jerome and Nicola are going.'

'That'd be a disaster.' Piers smiled at the thought. 'How about some take-away down in the city and then a walk along the river? That'd be safe enough.'

'It's a date. And we won't even need to change for that.' Casey rested her head on his shoulder. 'We have a lot to celebrate too.'

Sam grinned and grabbed Michael's hand as his parents rose from the table. 'C'mon, hop-along,' he said. 'I have to show you something on the computer. It's the best secret. I haven't even told Mum and Dad. I promised Nicola I wouldn't say a word. But I didn't promise her I wouldn't show anyone.'

'A game?' Michael asked.

'No,' said Sam. 'An email.'

'Is this about elephants, mate?'

Sam shook his head and tugged at Michael's arm. 'Just come and see,' he urged.

*   *   *

Nicola's senses were comfortably full of the person who occupied most of her thoughts. The scent of his aftershave filled the car and she was acutely aware of his restless legs and flexing fingers. At least holding a conversation had never been easier. He pounced on her slightest remarks. Not only were there no lapses, but she hardly needed to speak a word. That was OK. He would soon be lost for words.

Neither of them was familiar with the district or the café. The glass topped tables were spaced far from each other and tucked into intimate alcoves. Nicola's eyes were drawn to the small, elderly gentleman who was rising from his table to greet them.

It turned out that she didn't need to make the formal introductions she'd rehearsed over and over. 'I take it you must be Jerome?' the man said, proffering his hand immediately after greeting Nicola.

Nodding his head, Jerome looked from him to Nicola and back again. Her grin was so huge and her gaze so fixed on his face, as if anticipating a reaction she didn't want to miss, that he was perplexed. But only momentarily.

Perhaps it was the cockney accent or something familiar in the Englishman's craggy features but it all suddenly clicked for Jerome. Nicola watched his wary expression change in front of her eyes. As a beam of wonder suddenly spread across his face, she knew that he'd guessed.

'Hello.' Jerome's voice was full of soft incredulity. 'I know who you are.'

24

They started by telling Gareth Edgley all about their recent adventures. He was an ideal listener, making noises of sympathy or admiration in the right places.

'Now, how about you?' Jerome asked at last. 'Did you write any other books after those first two?'

Gareth shook his head and squirmed. 'My only scruple about meeting you kids is that I was afraid you might be disappointed. What happened after I wrote those books doesn't really bear telling. I'm afraid you'll find it very anti-climactic. Especially after what's just happened to you this week.'

'But you married Irene, didn't you?' Jerome fidgeted with the edge of his placemat. 'And set up a great outreach mission?'

Gareth heaved a sigh. 'The answer to both those questions is almost. I was engaged to Irene Bradford but she called it off with a couple of weeks to spare. And the mission didn't quite make it to greatness. I published those two books with some of the money we were given as donations by people who wanted to help our outreach. I honestly thought that it would be money well spent. It was supposed to be a wonderful way to bless more people.'

'And it was,' Jerome said quickly.

Nicola nodded and Gareth gave them both a pale smile.

'One of my colleagues thought differently. He was a man named Antonio. He features prominently in my second book. I used to call him one of my greatest friends. But when I published those books, Antonio thought I was losing sight of the greater vision. In his opinion I was spending money that could be used directly to bless the poor to glorify myself instead.' Gareth stopped briefly to thank the waitress who brought their cakes. 'Now where was I? I was talking about Antonio. If only he'd come to talk to me about all that, things might have worked out much better. Who knows?'

Nicola and Jerome looked uneasily at each other.

'What happened?' Nicola asked.

Gareth Edgley stared down at his black forest cake without raising his spoon. 'Shortly after I published my second book, I was rushed to hospital with an acute case of appendicitis. I came out to find that my little mission band was a thing of the past. The others had been talked around to Antonio's way of thinking.'

Nicola's stomach was sinking. Neither she nor Jerome knew what to say and Gareth gave them a forced smile.

'So there you have it. I felt hurt and hard-done-by, of course. I spent lots of time stomping around and asking God why that had to happen.'

'But what about Irene?' Jerome put in quickly.

Gareth gave a dry laugh. 'I see I'd better continue quickly with this. While we were still engaged, Irene joined our band with the best of intentions but those times were hard for her too. The nomadic lifestyle took more of a toll on her than she expected. She wasn't born for it. So she told me, "Gareth, I'm sorry but this is your lifestyle choice; not mine." I can still remember the compassionate way she spoke those exact words.' He raised his spoon and took a bite of cake.

'Irene died two years ago, but we kept in touch over the years. She lived a good life and I'll never forget her. To me, she'll always be that little girl with the snapping blue eyes and hair like a rippling wheat field. She settled down with Arthur and had five children.'

'Arthur?' Jerome's chest rose and fell, despite the sudden tight band that had clamped down around it. 'You mean Arthur Pratt?'

Gareth gave a wheezy chuckle. 'I see you really got into the spirit of my book. He was actually a very nice bloke. I've always regretted the spin I put on their relationship in those books. It was one of my greatest follies. My toes curl up with shame whenever I think about it, although they were gracious enough to treat it as a joke after several years.'

Nicola peered at Jerome. His face was impassive and gave no sign of his crumbling illusion.

'I never re-started the *Distributing Heaven* campaign,' Gareth said. 'For months I sank into hibernation, just wondering if all those years and all that work counted at all. It seemed that I'd offered God my very best and He'd chewed it up and spat it back at me. I questioned my faith; something I never thought I'd ever do. I wondered if the care and blessings I'd always put such faith in were nothing more than froth and bubbles. And do you know what I decided?'

'Would we want to know?' Jerome smiled but Nicola sensed that he was nervous.

'Don't worry. The worst part of this story is over. Those books were supposed to have been about turning points in my life, but those turning points I wrote about were piffling things compared to the one that was still coming.'

'So… what was it?'

'In the end I realised Antonio had been right.'

Jerome looked devastated at last. *'What?'*

'It's true. I certainly felt sincere about everything I'd written in the books. God had put me in positions to help others over and over, but I'd been thinking about my conceited self the whole time. I'd fallen into the trap of thinking I had to be great, whatever I thought that was supposed to mean. The *Distributing Heaven* outreach turned out to be a source of personal pride. There I was, thinking what a clever chap I'd been to set up the whole thing from scratch. I reckon God had to sweep it all away from me for my own good.'

Pride. A pulse raced in Jerome's throat as he thought how deeply he'd hidden his own pride. 'I think I understand exactly what you mean,' he said with a nod. 'God has had to work hard lately to get my attention on that. But you didn't give up doing acts of kindness, did you?'

Gareth began to answer around the cake he was chewing. Instead, he pointed to his mouth and laughed. He finished and swallowed. 'Not a chance. After God indulged me by letting me wallow in self-pity for a while, I began coming across folk who could use a kind word or helping hand, just as I always used to. But *Distributing Heaven* was over! Defunct!' He swept his hand through the air in a chopping motion to emphasise the point. 'But then I realised the acts of kindness I've done *post*-Distributing-Heaven have been far more meaningful.'

'Are you saying that you had to get really unhappy before you could get really happy?' The theory would have sounded like twisted logic to Nicola except that she'd just been through something similar herself.

'I don't believe it needs to be that way for everybody but it did for me. During those mission years, I was acting with kindness because I wanted to see a certain result. I had an expectation that people had to be grateful and happy so I could prove the importance of my mission. That caused more stress than you'd think. Because when people didn't seem as happy as I wanted them to be, I took it as a failure on my part.'

Nicola nodded her understanding. Jerome listened with the intent expression that meant that his mind was ticking over.

'I'm an old bloke. I can say this with no doubt whatsoever. The only way being kind has ever worked for me is when I let go of the result. I married a lovely lady and had two sweet kids of my own. And I became an auto-mechanic. And now I practise kind actions not because I set up a special group but because I want to be a kind person.' He smiled with the palms of his hands raised. 'Now it doesn't matter whether people question my motives or accept my gestures. I don't give a hoot. I'm kind and compassionate simply because I believe that's the sort of person God wants me to be.'

'Did those divine coincidences you wrote about keep occurring?' Nicola really wanted that to be the case.

'You bet they did! And I'm looking at two of them right now. Young lady, that morning when you saw me in the bookshop, I wasn't even supposed to be in the shopping centre. We only stopped so that the friend I was with could pick up some pain-killers for a headache. Browsing in that bookshop was just an impulse to kill time.' He shook his head. 'I was supposed to leave the next day. But as I told you in the email, my friend was so sick that he needed hospitalisation and I didn't feel I could just leave like that.'

'He's OK?' Jerome asked.

'The doctors say he will be but it was touch-and-go for a while,' Gareth said. 'What I hadn't told your young lady is that the very morning I met her I'd been in my motel room and I'd found myself saying, *If I ever really made an impact on anybody, I wouldn't mind a bit of a glimpse.* So you see you've both blessed an old guy's cotton socks off.'

'It's been fantastic meeting you.' Jerome leaned across to shake his hand. 'You've given me a lot to think about.'

Gareth tapped his pocket. 'I have something for you here. I'm glad I brought a copy over with me.' He passed Jerome a yellow-covered, dog-eared book entitled, *A Design of Gold.*

Jerome gazed down at the object he'd wanted more than anything and stroked its cover. Words seemed inadequate. 'Thanks very much. Will you please sign it?'

'Sure. Shove it back and tell me your full name.'

Nicola's head was whirling. She listened while Jerome spelled it out and Gareth repeated it.

'Not quite,' Jerome said. 'It's pronounced *Bow*man, like tying a bow, not taking a bow. Although, what does it even matter?' He caught Nicola's eye and laughed.

'Here, there's a message for you, too.'

Nicola peered over Jerome's shoulder as he opened the cover. Gareth's handwriting was thin, loopy and spidery.

To Jerome Bowman.

May you have blessings and prosperity as you weave your own design of gold. Never give up believing that you're making a difference right where you are. Remember that real greatness is just one small action after another, after another. And don't just believe in miracles. Rely on them.

Your friend,

Gareth Edgley.

Jerome gripped the covers so hard, his knuckles stood out white. 'Thank you.'

'You'd better thank Nicola too. I'm leaving tomorrow so her email got to me just in time. You know God loves you. He's proven it by working this out so perfectly. I hope you know that and never forget it. There's times when I did.'

'I think there's work I've got to do in that area,' Jerome said. 'But at least God's got my attention now.'

Gareth smiled indulgently. 'It does sometimes take a personal disaster to do that. But Jerome, when you're tempted to forget, you look at how much your girlfriend really cares for you and remember that God cares so much more. They both love you enormously.'

Jerome reddened and looked down at the floor while panic gripped Nicola's throat.

Gareth looked from one face to the other and shook his head with a groan. 'I just stuck my big foot in it, didn't I? Forgive me. I'm a silly old duffer who jumps to conclusions.'

Nicola couldn't bear to see Gareth Edgley looking so remorseful after his kindness to them. Keeping her secret was becoming almost impossible to bear anyway. Acting on impulse had worked for her on Thursday. Before thinking it over too carefully, she took the risk. *Maybe it's better this way,* she thought. *Less awkward than if it were just the two of us.* 'You were at least half right, anyway,' she said. 'I really do love Jerome and I wish I was his girlfriend.'

She watched Jerome with bated breath as he snapped up his head to stare at her. 'He could be fully right then,' he said softly. 'Because I wish you were my girlfriend too.'

Gareth began to chuckle. 'My instinct didn't fail me. Why don't you make it true?'

Jerome's raised eyebrows looked like a question. Nicola gazed straight at him and nodded, feeling as if she were melting to warm liquid. Jerome reached for her hand and cradled it between both of his. And she knew that everything was going to be OK.

*   *   *

When they left the café a wave of shyness swept through Jerome. He and Nicola leaned against the warm wall in the darkness and looked at each other by the light cast by a street lamp. They both laughed from sheer nervousness and kept their hands clasped.

'I don't know who blew me away the most, you or him.' It was not the most profound thing to say but he had to say something to dispel the sudden immense awkwardness he felt.

Her bright eyes were downcast. 'So you had no idea how I felt about you? I must have been keeping it to myself better than I thought.'

'But I would have loved to have known how you felt. Why did you want to keep it from me?'

Her lashes flickered. 'Because I couldn't understand how you could ever feel the same way about me. And you were my biggest guilt trip.'

She would never stop surprising him. 'Why was I a guilt trip?'

Nicola kept her face hidden. 'I don't know if this will make any sense to you. When Shane died, Karen said, "I hope that someday she'll feel the same way she made poor Shane feel." When I met you I thought that was just what had happened. That you'd been put in my life to break my heart and teach me a lesson for the way I behaved with Shane.' She shook her head with a wan smile. 'Especially when you looked just like my Personal Adonis.'

'Your *what?*' Keeping his shoulder against the wall, Jerome rotated slightly to face her better.

Her smile flashed. 'I won't tell you now. I'll show you when we get home. Sam and Laura know all about it so you might as well know too. I've just figured out that instead of being my biggest guilt trip, you're my most incredible blessing.'

Although it was more than he'd ever dreamed of hearing her say, he was embarrassed into speechlessness. Michael probably would have known how to respond and Gareth Edgley definitely would. Not knowing what else to do, Jerome squeezed her hand harder and instinctively glanced down at the book in his other hand. 'You're my biggest blessing, more like it. I still can't believe you asked everyone in that bowling alley if they'd seen us. And that you served Gareth Edgley in the shop. And because of you I've got this,' he said holding up *A Design of Gold*.

'It's all you ever wanted, isn't it?'

He looked up to see her eyes twinkling. And he tried to think of a way to tell her that Gareth Edgley's book was merely the second best treasure of the night.

'After all the time I spent searching for this, I don't know if I'm going to have the heart to read it,' he admitted.

Nicola's face flickered with concern. 'Why?'

'It's just that I know what happens in it. He gets engaged to Irene. And he meets that Antonio guy and sets up the mission. It's going to end as if everything's great. But all the time I'm reading it, I'll know that she doesn't stay with him and that Antonio turns the others against him. And that'll make me feel really sad.'

Nicola brushed her cheek against his shoulder. 'I know. I'd feel the same way. Have you ever thought of writing a book yourself?'

He hadn't, but the idea set off the spark of effervescence that he recognised. 'Hey, do you reckon I could?'

She nodded. 'You have a much more interesting sounding name than his, anyway.'

'You think so? I've never been all that fond of it. I always thought it's a bit weird.'

'No, it suits you to a tee. Sort of saintly but dashing at the same time.'

He burst out laughing. 'Thanks. I love these things you come out with. A dashing saint – how can I ever live up to that?'

'You don't have to,' Nicola chuckled. 'I've always thought that you're already like that but I didn't want to tell you before.'

'Why? I would've loved it.'

She shrugged with a light-hearted tilt to her shoulders. 'I couldn't just tell you things like that. It might've sounded dumb.'

'I don't think you could be dumb if you tried.'

'You've got to be kidding.' She suddenly turned serious. 'I was dumb when I tried to stop you kissing me.'

Jerome stiffened and rotated his shoulders back against the wall. 'I reckon I was dumb for not asking.'

'Well, why don't you ask me now?'

He swivelled back to look her in the eye. 'Are you sure you want me to?'

'Jerome! Are you teasing?' She smiled. 'You know, because of you, I know God loves me now. You're the biggest blessing He could have given me. So go ahead and ask.'

He could hear every beat of his own heart. The blend of moon and street lights shone on her throat. She waited motionless, like a marble statue. Her eyes were deep green oceans. She was more like an Amazon princess than anyone he'd ever seen. 'Nicola,' he said, clearing his throat. 'May I please kiss you?'

It was so formal it was hard to keep a straight face. 'I'm sure Prince Charming was never so polite,' she said with a teasing smile. 'Please, Jerome, don't keep me waiting any longer.'

He leaned closer and kissed her softly. Her lips were warmer than they appeared in the milky moonlight. So was her hair that swept down and caressed his face and shoulders. He wanted to laugh with triumph because he knew now without words that she didn't think he was just a callow boy. He could tell from her soft intake of breath and the way her hands rubbed his back and pulled him closer as if she couldn't get enough of him either.

The softness of her breath on his cheek made his pulse race. Jerome raised a finger to trace a line down her face, beginning at her temple and ending beneath her chin. He whispered, 'Getting this book isn't the best thing that's happened to me tonight.'

She paused to dash a tear from her eye but he didn't mind because he knew it was a good tear. He was going to show her how beautiful she was.

She was his design of gold.

Epilogue

Nicola was checking her emails and her heart leaped when she saw one from Karen.

'We were all happy to hear that Jerome and his friend were found safe and sound. Well done, to have figured out where they were. James and I would like to invite you both to come around for dinner next Friday evening. Laura will come too and we'll play a few games, just the way we used to. James is looking forward to meeting Jerome and it's about time I made James smile. But most importantly, I am sure it would have made Shane smile too. I've decided that doing things that would please Shane will help me recover as quickly as possible. Please let us know if you can make it.'

Nicola looked forward to introducing Jerome to her brother. They had enough in common to get along together famously. It was a great feeling to be able to acknowledge her love for Jerome to everybody and most exciting of all to think of having him there beside her. Just thinking about it in the privacy of her own room made her blush. There was nobody else in the world like Jerome.

Being back on good terms with her own family would make it easier for her to move back to her mother's house for the time being. Staying on as the Bowman's boarder with the way romance had bloomed between her and Jerome was now out of the question. But it was the most wonderful reason for moving out that Nicola could think of.

She picked up the last breakable item to slip safely among her box of soft clothes; her picture of Shane. Ridiculous as the thought was, Nicola couldn't help imagining more of a twinkle in his eye and a sparkle in his smile than she had given him, because things were beginning to work out well with her family again.

Karen was right. Her invitation was a good sign. Shane would have loved that.

If you loved 'A Design of Gold' check out:

The Risky Way Home

Had Casey Miller known the peril in store for her she might have turned down her dream job offer.

Things are definitely not as they seem. Her personal judgments are turned upside down as she finds herself drawn into a story of terror and revenge that began twenty years earlier. All the while her heart is torn between two men; suave, polished Eric and calm, reclusive Piers.

You'll be unravelling mysteries with Casey and rejoicing in the choices she makes as she finally discovers the home of her heart.

Also by Paula Vince

Picking up the Pieces

The "Quenarden" series of fantasy/adventure for young adults.

Quenarden 1: The Prophecies

Quenarden 2: The Castle of Light

Quenarden 3: The Dark Secret

Available through Appleleaf Books: www.appleleafbooks.com
Or your local Christian bookstore